I. M. TRAVIS
Mystery Man or Miracle Maker

GREG CASADEI

Copyright © 2023 Greg Casadei.

All rights reserved. No part of this book may be reproduced, stored, or transmitted by any means—whether auditory, graphic, mechanical, or electronic—without written permission of both publisher and author, except in the case of brief excerpts used in critical articles and reviews. Unauthorized reproduction of any part of this work is illegal and is punishable by law.

ISBN: 979-8-89031-812-1 (sc)
ISBN: 979-8-89031-813-8 (hc)
ISBN: 979-8-89031-814-5 (e)

Because of the dynamic nature of the Internet, any web addresses or links contained in this book may have changed since publication and may no longer be valid. The views expressed in this work are solely those of the author and do not necessarily reflect the views of the publisher, and the publisher hereby disclaims any responsibility for them.

One Galleria Blvd., Suite 1900, Metairie, LA 70001
(504) 702-6708

CONTENTS

Chapter 1   Contemplations 1
Chapter 2   Perspectives 11
Chapter 3   Uncertainty 16
Chapter 4   Battered 25
Chapter 5   Survival 32
Chapter 6   Revelation 36
Chapter 7   Resentment 47
Chapter 8   Conflict 53
Chapter 9   Truce 60
Chapter 10 Goodbye 64
Chapter 11 Wait 69
Chapter 12 Next 74
Chapter 13 Alone 79
Chapter 14 Salvation 90
Chapter 15 Setup 106
Chapter 16 Foiled 110
Chapter 17 Empty 117
Chapter 18 Awakening 124
Chapter 19 Miracle 130
Chapter 20 Despair 135
Chapter 21 Lost 143
Chapter 22 Recovery 148
Chapter 23 Beaming 154

Chapter 24 Discovery 160

Chapter 25 Encounters 169

Chapter 26 Seeking 181

Chapter 27 Fulfilled 190

Chapter 28 Wonder 198

Chapter 29 Rebound 205

Chapter 30 Robbed 211

Chapter 31 Angry 224

Chapter 32 Meeting 230

Chapter 33 Admissions 239

Chapter 34 Clarity 248

Chapter 35 Forgiveness 253

About the Author 263

CHAPTER 1

Contemplations

No one expects a car to drop from the sky. One fell, though, crushing Julia Cavatelli's van. Through abundant grace, she survives. Or does she?

☦ ☦ ☦

Mile marker 133 looms ahead. Robotic drivers westbound on Interstate 10 through Phoenix ignore the milepost. Not Julia. Each time she travels this interstate, the sign reminds Julia of her misfortune. Despite efforts to overcome, horrific memories plague her.

Closer, Julia tugs her seat belt and tightens her steering grip—knuckles white as ivory. Her shoulders seize like overdone steaks, and her temples pulsate like an angry cobra's heart. Perspiration dampens her bra, and she gags down a dry heave.

Julia's behavior concerns her friend Diane, one of few people in whom Julia confides.

"We're near, right?" Diane asks.

Julia's eyes are glossy and fixed. "Yes, yards ahead."

"You're tense."

"It's involuntary."

Julia hunches her shoulders and squints. Her recollection of crumpling metal cause cringes.

"But your accident happened months ago."

"Haunting memories ignore time."

Julia shrieks and rubs her right calf. Diane reaches for the steering wheel. She waves Diane away. "I've got it." She looks back and forth from the road to her leg.

"Cramps?"

"Yes, and I hate these spasms and cramps, especially when I drive. They hit me often and last too long."

Beginning over two years ago, on November 8, 2011, Julia cramps over twenty times most nights. They force her to climb from bed to stretch her calf until relief comes. As a result, she lives exhausted.

"Will you ever improve?"

"Yes, if God answers prayers."

"You have an edge there."

"I pray so."

Red lights dot West Valley Hospital's roof. Images of her trip there invade Julia's mind like pests at a picnic—she dreads them, but they always arrive.

She lies cinched to a backboard. Lights reflect off chrome cabinets, which line both sides of the ambulance. A focused paramedic sits beside.

A plastic collar stabilizes Julia's head. Although it is called a precaution, she hurts in ways not experienced since childbirth thirty years ago.

She remembers having two questions: *What's happened to me?* and *Where's Gino?*

"I expect your pain reminds you?"

Julia's head jerks—jolted from her trance.

"I'm sorry?"

"I said I imagine pain keeps memories of your accident fresh." Julia runs her hand on the thin four-inch scar on her throat, still pink and firm. "My pain smothers like our summer heat."

"I worry. You sound hopeless."

"I'm honest."

So as not to offend, Diane considers her next comment carefully. "Optimism helps, you know."

Julia snaps. "You sound like Gino."

"He still harbors hatred?"

Julia imagines Gino—her mate of forty years, bombastic and compassionless. *If you only knew.* "Yes, and I fear his actions if he finds the other driver."

Gino's obsession with the other driver nears unhealthy. While Julia tolerates his comments about her slow recovery, she finds threats against the other driver scary and unacceptable.

"He still talks revenge?"

"Every day."

"How do you deal with him?"

"I ignore the subject."

"I'm sure it's hard."

"You know Gino. He's ballistic if I mention my accident."

"Why? You're the one who suffers, not him."

Julia's condition worsens daily, which poses two challenges: first, how to salvage life with Gino, who believes she malingers instead of working toward recovery; second, how to convince him his inter-actions with her and his intentions toward the other driver further destroy, not rebuild, their union.

"My injuries affect Gino, and he intends to square with the other driver for the inconveniences he caused." After a contemplative pause, she adds, "Here's the truth, Diane. A horrible result awaits if I don't act on Gino—soon."

Julia regrets her limitations. She yearns for feeling whole, for days with smiles, joy, and mutual responsibilities—a time free of intense pain. But in matters of truth, facts from one's brain always trump heartfelt wishes.

Julia's tone fills with determination. "I must stop him, Diane. I must!"

† † †

It is August 2013. An intercom beeps in a quiet room. Gino Cavatelli tosses his pen beside his computer. *Now what?*

Irritability fills Gino's tone. "Yes, Julia?"

"I'd like some water please." She hates to bother Gino, but Julia relies on him for significant help since her accident.

He shakes his head and scrolls to the next computer screen. "Yes, of course."

After several minutes, the intercom beeps again.

"Gino—my water?"

His eyes roll. "I'm busy."

Subject to his anger—again—she relents. "When you get a chance, okay?"

"Sure." His disinterest hurts.

Julia's demands limit Gino's time to focus on his needs. His bitterness and hostilities crush her daily.

Back to his computer, Gino scrolls pages of Phoenix-area auto repair shops. The number of facilities suggests finding the other driver will not be easy. He slams his laptop shut and stares into emptiness. *When will I have free time to call these shops?*

Julia's mouth clicks dry with every lip movement. She reaches for and pulls back from the phone several times. Finally, parched beyond comfort, she pages Gino again.

"Gino—my water, please!"

"Yes, of course." He pushes back from his computer. Mumbles and clanks spill from the kitchen. *She can't even get her water?*

A soft glow from a television lights their bedroom. Julia's expression reflects need. Sorrow grips Gino. *She looks helpless.*

"Here you go." Water sloshes out when Gino plops the glass on a TV tray. "Sorry."

"You need not apologize." Julia grabs his forearm. "And thanks, Gino."

He looks at his arm, then her eyes—basset-like large and equally sad. She swallows her tears.

"You're welcome." He smiles, emotionless.

"Honestly?"

"Yeah. Why?" He pulls his arm away and cants his head, his eyes beady as if to challenge.

"I often think you dread helping me."

"I'm overwhelmed some days."

"I'm sorry."

Gino sits on his side of the bed and turns toward Julia. "It's not your fault."

Julia's medical and emotional conditions cause a *poor me* attitude, which Gino loathes. Rather than battle to restore her health, she surrenders to her limitations and their consequences. Fault or not, she disappoints Gino.

"But it bothers me."

"For no reason."

"But."

"Stop. You know how I feel."

Julia's heart grows heavy. "I wish my body allowed me to help more."

"In time, perhaps. Maybe not like before, but better."

"Until then?"

Gino looks back as he walks out the door. "I'll care for you." His comment weighs heavy. Julia sobs, her face buried in a pillow. She senses a lack of caring despite Gino's words and actions, which further crack their foundation.

Back to his computer, Gino scrapes his whiskers and contemplates his next move. *Surely, there's an easier way to find the other driver. Perhaps I'll get faster results if I call accident victims before body shops. Yes, I'll call them when possible.*

I must change Julia and find him. I must.

† † †

The officer's wife recoils from his touch. Heartbroken, she clutches her shoulders for security. Confusion covers both of their faces.

These days, her husband's once firm, comforting embrace feels mealy and cold. His tender, passionate kisses now feel stiff and empty. His sparkly eyes now look dull and distant.

Like her, he acts differently.

"What's wrong, Stella?" He lives oblivious to her reality. Stella Ellis closes her eyes and sighs deeply. "Nothing. Why?"

"You're different."

She points at him, and her voice quivers. "No, you're different. Your actions no longer match your words."

She picks up and tosses her husband's hiking magazine to an end table. With a disgusted headshake, she retrieves his coffee mug. *He never even picks up after himself anymore.*

"My reaction fits our household." She heads toward the kitchen with his mug.

He turns her by the shoulder. "Which means?"

Stella looks at her shoulder and smirks. "Nothing. I trust you enjoyed your day."

"Trust has limits, and why shake your head?"

"Always the optimist, right?"

"You overrate optimism."

"Thanks. You prove my point."

"Huh?"

"Look, I hope you feel good about your day, okay?"

He ignores her half-hearted tone. "Sure, why wouldn't I?"

He walks slump-shouldered toward their bedroom. He peeks back toward Stella. "I'm going to change."

His back toward her again, she mumbles, "I can only hope." The other driver's changes began on November 8, 2011. That night's events affect him more than he lets on—everywhere, with everyone.

Once a proud, focused patrolman, he now drifts like a rudderless ship in a boiling sea. Tall, with jet-black hair, thick chest, and chiseled features, he has a look that belies his suddenly timid demeanor. Through one event, he no longer exhibits the confidence new officers often admire in him.

In his bedroom, the other driver's eyes dart wall to wall. Once a haven from fear, walls now close in and threaten him daily. His damaged knuckle aches from recently punching his dresser over his failures.

He locks his weapon and dons comfortable clothing. A glint from his badge catches his eye. It reminds him of the pledge he violated and how he dishonored everything for which the emblem stands.

His fuzzy likeness reflects in spit-shined shoes. His stomach sours. *I long to find and apologize to those I harmed. Otherwise, I'm doomed to a life of misery.*

The patrolman scoffs at his image in the mirror when he leaves his bedroom. *Thank God my deceased father never witnessed my cowardice. I act in every way he despised.*

He slumps to their recliner, feeling down like most nights. He scans the newspaper for nothing in particular.

Stella sets silverware on the dinner table. "Comfier now?"

"Much, thank you."

"Supper's ready soon."

He flips the page noisily. "I'm not hungry."

Her heart sinks. "Again?"

"Sorry. I might eat later."

"Why won't you tell me what happened?"

"Not now, Stella." He raises his paper to block eye contact. Stella pushes down and nearly rips the paper from his grasp. "If not now, when?"

He pauses for composure. "Someday, I promise, but not today." He raises and snaps the paper straight.

Stella moves to their bedroom. She slams the door. The patrol-man lowers the paper and stares at the wall—again alone—to wonder how many he injured and how badly. Sadly, he excludes Stella from his list of victims.

His hands cup his face. *I must find everyone I hurt, apologize, and seek forgiveness. Only then does it make sense to come clean with Stella and the department.*

No matter how long my search, I'll find everyone. I must.

† † †

Two men at the front of the chapel resemble statues. They hope to appear unobtrusive but fail.

Tears of others splash on the floor like waves upon a shore. These mourners wish to know why Eddie Elder died. But understanding—like a fallen snowflake, perfect when created—often melts into a pool of uncertainty at a time like this.

A slight pale-skinned man approaches the chapel. Cemetery workers rake around and manicure headstones. The pale man smiles and nods. Caught ogling, they glance away and scratch the ground harder.

One caretaker elbows a coworker. "Happen to see what I see?"

"Maybe."

"The sunlight."

"I know."

A sliver of light pierces overcast skies and shines on the chapel visitor.

"The sun falls on the man and illuminates his way to the chapel."

"Like a spotlight from heaven," the second caretaker comments in reverence.

"You talk crazy—only a coincidence."

Another worker approaches. "Notice anything weird about the guy near the chapel door?"

"Yeah, light surrounds him."

They watch in awe as the man enters the chapel.

The first caretaker thrusts his hand skyward. "Whoa!"

An eddy of dark clouds engulfs the sunray. With a flash and swoosh, a black hole swallows the light. Workers stand in the overcast and look in disbelief.

The small man sits in the last pew and prays for those who weep. His heart aches—a cost of deep love and intense caring.

The stilted mannequins in the front move as if choreographed. They bow and face the casket and admire their handiwork: their measure of success—to act as if they care. In truth, they live with death and have grown numb to its sorrows.

Whimpers of tormented mourners turn to sobs. A widow sits somberly. She occasionally wipes her eyes with a tissue. A veiled woman on her right offers comfort, which the widow graciously accepts and appreciates.

Sorrow rips a highway patrolman's heart; he chokes back his emotions. His friend's death creates a void, which already gnaws at him. He prays for a Lazarus-like miracle.

The sad day continues when the two men secure the coffin's lid to seal James Elder's body for eternity. Everyone hates this moment.

The men bow again—a thoughtful act mastered well. With the lead attendant's nod, they return to both ends of the casket. Mourners dread their next move, when they wheel James Elder to a hearse—the dark death wagon vital to this morbid business.

The men roll the coffin to a side door. Distraught loved ones follow Mrs. Elder. The coffin cart's wheels screech in need of maintenance. Few people notice.

The pale man rises, which illuminates space around him. He leaves unnoticed through the door from which he entered.

Now graveside mourners drop handsful of dirt on Mr. Elder's casket. Some toss flowers atop the soil. The patrolman sobs behind dark glasses. Before mourners leave, they pay final respects to Mrs. Elder, whose expression hides her grief.

The small man approaches her from behind and rests his hand on her left shoulder. She turns and notices his wrist scar. She lifts her head, and her eyes meet his steel-blues. The mesmerized widow's smile expresses: *Thank you.*

The man nods and returns to the tree from where he observed the service. Peace and comfort overcome Mrs. Elder, who bows in thankful prayer.

Like cemetery workers, the pale man's work lies ahead. Without his assistance, a lost girl faces death in a California forest. If open to his help, he will save her tonight and countless others in the future.

Mourners walk from James Elder's grave site, and caretakers ready to fill his grave. One worker looks where the pale man stood. His face scrunches with confusion. The mysterious man, there an instant ago, departed, as if never there.

† † †

Many of these people face a date with destiny. Although unaware, each person's journey has begun—their outcomes known and unchangeable. Life happens as meant. It must.

CHAPTER 2

Perspectives

Not all days go according to plan for Julia Cavatelli, a bank vendor manager. Despite a dinner date on her calendar for weeks, a coworker coaxes her to help solve an urgent problem on November 8, 2011. Julia's mind says *no*, but her mouth says *yes*. She urges expediency.

Julia's decision surprises no one; coworkers rely on her often. Highly competent and confident, Julia completes twice as much work as her peers. Today's request, however, creates a nagging delay.

† † †

Gino checks the clock. He expects Julia's arrival, but mere minutes have passed since he last checked. He prepares her favorite meal but fears they might eat late, like most nights. Work demands or traffic often foils their plans.

To keep perspective, Gino relaxes in his recliner. *Thank goodness she commits to our family when home similar to work when there.*

Julia Cavatelli, in her late fifties, exhibits model behavior in every aspect of life. As an employee, few match her commitment or capacity. As a wife and mother, she worships her husband and two adult children. As a grandmother of four, she cherishes each and seldom misses their significant events despite other demands. She often defers her interests for theirs. As a friend, she gives much and expects little.

Gino looks at his yard. *I love our life together. After forty years, our marriage stands strong despite life's challenges. Many admire our relationship. No one compares to Julia.*

The clock gongs five. *Julia should arrive any minute—I hope.*

Gino lowers the temperature on his braising short ribs. He slowly inhales and enjoys the rich aroma and anticipates Julia's joy when she learns what awaits her.

† † †

Problem solved, Julia readies to depart. The clock reads 5:09 p.m.— over an hour later than she sought to leave. Not the master of time, she shrugs and reflects. *Relax and decompress for your drive home.*

Other coworkers approach as Julia grabs her purse.

"Hey, Julia."

Julia steps out of her cubicle. "I see trouble." Another coworker fumes. "Hold on there. Trouble?"

Julia's peers block her path. "Yes, your devilish looks signal no good." She glances at the clock with a nervous smile. *Of all days for another delay.*

Her heart announces growing tension. "So you stopped to chit-chat, or what?"

"We're off for a drink. Why not join us?"

"No, I'm already late. I planned to leave by four."

"You leave early? No way. You're here every day before us and at your desk when we leave."

"I know, thus my frustration. I seldom leave early, and when I try, I get bushwhacked into staying."

"You open yourself to requests because you never say *no*."

"You're right. I apparently removed *no* from my vocabulary here and elsewhere."

"So say yes again."

"No. See, I *can* say no. Besides, you don't need lousy company." Julia's friends try to persuade her and waste more valuable time.

Her voice stronger, Julia convinces them her *no* stands.

With her friends deterred, Julia stops at the restroom. She hates to use public facilities; but, of all days, today's use, a must, consumes more time.

† † †

Julia enters the parking garage. A chilly November afternoon, she warms her van. Her favorite Christian radio station airs a mes-sage about God's providence. Two commentators discuss a story of a girl previously lost on a family outing in California. Julia listens intently.

"Twelve-year-old Gwen Middlebond wandered from her family's campsite," the guest commentator says. "On her second night alone, a man appeared from the forest to help her."

"You said, '*a man appeared?*'" the program host questions.

"Yes. This man emerged from the forest forty or more yards from Gwen. She blinked and suddenly found him next to her."

"How?"

"No one knows, but Gwen insists this happened as described."

"I expect he frightened her. He showed up and covered space in milliseconds. He terrified her, right?"

"No, not at all. Gwen said even though the man seemed different, she never feared him. She referred to him as '*my friend.*'"

"She knew him?"

"No."

"Yet she called him a friend?"

"Yes, and officials who interviewed her said they believe her."

"You mentioned Gwen said the man appeared different. How?"

"She said the thinly built man had light, sort of pale skin. His blue eyes supposedly mesmerized her."

"A twelve-year-old said mesmerized?"

"No, my word based on her description of how his eyes affected her."

"I see."

"Also, the man apparently spoke softer, more comforting than other people she's met. The total of those characteristics enabled Gwen to feel safe."

"Remarkable."

"I agree."

"Anyone determine what the man said or wanted?"

"I guess not much."

"I presume he spoke for Gwen to comment on his voice, right?"

"True. Let me put it this way. What the man said satisfied what Gwen needed to hear."

"Like what?"

"He told her not to fear—he only wanted to comfort and help her. Perhaps a tall order under the circumstances, but he won her confidence, then asked random questions, like to distract her from feeling lost."

"Lost—or found?"

"What a fabulous question. I think the stranger held Gwen in his care. He knew where she roamed from, her location, and where she needed to return?"

The guest commentator continues his insights about Gwen's story, followed by the host's wrap-up perspective.

"For believers, we understand Gwen experienced God's providence. He extended it for her protection and customized it to her needs.

"No, luck played no role here, as some think. Instead, a loving God, through his grace and mercy, sent a miracle maker to return her to her earthly home. I find no other explanation.

"The indication here is we're never alone with God. We exist safe in his care. This message of hope changes lives forever for those who seek and allow transformation.

"If you'd like more information about God's love for you, call..."

Julia blots her eyes. She trusts God guides her every thought and action, a governing perspective held before the lost girl's story. She believes God's protection will cover her until she dies.

Refreshed, Julia latches her seat belt with a new perspective—a different feel about her day. In less than forty minutes, she will learn how dramatically some days change and how God's providence indeed works in her life.

The clock reads 5:24 p.m.

† † †

A man embarks on another family visit to San Diego in his dark blue SUV. The driver, whose job involves highway driving, struggles to keep perspective when on the road. Like most trips, he expects to encounter many lousy, lawless drivers. His predictable response includes a fist shake and a holler as they pass, "I'd ticket you if I were on duty, you reprobates." These outbursts calm him.

The driver mentally reviews his route. The clock reads 5:24 p.m. as he shifts into drive and begins a trip unlike any before.

† † †

The pale man rises from his knees after hours of hypnotic prayer. He knows when, where, and what events happen before they occur, and the identities of individuals involved.

Today, he focuses on some in his flock more than usual. While he holds the key to their destiny, a necessary calamity approaches. Complex variables intertwine for them, which requires the man to leave soon.

CHAPTER 3

Uncertainty

As usual on workdays, vehicles clog Jefferson Street. While Julia waits for a traffic break, annoying horns echo in concrete canyons created by skyscrapers. She taps her left foot faster. *More delays.*

After several minutes, she waves *thank you* to a kind driver, who let her onto Jefferson.

The clock reads 5:31 p.m.

Bumper-to-bumper traffic further delays Julia. As expected, however, traffic eases as cars peel off I-10 westbound onto the 101 northbound. She accelerates to sixty-five miles per hour and moves left to avoid traffic, which enters and exits the freeway.

Julia instructs her hands-free system to phone her daughter, Angela, who expects her call.

The clock reads 6:12 p.m.

† † †

After congestion on 101 south, the driver of the dark SUV expects relief on Interstate 10 west. The smell of a burger and fries clouds his concentration. He succumbs to temptation and fumbles with his *to-go* bag.

His brain warns him to wait to eat until traffic thins. His grumbling stomach, however, wins out over his weak mind.

The wrapper crinkles as the driver undresses the burger. He lifts one hand from the steering wheel to better tackle his task. Paper open, charbroiled aroma further entices. He eyes his burger like a shark a surfer, his thoughts far from driving.

He lifts his eyes.

"No…Damn!"

† † †

The clock reads 6:13 p.m.—133 minutes after Julia expected to leave work. She speaks with her daughter, Angela, over her hands-free phone system. Seconds before her life changes forever, she comments about her drive home. "So far so good, Angela."

Julia cringes when tires squeal.

To her right, dust and smoke billow skyward. Her head swivels and eyes dart right to left and back to find an escape route.

A storm of sparks follows crunching metal sounds.

Like in slow motion, a vertically airborne car falls trunk down and toward her. Julia tenses and awaits impact.

"I can't believe—"

The car smashes her van's hood.

The airborne car bounces off and away as the impact jostles Julia in her seat. Once stopped, sounds of destruction give way to eerie quiet—awareness to unconsciousness.

Julia regains consciousness seconds later. Smoke, fine dust, and an airbag engulf her. Her eyes rock in her head as she processes what happened, unclear if injured.

The airborne car rests on its roof after barrel-rolling two and one half times down the freeway. It smolders amid broken glass and mangled metal. The dazed driver wanders the highway.

Another wrecked car sits sideways and hisses like a forgotten kettle. Emergency flashers blink involuntarily.

Julia's cell phone lies on her floorboard, its line open.

"Mom, Mom! What happened?"

She hears no response. Her heart thunders; she calls out again. Dazed several seconds, Julia spots her cell phone and hears a faint voice.

"Mom, are you okay?"

Julia rubs the back of her neck and rotates her head slowly. Pain explodes in every cell of her body. Tears cloud her vision.

Angela directs daughter, Adriana. "Call Grandpa, and tell him Grandma's had a car wreck. Call him now!"

Angela screams again. "Mom, talk if you hear me." A soft voice responds. "Hello."

† † †

Gino's caller ID announces a call from Angela's house. "Hello."

"Grandpa, it's me, Adriana."

"What's up?"

Adriana speaks unusually loud, her speech fast and muddled. "Grandma's had an accident. It's her head."

"Slow down. I can't understand you."

"Sorry, I'm scared."

"I get that, but calm down so I can follow you. What about Grandma's head?"

Julia often suffers headaches due to neck spasms and nerve irritations. Gino surmises she aggravated her neck.

Adriana pants. "I don't know. She's had an accident, and it involves her head. Mom's on the phone with her now."

Angela motions to Adriana.

"Wait, Grandpa."

Gino listens to Angela's side of conversations with Julia and Adriana. She instructs her mother, "Hold on, Mom. Adriana, tell Grandpa I'll be at his house in seconds. After I leave, keep Grandma on the line. Hang on."

"Mom, stay on the phone with Adriana until someone helps you, okay?"

"Okay." Julia's voice suggests uncertainty.

"Dad and I should arrive there soon. Remember to stay on the phone with Adriana."

"Yes, okay."

Angela hands her cell phone to Adriana. "Here, talk to Grandma until medical help arrives."

"Okay."

Adriana returns to her home phone. "Mom's on her way."

No sooner is it said than Angela pounds on Gino's door. Pain attacks her forehead.

Angela yells with a terror-filled voice. "Dad, Dad! It's me, Angela. Let me in. Mom's had a wreck."

"Your mom's here, Adriana. I've got to go."

The girls, his two miniature dachshunds, bark and bounce out of control when Angela enters. They sense her tension and quickly find their blankets.

"Calm yourself, Angela. Breathe."

"I can't."

"Try!"

"Fine."

"What happened?"

Angela comments between gasps. "I heard a crash while on the phone with Mom."

"Damn it, calm down. If not, air won't reach your lungs, and you'll pass out."

Angela's shoulders relax, her chest expands with a long inhale, and her closed eyes twitch. She continues with subdued angst. "I screamed her name six, maybe seven, times. She never answered."

"Weren't you and she talking when the impact happened?"

"Yes, I mean no, I mean yes."

"What?"

"Yes, until I heard crashing sounds. Afterward, Mom never answered when I called for her. I only heard weird background noises. Moments later, Mom got back on the phone."

"Did she say what happened?"

"Only that a car flew through the air and hit her."

Gino shakes his head confused. "What do you mean flew through the air?"

"I don't know, Dad. She said, *'Someone hit me, and I've hurt my neck. I'm in the middle of the freeway and see other smashed cars.'*"

"Where did this happen?"

"Westbound on I-10 near the Avondale exit. Hurry! We've got to go."

† † †

The dark SUV flees the accident. Its driver stiffens and blinks back tears over the damage he caused. His heart pounds out of his chest; his wedding ring clatters against his steering wheel. He squints to focus through moist eyes. The driver's lack of visual clarity matches the fuzziness in his mind.

Elsewhere, a small man drops to his knees. *Do right. The eve of your today represents the dawn of your eternity.*

Bug-eyed, the driver checks his rearview mirror, turns on his dome lights, and glances several times to the back of his SUV. An ethereal voice with a message about his eternity short-circuited self-talk about the accident.

Unsettled, the driver processes much. *How did this happen? Why didn't I stop? I know better. What about the message—a voice so real. Should I turn around? I can't. I acted cowardly, illegally, and shamefully. I'll account for my sins in time. I'd despise another person if he did the same. I must stop. Yes, I will. No, I can't.*

The driver continues west.

Although miles away, crash images muddle his mind. So does the voice convicting him.

† † †

Gino's son-in-law calls with information from a 911 operator. A crash on I-10 involves a rollover, a detail previously unknown. Once Gino hangs up, he rubs a sharp pain in his temple.

Angela asks, "What about a rollover? What did he say about a rollover?"

Mindful of tone and pace, Gino relates his son-in-law's message, which adds to their uncertainty about what happened.

"Speed up, Dad. Mom needs us. I'm scared."

They experience painful silence until Gino asks a question. "Angela, was Mom coherent when you talked?"

She rubs her forehead, as if for recall. "Stunned, and I know she hurt, but, yes, I understood her."

Dash lights illuminate Gino's smile. "Good."

His comment angers Angela. "Good?"

"Yes. If Mom rolled over, she'd have been frantic and impossible to understand."

Angela looks to and from Gino and the road several times and comprehends his smile.

"Same if she suffered serious injuries."

Angela nibbles the side of her index finger. "I guess I never considered those points in my anxiety, but they make sense."

Gino looks ahead. *Thank goodness my points make sense. I now only feel the need to puke instead of losing all bodily functions.*

† † †

Gino slams his steering wheel. A highway patrol car blocks the westbound ramp to I-10. Emergency lights flash ahead. Without hesitation, he inches past the cruiser.

"Are you sure it's okay to go around?"

"No, and I don't care."

Gino assumes his chest pain and heaviness relate to stress. Thankfully, Angela misses him grimace and grab his chest as they approach the wreckage.

Now closer, the accident scene looks more grisly than Gino expected. His eyes dart wildly, and his mind races. *How could anyone survive this tragedy?*

Fear grips him.

The beam of a Department of Public Safety (DPS) patrolman's flashlight glares through Gino's windshield. To his left and ahead, cars and parts litter the interstate. It more resembles a junkyard than a freeway. An ambulance pulls away in the distance.

A patrolman approaches. Gino lowers his window. "Why'd you go around my patrol car?" the miffed officer asks.

"My wife was driving the van."

More relaxed, the officer says, "I'm sorry, sir. You may continue, but stay on the shoulder."

"Yes, sir."

The patrolman clicks off his light and moves to resume traffic control.

"Excuse me," Gino calls out before the officer takes many steps.

"Yes."

"Do you know my wife's condition?"

"She's in the ambulance." The patrolman points to taillights, which fade into darkness. "She complained of head and neck pain, so paramedics felt it best to take her to West Valley Hospital. She didn't appear to have cuts or broken bones, however."

Speechless, Gino follows the dimming taillights until out of sight.

"Wish I had more information for you, but I don't."

Gino thanks the patrolman and drives even with his mangled van. The setting, too unreal to be real, resembles a scene from a *Mad Max* movie.

Gino gazes in weak-kneed disbelief. Angela grabs his arm for support. Her eyes scream of a broken heart.

Drivers inch past the wreckage and gawk. They revel in the misfortune of others. Sadly, there exists a broad and troubling appeal in misery.

Despite the officer's request, Gino exits his car and creeps onto the freeway to check his van. A man in reflective vest hollers at him from several yards away. "Excuse me, sir. Where are you headed?"

A DPS chaplain faces Gino, who points to his mangled van. "I'd like to check my damage."

"It's dangerous out here, so you need to wait until a wrecker moves it to the shoulder."

They walk together to Gino's Rodeo, where Angela awaits.

"I appreciate your cooperation."

"Sure, Chaplain. May I ask a question?"

"I'll answer if I can."

"I'm curious if the driver of the rolled vehicle survived? The car's a disaster."

"Paramedics said she did, but she's pregnant. They gave no word on her baby."

"Horrible."

"Yes, they transported the driver to the hospital for a thorough checkup."

"Look at her car."

"Yes, totaled," the chaplain offers.

"I'm amazed how the roof collapsed everywhere except over the driver. If not, her trip might have been to a morgue."

The chaplain makes the sign of the cross. "Amen."

"I'll keep them in my prayers."

The chaplain offers an affirming smile. "Prayer helps. Listen, I must leave for a fatality on Northbound 51. I stopped here because of the carnage. I thought I might be of service."

"I understand." With a wave of his hand, Gino adds, "This scene suggests someone died."

"Yes, but praise God, all injuries appear minor."

"I don't know how."

"Nor I. I pray your wife recovers from her injuries soon.

Gino watches the chaplain walk away. *We both have tasks ahead. Mine—to ease my daughter's fears over life's unexpected reality. His—to dry a grieving family's tears over life's undeniable frailty.*

†††

The troubled driver, who races west on I-10, seeks distance. And like victims in the bellies of ambulances, he mulls his suddenly uncertain future.

He continues west, unsure of what to do next. He foresees darkness no matter what he decides.

† † †

The frail man slumps in prayer. His assistance tonight has begun his involvement with accident victims. Much must happen over two years before everyone lives whole again. He knows what comes next. Others do not. Today, however, turmoil creates uncertainty sure to grow in weeks and months ahead.

It must.

CHAPTER 4

Battered

Chain binders tightened, Gino's battered van heads to a salvage yard. Angela grabs her father's arm. "Sad, isn't it?"

"No. I can buy a new car. I can't replace your mother. Let's hope paramedics assessed her condition correctly. Let's get to the hospital."

West Valley Hospital sits five minutes west on Interstate 10. Red lights dot its roofline to guide Air Evac pilots. Gino thanks God Julia rode in the back of an ambulance, not the cavity of a chopper.

People in the emergency waiting room huddle around a small pale man. He speaks alternately with each. All listen, riveted. None appear sick or injured.

Gino snoops while Angela learns Julia's location. The scene reminds him of biblical accounts of followers seated at Jesus's feet in rapt attention. The small man captivates everyone, to include Gino.

Angela and her dad head to Bay Two.

"Ang, did you see the light-skinned guy in the waiting room?"

"No. Why?"

"I wondered if he seemed odd to you."

"Odd? How?"

"Slow down, Angela." Gino looks back at the waiting room door as he struggles to keep pace. "So you didn't notice?"

"Notice what?"

Gino shakes his head—bewildered. "I guess nothing."

Angela opens the curtains to Bay Two with a sideways tug. Gino follows, afraid of what he will see.

Julia lies with eyes closed. A machine monitors her vitals. Readings flutter near normal per Angela, who is a nurse. Gino trusts her judgment.

Groggy, Julia stirs with a half-smile as curtain rings scrape in their track. "Where have you been? I expected you sooner."

Gino and Julia embrace long and lovingly. He moves aside to give Angela better access. "We got here fast as we could. The cops made us wait to empty our van."

Angela hugs her mother, surprised she looks so good. "How do you feel, Mom?"

"My neck and low back hurt a lot." A tear trickles down her cheek. "Thank God he spared me to tell you."

"You're not—"

Julia shrieks, and her right leg jerks.

"Mom, what's wrong?"

"Julia?"

"Leg spasms and cramps."

Gino's grimaces. "Your calf feels stiff as steel. Look at your gnarly toes."

Julia's back arches. She tugs mattress edges. "I don't need to look. I feel."

Eyes closed and top teeth over her lower lip, Julia waits for relief.

Angela nudges Gino aside to assess her mother's calf.

"You have crazy legs, right, Mom?"

"Yes, but never this problem."

Angela pushes Julia's right toes back without impact. "Sorry, Mom. I thought this might help."

Julia exhales deeply as her cramp resolves. "What a long one."

"You've had others?"

"Yes, Ang. These spasms started right after I saw the doctor."

"So the doctor doesn't know about them?"

"No."

"What did the doctor say about your condition?"

"He checked me over and ordered a total spine scan because of paramedic input."

Gino offers, "Maybe the scan will show what's behind the cramps."

Angela asks more medical questions, which Julia cannot answer.

However, she reveals much about her emotions during the accident.

"I thought the car would crush me, and I didn't get to say good-bye to anyone."

"Horrible."

"You can't imagine."

She bends and hugs her mother. Their tears mingle briefly.

"You all flashed in my mind."

Gino stands beside Angela. He dries Julia's tears with his handkerchief and offers it to Angela.

† † †

Julia waits for test results with her family. Another spasm and cramp shatter her comfort.

Through conversation, Gino realizes he failed to call their son, Dominic, about the wreck. As they talk, Dominic expresses both concern and optimism about his mother's condition.

Gino offers reassurance. "Mom might be her bubbly self in a few weeks. You want to talk with her?"

"Sure, but only for a minute or two. Mom needs rest, not conversation."

"She wants to speak with you. Hold on."

Julia asks about Dominic's day, deferring talk about her ailments. Once confident his mom is okay, Dominic insists she rest.

A handsome DPS officer arrives soon after Julia's call. She finds his five-o-clock shadow an asset.

"Sorry if I interrupted, folks," the officer says.

Julia smiles. "You're not."

Gino points to an empty chair. "Please, sit."

"I'll stand if you don't mind. I won't be here long."

After Gino settles in the chair, the officer says, "I'm officer Rozelle with DPS. I'm investigating officer for tonight's accident on I-10 and Avondale."

Julia introduces herself and her family. After more introductory comments, Officer Rozelle discusses the crash.

"Here's what I know so far. Please understand I don't have many details yet."

Julia nods. "Sure. Any information beats what we know now."

"Understood." He pulls a small spiral notebook from his shirt pocket. "I spoke with four witnesses and asked each call me tomorrow for a detailed statement. How about you tell me your recollection of the accident."

Julia relates what little she recalls. Officer Rozelle jots notes. Her information helps little.

Once she finishes, Officer Rozelle offers information about the wreck gleaned from witnesses thus far. "Once I complete my investigation, I'll provide a DR number you can use to find my report online. The department also sends out hard copies on request to par-ties with a personal or legal interest in accident details."

Julia nods again. "I see."

"Once finished here, I'll visit with the other two drivers. Each went to a different hospital."

Gino questions the officer's facts. "You said the accident involved four cars, and each driver went to the hospital. But you said you're off to see two drivers. Did you already meet with the fourth?"

"You're right, sir. Witnesses said a dark SUV occupied the far-right lane. The driver started the chain reaction, then fled."

"What?" Gino asks, in rage.

"Yes, sir, the driver left the scene."

"Did DPS stop him?"

"No, sir—too much time passed between impact and our arrival."

"Did anyone describe the car?"

"Not in detail."

Gino leans forward; his right foot taps wildly. "His SUV must have severe left-side damage. You surely check body shops, right?"

"Mr. Capo—"

"It's Cavatelli."

"I'm sorry, Mr. Cavatelli. I'll look for the vehicle and driver during my investigation."

"What steps will you take to locate him?"

"We use established protocols. Let me assure you I'll make vigorous efforts."

"Will you document your actions?"

The officer's tone sharpens. "No, I'll report accident facts and driver information. If I find him, I'll include the driver's information along with the others. If not, I'll note I couldn't locate the fourth driver."

"I hope you find the son of a—"

"Gino!" Julia yells, embarrassed.

"I'm sorry, but this pisses me off."

"Yes, sir."

"How long will you look for him?"

"As I said, I'll follow a process, which lasts as long as it takes. You'll get my best effort."

Gino doubts but placates the officer. "I have no doubt." He stares down and shakes his head in disgust. Unbeknownst to him, he forms a fist with his right hand, which bounces on his right knee.

"I want you to know everyone should survive. Paramedics said, although battered, none of the injuries appear fatal."

"Not even the driver of the rollover vehicle?"

"Correct. Notwithstanding the car's condition, we expect her to be okay."

Angela slumps in relief. "Thank goodness."

"Yes, ma'am, we're all thankful. The destruction reflects evidence of violent collisions with massive energy releases. We often see critical injuries or fatalities in similar accidents."

Julia's furrows her brow. "Officer Rozelle, you said you talked to four witnesses."

"Yes, ma'am."

"Was one named Travis?"

Officer Rozelle checks his notebook. "No, ma'am, no one by that name."

"But he was there. I talked with him. He helped me."

The officer stiffens and looks away. His expression conveys much; a half smirk betrays his silence.

Gino notices. "What's left unsaid, Officer?"

"Accident victims often say they encounter someone at the scene, which we can't verify. I reacted because of similarities between your wife's question and inquiries and comments I've heard before."

Angela's eyes grow full-moon round.

"Yes, ma'am. I'm shocked every time I hear these inquiries. Perhaps I shouldn't be—I hear them often."

Angela turns to Julia.

"Mom, who's Travis?"

She pauses.

"I'll tell you later."

† † †

The SUV driver chokes down bile, the burning punishment for the mess he caused earlier, or so he believes. He mentally replays the accident with hopes of placing blame elsewhere. The story ends the same, however. He started a wreck and fled like a coward. His failures number many.

He failed to uphold standards he expects others to obey.

He failed to display principles of human decency.

He failed to abide by his belief actions are right or wrong, black or white, not gray.

With past mistakes, he assumed responsibility and took corrective actions. But tonight, he disowns his behavior and its consequences. A voice in his mind provides frequent reminders.

The driver passes Dateland, Arizona. An odd name, it reflects why the tiny community exists—to farm date palms. Aside from sweet fruit and good pies, Dateland marks one hour left to Yuma.

Emotionally battered, the driver needs rest and opts to stay in Yuma. At 180 miles west of Phoenix, he feels safe there.

He finds a budget motel off Sixteenth Street and collapses on the swaybacked bed. The room smells musty—its walls stained with who-knows-what.

The driver needs sleep but has much to do. He crafts an excuse for his Yuma layover. His wife expects him by midnight, and he never stops on trips to the coast. *She'll find my delay out of character, but I've forsaken character in all I've done tonight. What harm is there in one more mistake?*

He rubs back and forth across his lips with his left index finger. *The impact of lying to my wife carries serious consequences, but I have no choice. I'll do what I must and worry about recovery later.*

He tosses. *But how will I sleep? My emotions eat me alive. My insides are raw. There's little left to consume. I'm near empty. It's empti-ness for which no fuel exists but rest.*

He rolls over and lifts his cell phone from the nightstand. He dials his wife's number and inhales and releases his breath slowly through puckered lips.

His wife, her voice sweet as ever, greets him lovingly.

"Hello, honey."

"Stella!"

CHAPTER 5

Survival

A doctor enters Bay Two. Tall and lanky, and with a stethoscope around his neck, he looks the part. His easygoing style and clear communication calm everyone.

Gino moves to the edge of his seat and hangs on the doctor's every word.

"The CT scan shows no mechanical damage in your spine to account for your neck and head pains—no fractured vertebrae, proper disc spacing and so on. So, structurally, your neck looks solid."

Julia shifts her position to ease her pain. "Great."

"Given your spine's condition, I attribute your pain to how you knocked about after impact."

"I don't remember much before I blacked out. I assume I bounced around."

The doctor and the Cavatellis discuss Julia's condition until he answers every question. Best news of the day—he expects her to heal in time.

"Now, for your low back, I'm afraid I have bad news." Gloominess fills the bay before the doctor continues.

"You have stenosis, a condition where bony spinal canals gradually narrow. This condition causes pinched nerves."

"What do we do about sten—"

"Stenosis—s-t-e-n-o-s-i-s. We do nothing tonight or the next few days or weeks. Unlike your head and neck, however, stenosis worsens with time."

The doctor continues to explain spinal stenosis and discharge instructions. He directs Julia to follow-up with her family physician as soon as possible.

Julia raises the issue of spasms and cramps, which the doctor also refers to her primary care physician. He surmises this condition relates to localized trauma.

The doctor prepares to move on. "Allow me a few minutes to finish your paperwork, and we'll get you out of here. I shouldn't be more than twenty or thirty minutes."

"That will be fine."

Gino lifts his head and smiles. Love fills his heart. Julia used her mother's favorite answer to questions of choice. Her passing devastated them both, but Julia acts more like her every day.

"Good. I hope you get well soon. You'll feel worse tomorrow, but you should improve soon after."

The doctor nods toward Gino and Angela as he exits the bay.

They return his pleasantries.

"What's wrong, Gino?"

"You writhe in pain, others lie in hospitals, and the responsible driver relaxes who-knows-where. You don't deserve this."

"Let's focus on Mom getting better, Dad. We can't change what happened, so why not concentrate on what we can influence— Mom's recovery?"

"I agree. My survival doesn't seem to be an issue, and I'll heal. Let's get me well, set up insurance stuff, and put this behind us with-out too much drama."

Julia waits for Gino's comment. Hearing none she probes. "Tell me your thoughts, Gino."

"Why?"

"Because I asked."

"I wonder why the coward fled."

"I expect Officer Rozelle to find your answer."

"I won't rest until then." Gino resumes a pose reminiscent of Auguste Rodin's bronze sculpture *The Thinker*. He straightens his posture. "It's time to talk about Travis."

† † †

The exhausted driver tosses in bed. The wall air conditioner groans from years of overuse. He questions why, instead of cozy in bed next to his wife, he lays awake in a two-bit motel, making up lies. Since lies beget lies, he builds the web needed to cover his earlier tracks. His need to deceive sickens him. *Has my life become a series of lies, destined to continue until I own up to my actions?*

After he broods longer, he uses faulty reasoning to validate his deceptive behavior. *I stand to lose much with the truth—my family, my job, and my reputation as a man of integrity. Funny, I must lie to preserve my integrity. What a joke!*

He rolls again. Crinkly sheets take his mind to dark places. The clock reads 3:42 a.m. Random thoughts bounce in his head. *What happened to me? Will one senseless act forever define me? God, help me. I'm not a bad person, at least not as bad as my actions tonight. But others likely see me a monster. Who causes a wreck and runs but a loser?*

The driver falls to his knees at the side of his bed. He clasps his hands.

"Lord, help me atone for my horrible mistakes, their devastat-ing results, and my lies. You owe me nothing, Lord, but I owe many. I'm a coward, however, a weak, worthless chicken who needs guid-ance to know how to proceed, strength to do so, and forgiveness when I do what's right.

"No. You don't owe me, but I wouldn't mind a little sleep for survival tonight. I'm exhausted.

"Thank you, Lord, and good night."

He remains on his knees with a sense of unworthiness.

† † †

The pale man considers pleas from troubled souls, to include a tormented driver. Sensitive to all, he responds to each in his time, not theirs.

For now, he allows the troubled driver to stew in anguish to learn guilt is a burden earned—forgiveness a gift given. However, sensitive to the driver's immediate need for survival, the pale man grants one request. He closes his eyes and murmurs *sleep...*

† † †

Suddenly groggy, the driver makes the sign of the cross and returns to bed. He pounds his pillow, rolls to his back, intertwines his fingers, and places his hands on his chest. He closes his eyes and falls into a deep sleep in seconds.

CHAPTER 6

Revelation

Despite raw emotions, Julia discusses Travis with Gino and Angela. She chooses her words carefully. Eyes fixed and glazed, she says, "After impact, I sat stunned unaware if hurt or not. Everything got fuzzy."

Gino shakes his head in disbelief. "I imagine so."

"Adriana stayed on the phone with me, but, honestly, I don't remember what she said."

Angela clarifies. "She kept you alert until help arrived."

"Probably."

"I told her to stay on with you."

"While we talked, a man named Travis knocked on my window."

Julia glides her hands down her cheeks. "His skin white as alabaster—pale, almost ashen."

She forms her hands as if compressing a basketball from its sides. "Lean, perhaps frail."

She places her fingers under her eyes. "Travis's eyes, pleasant and intense, captivated me. I found it hard to look away."

She splays her hands upward and outward. "His beautiful aura."

Gino's face contorts. "Aura?"

"Yes, soft glow."

Gino looks down and away to hide mounting anger. "You screamed, right?"

"No need to."

Gino's eyebrows arch.

Noticing her dad's disposition change, Angela intercedes, "What happened next?"

Julia plumps her pillow.

"I rolled my window down a few inches. Travis asked if I felt okay."

Julia cups the sides of her neck. "I told Travis my neck and head hurt a lot."

"Did you feel pain anywhere else?"

"I couldn't tell Angela—too stunned I expect."

"Did he leave then, Julia?"

"No, he said, *'Shut off the van.'* I tried but couldn't."

"Who turned it off?"

"Travis motioned and hollered, *'Roll down your window more.'*"

"And?"

"I did what he said. No questions. No concerns."

Julia's response astonishes Angela. "What do you mean?"

"I rolled down my window."

Angela squints her eyes and tilts her head. "You did?"

"Yes."

"You opened your window for a stranger?"

"Yes, and I'll tell you why. While I warmed the van in the parking garage, I listened to the radio and—"

"You always listen to Christian radio."

"True. And, today, commentators spoke about a lost girl in California's mountains."

"How does this relate, Mom?"

"Travis looked like the person described on the radio—his characteristics too unique to be common."

Gino grouses. "It sounds far-fetched."

"I understand and didn't expect you to believe me."

"It's not a question of belief, Mom." Angela leers, disappointed with her father. "Apparently, the guy helped you, and that's what matters to me. If he's helped others, I'm happy. I don't get it, but good for him."

Gino's attention drifts. *I won't challenge Julia's delusion. Besides, she might be right based on Officer Rozelle's comments.*

"What happened when you lowered your window?" Angela asks.

"He reached in and tried to shut off the van but couldn't."

"So the van continued to idle? Who shut it off?"

"I'll get there in a minute."

"Okay, you opened the window, and he tried to help."

"Yes, then a second man came up."

"A second man?"

"Yes. The second guy helped but didn't stay long. He shut off the van somehow, then went to another car."

"So Travis left beforehand?" Gino asks.

"No."

"Did the men talk?"

"No. In fact, the second guy acted like he and I were the only two there. He asked if I needed help, and I said the van wouldn't shut off. He reached in and forced the key to *Accessories*."

"That's all?"

"Yes. And Travis stood beside the second guy while he helped me."

Gino's confusion grows. "You think it's possible they saw each other and, at the moment, merely failed to acknowledge one another?"

"You tell me. You're the mystery solver."

Angela rubs her chin. "Travis stayed?"

"Yes, and once the second guy left, Travis asked, *'Do you mind if I sit in the passenger's seat until medical help arrives?'*"

"Whoa, whoa, whoa! Tell me you didn't, Mom."

"Yes, I did. I said yes."

"Yes, what?"

"I allowed Travis to sit in the van."

"What were you thinking?"

"I don't know. Travis acted kind, so I never felt fear."

Gino throws up his hands in disbelief. "I can't believe you took those risks."

"I knew he wouldn't hurt me."

"How?"

"I don't know."

Angela paces. "So he got in the van? You let him in the van?"

"Yes."

Angela turns from Julia and thrusts her hands toward the ceiling. "I can't believe this."

"Let me continue, Angela, please."

Lips tight in disbelief, Angela closes and opens her eyes slowly. "I'm sorry, Mom, and I mean no disrespect, but this revelation sounds crazy."

"I acted out of character, I know."

"You realize this situation could've ended badly."

"I suppose, Ang, but let me go on."

"Yeah, I want to hear more." Gino hopes additional details will ease his tension.

"So Travis walked around and sat in the passenger seat once he moved the airbag and other crash debris."

"Crazy."

"Yes. Then Travis smiled. I felt odd, almost possessed."

"Possessed?" Gino's face reddens with anger.

"Not like you think, Gino. He's Travis, not Bela Lugosi."

"I understand. But possessed?"

"Okay, maybe I used the wrong word. Perhaps *vulnerable* better describes how I felt."

"Oh, *that's* better."

"Let me explain. I know you think something bad happened, but it didn't."

"Thanks for the credit, Julia."

"I respond to what I hear."

"Let her talk, Dad, or we'll never know what happened."

"Sorry. I'm a cynic and grow angrier by the moment."

"About what?" Julia asks.

"That a coward's actions caused your exposure to this Travis guy."

"Gino, I know your concerns about safety, but Travis helped me. May I finish?"

"Continue, Mom." Angela's side glance to her father goes unnoticed.

"We talked. Remember, Adriana, still on the phone with me, heard it all and…"

† † †

"Ma'am, I'm here to help until paramedics arrive."

Julia's voice cracks. "The other man didn't say a word to you?" Her hand trembles on her chin.

"Let's focus on you."

"What about the other guy?"

"I am here to calm you."

"The other man?" Julia's pressing fails to derail Travis.

"He concentrated on you, not me."

"But he didn't see you."

"Laser focus causes one to miss insignificant details."

Her face moistens with tears. "Do you know what happened?"

"Let's calm you before I answer."

"I'm confused—so much happened so fast."

"Yes, common in accidents."

"You saw?"

"May I use your name as we talk?"

"Yes, of course—Julia, I'm Julia. Did you see my accident?"

"My name is I. M. Travis, but you may call me Travis. "Julia, may I rub your hand to comfort you?"

"Rub my hand?"

"Yes. Comfort dries tears, and I need you calm."

"I guess. Yes, that will be fine."

† † †

Gino lectures again on the dangers of strangers, his disappointment in Julia's actions evident. Her foolishness, he admonishes, left her vulnerable to disaster. Harsh beyond reason, his words sting, and anger Julia.

"I'm not your child, Gino."

"But you are my wife, and I'd like to keep it that way."

"Do you want to hear more or not? I'll stop if you prefer." Angela scowls at her father. "Of course we do, Mom."

"Gino?"

"Yes, of course. So you opened your window, let the guy in the van, and allowed him to fondle your hand?"

"He didn't *fondle* my hand, Gino. He held and rubbed it."

"Semantics."

"No."

"Dad!"

Gino nips at the inside of his cheek.

"I found his request odd, but Travis, soft mannered and kind, I said, *'Okay.'* Besides, I needed comforting. So Travis moved his hand toward mine. I met him to hold hands on the console."

Gino nibbles his index fingernail.

"He moved his hand slowly with care, consideration expressed in every action and word spoken."

Gino's mouth puckers—his eyes roll. Angela's frown and headshake signal him to stop before Julia notices.

"So he held my right hand in his left and gently stroked the top in a circular motion. I believe this was to distract more than…"

† † †

"Your hands feel soft."

"Lotions, Julia?"

"Creams don't make hands this supple."

"Good genes perhaps."

"I don't know about genes, either, but something is different."

"I often hear this, Julia."

"I'm sure," she says with a faint smile.

"See, Julia. You already feel better."

"You know what, I do."

Her heart warms like her hand. "Were you on the freeway when the accident happened?"

"Julia, I am here to comfort and assure you that you will be fine." Her shoulders slump as she blinks long and slowly. "I feel relaxed and secure."

"Yes, Julia. I knew you would."

† † †

Gino feels stuck in a personal *Twilight Zone* episode. Her story sounds unlikely, if not unreal. He considers she might have a concussion, although she never said she hit her head.

Julia continues and snaps Gino from his dissection of her story.

"Travis used my name a lot. He said he would, I guess to validate I survived."

"I'm glad your hand is all he stroked."

"Gino, I hate your crass and inappropriate comments."

Angela shakes her head. Gino shrugs. Julia frowns, disappointed.

"I'm sorry, Julia. Please forgive my misplaced attempts to lighten the mood."

"Apology accepted, Gino. But please, no more."

"What kind of questions did Travis ask?"

"All sorts, but few related to the accident."

Angela asks, "What did he say about how the car hit you?"

"He knew how impact happened."

Angela's brows show confusion. "But you said he didn't see you crash."

"Right."

"Did he say someone told him what happened?"

"No, and he said, *'I knew your thoughts as the car dropped on you.'*"

Gino smirks. "He's a mind reader too?"

Julia resigns to Gino's sarcasm after heaving a deep sigh.

"Let me explain. While the car fell, I said aloud, *'Well, Jesus, I always wondered how I'd die. Now I know. A car's going to crush me. It's not how I envisioned my death, but please know I'm ready.'*"

Gino and Angela look at each other dumbfounded.

"In a blink, I found myself in the middle of the freeway—dazed and in pain."

Gino's jaw drops. "Ready for what?"

"To die, of course—I'm at peace and wanted to tell Jesus I'm ready to go."

Gino leaps up and grabs the sides of his head, eyes shut, as if to deny reality. "I can't believe this happened. *Ready* to go? What about Ang, Dom, and the grandkids. What makes you think we share your readiness?"

"That's why I felt troubled. I didn't say my goodbyes."

Gino lowers his arms and slumps in his chair. Thankfully, his blood pressure likewise drops.

Angela turns away, pondering, "But how did he know your thoughts? It's impossible."

"I'm not sure, Angela."

Gino eases his suspicions about Julia's mind. Her story is logical, her clarity perfect, and her conviction unquestionable, Gino concludes events happened as stated.

"What happened next, Mom?"

"I asked Travis a question…"

† † †

"Did you see my accident, Travis?"

"No, Julia. I came to comfort you."

"But you arrived so fast?"

"You thought you'd die tonight but didn't."

"Thank God."

"You place your thanks well, Julia. And you will not die anytime soon or because of your accident. Your time has not yet come."

"How do you know? And what do you mean my time has not yet come?"

"Call it a hunch if you please, but you lack fatal injuries."

"Not fatal, but I hurt—a lot, and I worry about other drivers."

"I know, and the depth of your concern reflects the tenderness of your heart."

"You're kind to say so."

"I respond to what I see."

"If you didn't see the accident, why did you stop?"

"Julia, I intend to stay until medical help arrives if that's okay."

"Of course, and you never answered."

"You felt God wanted you tonight."

"How'd you know?"

Travis smiles and again rubs her hand.

"How many grandchildren bless you, Julia?"

"Four. I wanted God to know I was ready."

"I know."

† † †

Gino fears more questions might rasp a nerve. He defers most but must ask one now.

"Please don't blow up, but if this wasn't a full-blown dream, are you sure you didn't imagine this Travis guy?"

"This happened, Gino. As sure as I am here in West Valley Hospital, this was real. Hear me out."

"There's more?"

"Yes. I asked Travis several times if he saw the accident, but he answered the same—no. But he exactly did what he said he would do."

"Did he ever offer medical help, Mom?"

"No, only provided comfort and asked questions."

"What do you make of this, Julia?"

"I don't know, but I believe the accident and Travis happened for a reason."

Gino nods. "You know I share your view, but it's hard to understand the purpose."

Julia stares ahead. A tear trickles toward her neck. Gino wipes it with his thumb.

"I'm so sorry this happened."

"You should've been in the van."

"What happened next, Mom?"

† † †

A paramedic leans in the passenger door. All business and energized, her behavior suggests control in the face of chaos. She shines her flashlight in the van. "Are you okay, lady?"

"I don't think so. My head and neck hurt horribly."

She motions her light down the freeway through the wind-shield. "Are you well enough for me to help other drivers first?"

"I believe so. The rollover driver likely needs more help than me."

"I'm glad you understand. I'll return fast as possible unless someone arrives sooner."

"Okay. I should be fine."

Julia watches as the paramedic moves to the rollover. Her image changes color with emergency light flashes. Julia looks back to Travis.

"She has much to do, Julia. Waiting exhibits kindness."

"It made sense."

"Not everyone chooses like you."

"Sad."

"Yes, especially since the rollover driver needs immediate attention."

"How do you know?"

"I'm blessed."

† † †

Gino and Angela struggle to make sense of Julia's story. Although sequentially logical, each detail makes her message bizarre.

"What did the paramedic say to Travis?"

"Nothing. The paramedic leaned over Travis but never asked if he needed help. She had to have come within inches of his face and never said a word."

"You don't mean to say—"

"I don't *mean* to *say* anything, Gino. It's what happened."

She turns from Gino angry; he still questions her veracity.

"I'm sorry, but please appreciate how hard it is to comprehend this revelation. Angela and I didn't experience your accident, so we can't understand how or why this happened."

"I never said *I* understood what happened." Dried tear tracks cover Julia's cheek. "I offer you what took place."

"I'm sorry. I know I seem to doubt you, but I don't. I hope you'll continue if there's more."

Julia thinks a minute. Her voice barely a whisper, she says, "When the paramedic left, Travis asked more questions and rubbed my hand again."

Silence unsettles Gino. He looks at Angela, who shrugs.

"A minute or two later, another paramedic arrived, this time at my window. He asked if I was okay. I told him where I hurt. After the seconds it took to answer, I looked at the passenger's seat. It was empty."

"Empty?"

"Yes. So I turned my head carefully and checked for Travis in and outside of the van. He wasn't there—but gone, as if vanished— gone, as if never there."

CHAPTER 7

Resentment

Officer Rozelle taps his pen, which irritates a coworker who dictates a report. Seldom inconsiderate, Rozelle is often preoccupied since con-ducting a November 8, 2011, investigation. He disavows problems but fools no one.

Rozelle examines Julia Cavatelli's accident diagrams again. He memorizes facts for when he communicates with Mr. or Mrs. Cavatelli. His report, although detailed, lacks one vital piece of information—the other driver's identity. He expects Gino to resent and question this omission and his efforts to find the responsible driver. Today, clarity a priority, Officer Rozelle practices his pitch until well rehearsed.

The officer dials the Cavatelli's home phone. His stomach churns more with each ring.

"Hello, Gino here."

"Mr. Cavatelli, hi, it's Officer Rozelle."

"How are you, sir?"

"Fine."

"Great. Same here—mostly." Gino grabs a pen and paper. "How can I help you?"

"I issued my report this afternoon." The officer's tone is out of character—monotone.

"Good."

"Yes. If you have pen and paper, I'll give you my DR number." He sounds cautious.

"Are you okay, Officer?"

Rozelle artificially injects life in his voice. "Yes. Why?"

"You sound different."

"Just busy." His response lacks conviction.

"I've got pen and paper, so shoot."

"Before I address the report, let me tell you of an encounter I had while I worked this case."

"Oh?"

"Yes, it's unusual, to say the least."

"I'm not surprised when Julia's involved."

Unclear on the background of Gino's comment, Rozelle ignores the slight.

"I'm not sure what to make of this encounter, but I'll do as asked."

"Asked?"

"Yes. I spoke with a man who evidently knows Mrs. Cavatelli."

"Seriously?"

"Yes, and he asked I give *you* a two-part message."

"Me?"

"Yes, you."

"Okay, I guess."

"The first part is, and I quote, *'The stench of hatred nauseates the soul.'*"

"That's the message?"

"Partially."

"He phoned you this?"

"No, I talked to him in person."

Several seconds pass. "Hello."

Gino sighs. "I'm sorry. That message causes me to think."

"Anything we should discuss?"

"No. Please tell me the second part."

"Again, I quote: *'Abide by what is right to enjoy life fulfilled.'*"

"Your friend sounds like a philosopher."

"Not a friend, but, yes, deep."

"I'm curious. Can you describe this person?"

"Yes. The man stands five feet eight, maybe five feet nine, with stunning gray-blue eyes. His complexion, somewhat light, looks odd compared to other people. But he carries himself and talks with calm confidence—peacefulness. He stirred me in weird ways inside."

Officer Rozelle hears a loud exhale. "Do you know him?"

"Not exactly."

"Well, I still obsess over my experience."

"I understand he makes quite an impact."

"Perhaps an understatement."

"No doubt."

"I apologize for the sidetrack, but I promised to deliver his message."

"I'm glad."

"I appreciate your indulgence."

"Please, the report."

"Okay. Report number: DR-11-1751. My staff sent Mrs. Cavatelli a copy via mail today. The report also resides on our web-site. Follow directions on our site, and enter the DR number where indicated."

"Did you find the other driver?"

"No, sir."

"What?"

"I didn't find the car or learn the operator's identity."

"You're not serious."

"I'm afraid I am.

"Mr. Cavatelli, are you there?"

"Yeah."

"I hear disappointment."

"Oh?"

"As much as you, I wish I found the person, but I didn't—no excuses."

"Tough break for you."

"You're angry."

"Nah." Disrespect fills Gino's comment.

"You are."

"Let's move on. Answer this question. How hard did you look? I mean, did the fact no one was seriously injured influence your efforts?"

"Not in the least." Rozelle hides his resentment over Gino's insinuation.

"So you looked as hard as you would've had someone died?"

"Mr. Cavatelli, I tried, but, *truthfully*, I came up short."

The officer's words intrigue Gino. *Why stress* truthfully? *In law enforcement, truthfulness should be a given. Does he hide the truth?* "Please tell me what you found, and I'll tell Julia."

Officer Rozelle summarizes the accident in detail. He deftly dodges Gino's questions about the fourth vehicle's driver. Gino's resentment for this person, and perhaps the official who failed to find him, is evident in his voice.

"You consistently refer to the fourth driver as *he*."

"A generic reference, the operator's actual gender is...uh, unknown."

"I see." Gino disbelieves. The officer's stammer further damages his credibility. "How sad."

"Sir?"

"The person who caused the chain reaction gets off *scot-free*."

"Possibly, but everyone accounts for their actions in time."

"Maybe, but I'm sick over this—yet another case where a person escapes personal responsibility for his actions. This trend makes me crazy."

"I understand your frustration."

"I'm not sure you do. My taxes pay for competent law enforcement, yet this driver skates. It tempts me to take matters into my hands."

"We need to watch such talk, sir."

"I'm frustrated."

"I wish you'd appreciate how hard I tried to find the responsible driver."

"Did you check body shops?"

"Mr. Cavatelli, I used every investigative tool in my kit."

The two men discuss the investigation a bit longer. After, Officer Rozelle responds to all of Gino's questions and comments. He finally acts satisfied.

"May I ask about Mrs. Cavatelli? How's she doing?"

"Still battles bad neck and low back pain, severe headaches, and nightly muscle spasms and cramps. Our family doctor suggests she might take months to recover fully."

"But her doctor expects her to improve, right?"

"Yes, but, in the meantime, work kills her, and she goes to bed right after supper most nights. These changes add stress to our relationship."

"I'm sorry. Please let your wife know I asked about her."

"She'll appreciate your interest. Say, can you tell me more about vehicle two?"

"If I can."

"The pregnant driver—what happened to her baby?"

"She lost him."

"No."

"I'm afraid so."

"A boy?"

"Yes."

"I'm sick."

"It's sad. As you'd expect, the mother struggles emotionally."

"This will break Julia's heart, and it increases my resentment toward the other driver. He's a murderer."

"I get how you feel, but please be careful with labels."

Gino composes himself. "I'm sorry for my poor choice of words."

"I wish I had different information, but I don't."

"Officer Rozelle, facts are yours to report, not to change."

"I'm glad you understand, sir." Officer Rozelle appears unaware of Gino's disbelief.

"I do." Gino must end the call before he makes comments he regrets. "And thank you."

"You're welcome. Have a great day, Mr. Cavatelli."

This conversation perplexes Gino. *I can't believe he couldn't find a damaged SUV. Perhaps a tough task, but I'm furious he failed. My investigation will succeed where Officer Rozelle's failed, and I'll bring closure to this horrible chapter of Julia's book, a chapter that requires more pages.*

Although his situation frustrates him, Gino counts his and Julia's blessings. If she traveled a little faster, or if the vehicle that fell on her had been ahead further when hit from behind, the car would have crushed Julia's roof. She came within a literal whisker of death.

† † †

Three weeks after Officer Rozelle's accident report, Neurosurgeon Rod Nowiski wraps up a C4-7 anterior fusion, fixation, and plating surgery on Julia Cavatelli's cervical spine. Her surgery was a success, and Julia's cervical spine no longer leaves her vulnerable. The doctor expects Julia's head and neck issues to resolve after therapy.

Julia needed surgery after her primary care physician referred her to Dr. Nowiski because of persistent neck pain and headaches. The doctor's review of Julia's MRI showed cervical spine bruises at three levels, which the hospital CT scan failed to detect. He cautioned Julia against jarring events or hard sneezes, either of which could have left her permanently paralyzed. Despite low back pains, Julia's cervical spine became Nowiski's priority.

Presented with options, Julia asks, "When can we schedule surgery?"

† † †

Julia gains strength and stamina during her recovery. A full return-to-work now looks feasible. Pain persists, however, and she still does little more than her office job.

Gino loathes people bent on self-pity who yield to failure. Although he cannot change Julia's condition, he commits to two objectives: to drive Julia to higher functionality despite her limitations and to get even with the person who caused her circumstances.

The other driver's actions ruined Julia's health and stressed their relationship. Without question, cracks, which never existed before the accident, now threaten their foundation.

Gino resents.

CHAPTER 8

Conflict

Julia's hot, uncomfortable, and restrictive neck brace limits how far or fast she turns her head in either direction. As a result, Gino chauffeurs her where she must or wishes to go. Less than thrilled, he does what he must.

After Julia's return to work, Gino loses three hours every day taking her to and from her office. He suppresses complaints about his burdens but boils inside. He fools no one.

Beyond travel demands, Julia expects Gino to coddle her, which only reinforces her condition and feeds Gino's rage. He refuses to buckle to her desires, which Julia finds harsh and loveless. Gino believes his behavior promotes Julia's recovery and return to *normal*.

As Julia's needs increase, Gino's disdain for the other driver grows. Beyond irresponsible, he stole Julia's joy and happiness and robbed a measure of quality from their lives. Their relationship has become contentious, and conflict invades most days.

† † †

Hands on hips, Julia arches her back slightly. "My back kills me. It's even a chore to undress. Why did this happen to me?"

Gino comments from an adjoining room. "When doesn't your back hurt? You complain all day."

"I complain because I hurt. You should care I'm in pain."

Next to her now, Gino assumes his best theatrical form. "It wears on me: *'My back kills me. My head hurts. My legs cramp.'* It's all I hear all day, every day."

"It's the truth."

"Fine, but enough already."

Julia enters her closet to hang clothes. "You're terrible."

Gino follows. "Maybe so, but why must your misery always become my pain?"

"That's just like you. Make my condition about you."

"You miss what I mean."

"And what do you mean by *'all day, every day?'*"

Gino sits on the side of his bed to remove his shoes. "It's self-explanatory."

"And inaccurate. I'm not with you all day, thank goodness. I'm with people who care I hurt. Unlike you, they show compassion."

Gino does not look up from his shoes.

"I'd appreciate more understanding from you."

Gino rises from his bed. "Really?"

"Yes, it's how loving husbands behave. They care and offer comfort."

"Yeah, yeah, and, yeah, again."

Julia closes her eyes and lowers her head.

"Listen, I care, but I'm no *Travis*. I have limited patience."

Julia shakes both fists, her elbows tucked to her body. "You're so brutally honest, Gino. And you're right. You're not at all like Travis."

Marrow boils in Gino's bones. "Great. Use my words against me, right? It's bad enough yours rile me, but now you use my words to chap my rear."

Julia turns from him. "You're incredible."

Gino tugs her shoulder. Julia resists, so he frees his grip to avoid further harming her back.

"Look at me, Julia."

"Leave me alone."

"Look at me, damn it!"

"Why should I?" She snaps around to face him and gestures to her face. "Do you want to see this?"

"Don't be silly—of course not."

"Are you happy when I cry?"

"You're ridiculous."

"You love to revel in my despair, don't you?"

"Right."

"Just once, show you care."

"I do care. But dwelling on your circumstances doesn't help. You must deal with your pain."

"You don't understand. I could cry every minute I'm awake."

"Julia—"

"What I do is never good enough, right, Gino?"

"Please—"

"No, you add to my pain through cutting comments."

"You've got—"

"I'm miserable without your remarks. But you can't let up. You always have to—"

"Stop it!"

Gino's right index finger trembles inches from Julia's face. "Just stop. You talk insane."

"Oh, do I?"

"Yes. Look, your pain grows despite our wishes and prayers. To focus on it won't make it better, and your continual emphasis on negative magnifies and breeds more of the same."

Julia understands Gino's point, but her defensiveness persists.

"You know about negativity, Gino. It's what you most often offer—negative."

His eyes turn beady, his upper body tenses.

Julia's eyes fill with tears. "I wish you'd experience just once what I endure daily. Maybe you'd understand and care more."

"Let's face it, Julia, you've allowed the other driver to ruin your life. You *must* accept your lot and move on."

She wipes her cheeks. "No, I don't. And, no, I won't."

"You must."

"And he's ruined our life, Gino, not just mine."

Gino turns away. "True."

"Look at us," Julia pleads.

Gino faces her, his hands on hips.

"We can't talk anymore. We can't do what we once could."

"That's part of the problem." Gino paces.

"We argue all the time," she adds. "It's all we do well anymore."

"You're right."

"Life's so different than before the accident. We've let conflict over the crash tear us apart."

Gino sighs and rubs his temples, eyes closed. He approaches Julia, wipes her tears, and caresses her shoulders tenderly. He softens his voice and slows his pace. "You're right, so why can't we accept our new reality and define changes we need to survive?"

Defeat and desperation weigh heavily on Julia. "I can't—it's hard."

"Nobody said it would be easy. Look, we knew spine surgeries were rough."

"I know, but I had no choice."

"True, but you have a choice now."

"I suppose."

"What we can't do is let your physical pain cause emotional destruction in our relationship."

"True."

"Look, you have a bad hand. Play it, Julia. We can only make the best of our situation."

"I try."

"At some point what you have has to be adequate. The absence of wants doesn't mean you lack needs."

He returns to front Julia. Pain etches her face. "It's easy for you, isn't it, Gino? It's always been easy for you. You're not the one who hurts all the time."

Gino's voice cracks with frustration. "Julia, you don't see me."

"What do you mean?"

"You don't see how much I hurt—for you! How much I wish I could take away your pain."

"Is that so?"

"Yes, I pray I could."

"I'm sure." Disbelief spills from her tone.

"See, you're so obsessed with your situation you can't see others suffer too—for you."

Rigid again, she moves to their great room. Gino tags close behind and continues his exposition.

"Life doesn't have to end, but you allow it through inaction. I'm sorry you feel crappy, but I can't fix it. Only you can work on your condition."

She spins toward and charges Gino. Her fists shake again, this time close to Gino's face. He thrusts his head back to avoid contact. "No. You're not sorry. My pain doesn't faze you."

Gino steps backward. "Don't you think you're a bit dramatic? I only tried to make a point, not to make you mad."

"*Dramatic! Make a point.*" Her voice rings as loud as Gino's previously. "My neck surgery was dramatic. How my low back hurts is dramatic."

"Julia—"

"Why do I always feel alone when we're together?"

"Because togetherness means more than physical proximity."

"I've heard enough. In fact, you've said too much." Julia moves back to their bedroom.

Gino follows. "Sure, run away. It's what you do best—run to the bedroom."

"Leave me be."

"You don't accept your back will never be the same. Sure, run to the bedroom—your haven of endless self-pity. You can cry all you want there."

Julia slams the door.

She screams, "You're an insensitive bastard, Gino!"

Tears follow.

Gino listens.

They both are tired of conflict.

†††

Couples across the world analyze their lives, and Travis marvels at how many choose misery over majesty. He recognizes a seismic shift away from contentment.

People with pure joy thank God he continues to refuel their hearts with love. They seek him, expect him, and respond to his lead. Travis rejoices in their faithfulness.

Troubled souls disavow or ignore him, harden their hearts to his good, and question and curse their self-imposed *misfortune.* In truth, they misapply free will. Travis mourns in their senselessness.

Tonight, Travis prays for several people in Phoenix who grapple with conflict. Because of a single event, disharmony blocks joy. Helplessness, hatred, guilt, and uncertainty rule one or another. Travis uses these emotions to teach.

Every conflicted person involved in Julia Cavatelli's accident feels hopelessness. Personal transformations will occur, but not before Travis embeds valuable lessons into their heads and hearts. Until then, Travis aches over their conflict and pain needed for instruction.

† † †

The other driver stares at his ceiling. He cannot sleep—an inescapable pattern that started on the night of the accident. His memory haunts and causes him to cringe.

Metals crush.

Glasses explode.

Motors hiss.

Faces contort.

Bodies jostle.

Moans and screams become sobs.

Cars careen off each other. One launches skyward and lands on a van.

These horrific images and sounds started on November 8, 2011. They fill his mind, as does a recurring voice, which offers guidance on how to seek love, joy, and forgiveness.

These intrusions caused by his actions haunt and cripple the other driver emotionally. They also increase his desire to apologize to those he harmed. Failure-related fear counteracts his urge to atone.

He lives in conflict and plumbs the depths of his soul for answers.

Stella Ellis waits for her husband to come clean. She no longer believes his story about their SUV's breakdown. Their vehicle was too new and too well maintained to fail.

She lives with conflict over what to do. Her husband, in a dangerous state of despair, avoids all offers of help. Without assistance, he cannot function, and in time, his collapsing world appears destined to cause irreversible damage.

† † †

Julia, alone in her bedroom, dips deeper into despair. She relives the night's ugly events and questions if Gino might be right. Julia *wants* an apology and needs treatment for her emotional wounds. She found Gino harsh and heartless, and she does not feel he will offer one. He seldom does.

Gino, alone in his *great* room, dips deeper into anger. He searches for a better way to deliver his painful message. Gino wants to apologize and treat the wounds he caused Julia. He does not feel she will find his contrition sincere. She seldom does.

Unbeknownst to both, they want the same outcomes but misread each other's motives, or they misinterpret what each other means. In either case, conflict grows.

After an hour, Gino slips into bed, careful not to disturb Julia. He turns his back toward her, but sleep eludes him—troubled by frequent events.

Julia cannot sleep, either. She fights pain. She stares at Gino's back and considers his words from earlier.

They both have much to think about to neutralize the night's conflict before they rise again.

CHAPTER 9

Truce

The next morning starts as the previous night ended. Neither Gino nor Julia speaks or acknowledges the other.

While she readies for work, Gino studies the accident report and prepares to call each injured driver and the only witness to respond to Officer Rozelle. Any information they offer might help his search.

When ready to leave for work, Julia orders, "Let's go."

Gino follows her out their front door without comment.

Their drive downtown feels chilly. Neither Gino nor Julia know how to break the ice, although both want it crushed. Without a truce, their battle might last days.

Gino stops at a familiar curb. He peeks toward Julia, who slams the car door without a glance or goodbye. Her actions show how much she hurts. He rolls the passenger window down to call her back but stops. He raises the window and honors Julia's need for time and space.

† † †

The buzzer alerts Gino to pick up Julia from a coworker's house. He loses another hour, which angers him, but since Julia's accident, Gino no longer controls his time or activities.

He arrives before the ladies to preclude wait times for Julia, a consideration she takes for granted. Energy spills from the car after

Julia opens the door. The women use daily commutes home to solve world problems, which always ends with a laugh. Julia relaxes her façade, however, once in their van. The impact of exhaustion and pain paints her face.

Back to work two months postsurgery, Julia slogs through her tasks and prays for the past. Her neck no longer the problem, Julia's lumbar back pain now rules her existence. Her spasms still interrupt her nights, and she never gets healing sleep.

Gino looks toward Julia. She turns away, not wanting him to know she was watching him through the corner of her eye. He honks goodbye to Julia's coworker and turns for home. Neither he nor Julia knows how their night might unfold.

After several minutes, Gino swallows hard. "I'm sorry for last night."

Julia faces him. His profile looks less tense than before. "Me too, but this happens so often."

"I know." He glances back and forth from the road to Julia. "I'm miserable about it and couldn't sleep last night."

"Me neither." A lump fills Julia's throat. "So what do we do?"

"We call a truce and sign it with a hug and kiss before our feet hit the ground."

She smiles, at a loss for words.

"We acknowledge everyone cares about your pain—your condition. Your family, your friends, your doctor—we all pull for your recovery."

"You think so?"

"I know so."

"You forgot me, you know."

"It's a given you want to improve."

"I'm glad you used *we* instead of this being my dilemma alone."

"You know we're in this together."

Their eyes meet. Julia waits for more.

"We focus on what you can do, not what you can't. To do otherwise blocks progress."

"But how do I manage my pain? I haven't taken pain meds since right after surgery, and I don't want to start now."

"I agree, and I lack a solution. I refuse to accept answers don't exist, however."

"How do we find them?"

Gino considers his response. For the first time since her accident, Julia appears open to taking steps forward. He must seize the opportunity. "We develop strategies with agreement activities need not be all or nothing."

"Tell me more."

"You need balance."

"Balance?"

"Yes. Let's use sewing as an example. You sew as long as possible and rest when you must. You sew again once rested, pause when needed, and so on."

Gino glances toward Julia with a smile. She shows little enthusiasm. He breaks the silence. "Well, any thoughts?"

"Yes. I know you're right, but it's hard."

Gino nods agreement. "Sure, but you'll stay stymied if you greet each day with, *'My aching back!'* You need to wake up, acknowledge your pain, and move forward—not idle in neutral but press ahead. Even neutral keeps you stifled, so strive to move forward each day."

Julia drops her head and places her hands over her eyes. "I'm sorry I caused all this trouble."

"You didn't. The *other driver* caused our situation, not you."

Gino's tone reveals the depth of hatred for the other driver. He scares Julia.

"I promise to try harder if you commit to greater understanding on days I fail."

Gino senses success. "Deal." He thrusts his right hand toward Julia's. "Try to live life—that's all I ask. Play the cards you have. You don't have aces, but you don't have deuces, either. Your hand is worse than some people's. It's better than others."

"Deal." Julia's smile suggests relief.

She grabs Gino's hand. He looks at their clasped hands, happy she accepts his truce.

Once home, Julia rests hers and Gino's hand atop the van's console, the place Travis held hers after the accident. Gino hopes his efforts to comfort Julia today prove as successful as Travis's on November 8, 2011.

†††

It is months later, and Julia's low back worsens daily. Pain radiates down her right leg, which makes many aspects of life difficult. It dampens her enthusiasm and restricts her abilities, so she settles for inactivity and self-pity. She exists as a tightly woven basket case.

The more Julia hopes and expects Gino to understand, the less patience he shows. As a result, she goes to bed alone each night and prays for restorative sleep and strength for the next day.

Most nights, she fails.

Gino stews over many issues alone on nights Julia retires early. He prays for deeper perspective and an attitude needed to restore their crumbled relationship.

Most nights, he fails.

His and Julia's relationship, which once needed patches, now needs rebuilding. Defeat at their doorstep, and unlike Franklin Delano Roosevelt, their new deal—their truce—failed.

CHAPTER 10

Goodbye

Sam Ellis hugs Stella goodbye. His phony smile masks his heart. As usual, she sees through him.

Outside, he inhales, hands on his hips. His exaggerated breath serves his weak emotions more than his healthy lungs.

Trees Sam Ellis planted as saplings rise to the sky mature. Bushes he manicures weekly stand with every leaf in place. This yard he loves and labors over on weekends represents much of his life in this home. His longing look fits the day.

Before he boards his cruiser, Sam Ellis reaches for his hip. His pistol, its metal cold and smooth, nestles securely in a black leather holster. It is a tool of his trade on the force that he will fire for the first time today away from a firing range. The certainty about his gun use amuses Sam Ellis. He could never predict its use on regular days. Today, however, a day unlike any other of his life, he has no doubt.

Officer Ellis slips into his cruiser. He checks himself in his rearview mirror. His image repulses and conflicts him more than usual. He accepts his role in the accident, which carries a self-imposed life-long sentence he refuses to serve.

Sam Ellis settles behind the wheel and waves goodbye to Stella, his wife of twelve years. She watches through parted drapes. Ellis remembers the day they purchased those window covers—the only time in their life together he enjoyed shopping. She made the day special, a feat she did more often for him than he did her.

Officer Ellis backs up and offers Stella a goodbye beep. She looks worried as if she senses her husband's troubled mood. He pulls away with another wave. Her return hangs in the air until she slumps into their sofa, distraught.

† † †

Sam Ellis drives westbound on Interstate 10. For several reasons, he hates the stretch near mile marker 133. He cups his holster as he passes. His revolver rests secure.

After nineteen minutes, he exits I-10 onto Highway 85. Overrun with remorse, he needs uninterrupted thought. A remote dirt road he knows off the highway ensures privacy.

Officer Ellis switches on his light bar and pulls onto the right shoulder. After traffic clears, he turns left onto a dirt road, which leads to the Gila River water preserve. Few know of the seclusion at the back of this area, so no one should bother him there.

Once alone, Sam Ellis parks and allows his car to idle for air-conditioning. Stress-driven sweat beads glisten on his forehead.

† † †

Stella Ellis finally rises from her sofa. She could not have known the finality of her husband's goodbye this afternoon, unaware of his plan to exterminate the demons that plague him over the accident he caused. In fact, she does not know he caused a wreck—a secret he has hidden from her for months.

† † †

Sam Ellis sets an envelope, which bears Stella's name, on the passenger's seat. He thinks about what he wrote.

> *Dear Stella,*
>
> *There are gifts and wonders in life one earns and deserves. There are others that defy explanation. Your love falls into the latter category. I can only say thank you from the depths of my heart.*
>
> *I also thank you for your unyielding support. I've given much to challenge your commitment, but you never wavered. Lesser women wouldn't have sacrificed as you have.*
>
> *Thank you, Stella, my love. You've been better for me than I've been for you. You're simply a better person. You always have been—always will be. I'm sorry for this with every fiber of my being.*

He imagines Stella reading his letter—her face twisted ugly from crying, her heart broken. He shudders as if to shake raw images from his mind.

> *Finally, thank you for the most precious gift imaginable—Wendy. She's the sweetest soul alive, filled with your big heart and love-filled spirit. I can't describe my love for her in human terms. It is love like God has for his children.*
>
> *My love for both of you makes what I'm about to do hard. You deserve better than my selfish act, but this will be my final failure.*
>
> *I'm sorry, Stella, but know what haunts me doesn't relate to you or Wendy. It's sad you will both be most affected by its occurrence.*
>
> *I could write more but fear you'll find my words empty, so I won't. Please trust I've looked for other ways out. I*

dis-covered none. So while I've not asked forgiveness from others, I ask for yours. Forgive me.

With love for you both—goodbye.

Sam (Daddy)

Sam Ellis straightens the envelope, so it lays parallel with upholstery seams, a sign of his anal nature. A droplet falls from his cheek to his thigh—perhaps a tear, maybe sweat.

With his letter straight, he laughs uncontrollably. *Oh, had I'd been so careful about details on November 8, 2011.*

His right hand loosens the strap on his holster. He breathes shallowly and rapidly, and his heart thunders aloud. In seconds, his empty hand moves back to his steering wheel.

He retrieves from his glove box a Circle K napkin put there when he last bought coffee. He dabs his brow, which saturates the wipe. His eyes rock left to right.

Sam Ellis stretches his neck left, which cracks due to arthritic changes. He blinks in harmony with his heartbeat—sweat burns his eyes. He swallows hard—parched.

He reaches for his holster again—his palm uncharacteristically sweaty. His hand shakes as it meets his pistol grip. With a slow, uncertain motion, he unsnaps the holster again and slips the revolver out. It feels uncomfortable.

Nerves overwhelm him, so he jams the pistol back in its holster and exhales a cleansing breath. With a scratchy swallow, he readjusts Stella's letter on the seat. It slid slightly with his jittery movements. With a minor adjustment, it lays perfect again. The letter's placement represents the only acceptable aspect of Sam Ellis's life.

With a slow breath and a swift, seamless movement, Sam Ellis removes his revolver. His right hand trembles while he adjusts his grip. He lays the pistol on his lap and sobs and laughs simultaneously thinking of Stella and Wendy. His expression slowly fades from an odd smile to forlorn stare with thoughts of how his actions will crush them.

He sniffles and wipes dribble from his nose. He cleans his left index finger on his trouser leg, which creates a sheen. Any other time, Sam Ellis would find a dirty uniform unacceptable. Today, however, he abandons all standards.

Officer Ellis grips his revolver. He raises it slowly toward his head. Tears stream his face as he cries a final farewell to Stella, Wendy, and the others he harmed. It proves how easy apologies come when those affected are not present.

He places the revolver to his temple. Nervous tremors cause it to bounce against his head.

He swallows again and smells his breath, foul from tension. He cocks the hammer with his right thumb. In an instant, his agony will fall upon Stella and Wendy.

"Goodbye, Stella. Goodbye, sweet Wendy. Forgive me."

CHAPTER 11

Wait

A lumbar MRI confirms Julia needs an L3-S2 fusion, fixation, and plating surgery to fix her low back. She faces a longer, harder, and more painful recovery than for her neck surgery.

Julia needs strength but shows weakness.

Gino needs endurance but exhibits exhaustion.

Both need relief but must wait.

Gino wrestles with a familiar problem. With another surgery on Julia's calendar, he must suspend his search for the other driver. Her needs come before his, but Gino refuses to abandon his plans. For now, however, he must wait.

† † †

Julia's distant behavior bugs Gino. Conversation seldom helps. He tries to get her to open up regardless. "I'll pay for your thoughts."

"Guess." Julia avoids discussions about reality whenever possible.

"I don't know. That's why I asked."

Julia faces him and grabs under her chin. "My neck's still not healed, and I must face the knife again. I don't know how much more I can take—how much longer I want to endure."

"What else can you do? You already agonize in pain every day."

With exaggerated, ghoulish motions, Gino adds, "You're zombie-like when you get home, which I understand."

Julia's sagging face reveals the extent of her depression.

Gino rubs her hand. "So you have no choice. You must have surgery—now. Remember what the doctor said at West Valley Hospital?"

"Yes. I hear the doctor's words with each pang of pain."

"So let's get this behind us."

"Us, Gino—behind us?"

"Yes, *us*. Your circumstances affect me, and vice versa. Your backaches cause pains in my rear."

"Nice." She turns from him. "You're always Mr. Sensitive."

"I'm stroking your hand, aren't I?"

"Yes, but I've had better hand rubs."

Gino executes a princely bow. "Touché, my lady." He rises and theatrically motions as if gaffed with a dagger.

"Awe, did I smite thee, kind sir? I retract lest ye find me a horrid wench."

Gino grins. "It's good we joke about this, isn't it?" He turns somber. "Absent our rocky relationship, comic relief would be funny."

"Yes, it's good, but I think we do better today than a month ago."

"Do we, Julia? Are we better, or do we merely tolerate better?"

"I can only relate how I feel, and I say, yes, we've improved."

"I guess, but here's how I see our situation. I'll use an analogy: *Pressure in our teakettle nears the whistling point. It'll take little more heat to make it boil over.*"

Julia nods in agreement. "I know what you mean, but we man-age our differences better."

"Better is good, and it's why you need surgery—to get better."

Julia's face shows strain. "But I'm scared, Gino." Her tone matches her face. "I don't want to be cut again. I fear the pain of recovery."

"But you're in pain now. If surgery works, you'll only have several more months of it. After, you'll be better."

"That day seems far off with a massive cost to get there."

"Look at it this way: it's pain you'd have either way. So you'll either hurt forever without surgery or for a finite period once recovered from the operation. For me, it's a no-brainer. Then again, I'm not the one to go under the knife."

"I know I have to do it, but I don't look forward to it."

"Who would?"

Julia weeps. "And I don't want improvement. I *need* restoration."

"Let's not speculate about how you'll feel postsurgery. It's senseless."

Julia slumps. "Yes, I have no choice but to wait."

† † †

Julia has been in surgery for five-plus hours. Based on estimates, Dr. Nowiski should finish soon. Gino and others wait for his report.

The surgery waiting room phone rings an hour later. A pleasant nurse seeks Gino.

"Mr. Cavatelli, your wife tolerated surgery well. There weren't any complications. After Dr. Nowiski closes her incision, he'll talk with you. It might be another thirty to forty-five minutes."

"But she's okay?"

"Yes, fine. Mrs. Cavatelli will go to recovery for an hour or more. The time depends on how fast she wakes. You can see her then. Do you have any questions?"

"No." Joy fills Gino's heart and voice. "I'm relieved."

"I'm sure, Mr. Cavatelli."

Gino's tension partially resolved, he looks forward to a visit with Julia in her patient room. But, for now, he must wait.

† † †

The revolver's hammer nears the chamber. A restless round waits. The hammer strikes the firing pin. The impact ping sounds like an orchestral gong in Sam Ellis's mind. In a nanosecond, he enters eternal silence.

A flash and curly cued smoke ring accompany the weapon's internal explosion. Sam Ellis squints. *It is time.*

The round spins violently through the barrel toward a human temple.

In a final instantaneous expression of sorrow, Sam Ellis screams, "I'm sor—"

† † †

Gino checks his cell phone. His toe taps out of control. It has been forty-five minutes since the nurse's call, although it seems longer. *Julia should be in recovery by now. Why hasn't the nurse called again? Why hasn't Dr. Nowiski seen me?*

He waits. Troubled.

Others notice.

A person catches Gino's attention from across the room. Not there a moment ago, Gino searches his memory to identify the man. Few people have such distinct features. The man smiles and nods at Gino.

Others there try to ease Gino's tensions. However, their chitchat irritates rather than helps. Gino, fresh out of fake smiles and interest, focuses on Julia alone.

Dr. Nowiski remains a no-show one-hour postsurgery. Worry builds at seventy-five minutes. Even the chitchatters now sit quietly. Each additional minute wrenches Gino's innards harder. No joy. Just tension. No calm. Only anxiety. No confidence. Only speculation. Even so, they have no options other than to wait longer.

† † †

"Stella!"

Startled awake, Stella looks at Sam through sleepy eyes. She flips on a lamp to find Sam panic-stricken, drenched, and ghostly pale.

"Are you all right?" He appears more distressed than usual.

Sheets rise and fall rapidly over Sam's chest. "I had another nightmare. It was real and ugly, as usual. I had no way out."

"No way out of what or where?" Stella knows he won't divulge what causes his angst.

He turns to face her. "You know, out of nightmarish situations and images."

"Well, you scared me. I thought you were suffering a heart attack, having a stroke, or passing a kidney stone."

He cracks a quick, nervous smile. "I'd take a heart attack over brutal and frequent nightmares. At least with a heart attack, it might be one and done instead of a repeated horror show."

"What torments you so, Sam? I swear you dream every night."

"I don't dream. I suffer the same frightening nightmare over and over. One of these times, I might not wake up."

Stella married Sam years ago, but he is not the same man. He no longer opens up to her.

"What does it mean?"

He looks at the ceiling and then Stella. "Let's say it wouldn't be good and leave it there." His voice is soft and calculated. "It scares me to death."

"But what can be so terrible it terrifies you every night? Your job frightens most, yet you're never afraid. You hike in remote areas, and you're never scared. But you're like a child because of a nightmare?"

"You don't understand. This torment relates to real life, not fantasy."

"What is it? Why won't you tell me?"

"I can't. Not now—maybe never. It's painful."

"You must escape this demon and its impact. If not, you'll go crazy, and you're taking me with you."

"I know you're right, Stella, but demons die hard."

"Then let's talk. You can't slay a dragon if you don't lift a sword."

"I know."

"And you can't relegate a demon to hell if you don't confront it."

"I know already."

"You've got to deal with your issue. It affects us, not just you."

"Stop!"

"You're a changed man, Sam, and not for the better."

Sam whispers, "I'll discuss this when I can. I promise."

Stella turns forceful. Her voice trembles. "Why won't you let me help you? I'm your wife, an ally, not the enemy."

"Stella, bear with me. I'll be okay in time. For now, please, hug me and wait for my cleansing."

CHAPTER 12

Next

Dr. Nowiski, at the door to preop, spots Gino and his throng and moves there briskly. Calm but focused, the doctor acts as Gino expects based on Julia's first surgery.

The friendly man across the room departs. Gino watches him out. So do others, all of whom whisper among themselves once the pale man is gone.

The doctor drops to his knees amid Gino's group for privacy in the partially filled waiting room. Family and friends gather around, anxious to hear about Julia. Dr. Nowiski scoots closer, careful to honor personal space. Strained faces reveal the enormous cost of his delay.

Dr. Nowiski speaks matter-of-factly. "Mrs. Cavatelli's surgery went as expected. Once in the operating room, we…"

This message moves Gino. *I expect this kind of detail from Dr. Nowiski. A lauded neurosurgeon, he has a remarkable ability to communicate medical information in layman's terms, a trait patients and families like most about him.*

"All was well until staff extubated, or removed, her breathing tube…"

Gino's mind races. Until—*such a simple yet powerful word. It often precedes disaster. Whatever Dr. Nowiski says next supersedes what he said before* until. *I'm not ready for next.*

Dr. Nowiski's eyes meet Gino's. "For some reason, your wife had a seizure…"

Gino's emotions flurry. Seizure *replaces until as the day's cruelest word. From the nurse's, 'Your wife tolerated surgery well,' and, 'There weren't any complications,' to the doctor's, 'For some reason, your wife had a seizure.' How Julia must have thrashed throughout her seizure. My mind's eye breaks my heart. I must be more sensitive to her pain—if she survives. My world feels upside-down.*

His thoughts turn dark—his expression crazed. Images of a family in grief, not his, replace thoughts of Julia. *You and your family will grieve when I finish with you, you irresponsible monster. You caused this, and I'll find you if it's the last thing I do. You'll answer for the accident. God strike me dead if I fail.*

Dr. Nowiski continues. "She was fighting a losing battle on her own…"

Gino's eyes throb. *She was fighting a losing battle, and now my fight begins. I'll cause you as much misery as you've caused us. You're unworthy of life as you know it.*

"A nearby anesthesiologist reinserted her breathing tube and manually pumped air into her lungs. She continued until staff got your wife back on a ventilator."

Gino imagines other images. *I remember Dad on a ventilator after his quadruple bypass surgery. Although alive, he looked dead. I'm not sure I can handle Julia on this machine or what Dr. Nowiski says next.*

"The anesthesiologist also injected a drug to correct your wife's spiked blood pressure. A nurse found me, and I returned to monitor activities."

Gino's heart races and mind jumps again. *My blood pressure soars with this news. The only medicine for me is payback. I'll find you and even the score. Being Italian, I know well how payback works. A biblical principle—an eye for an eye and a tooth for a tooth—justifies my intended actions.*

"Her blood pressure stabilized within minutes. And because we pumped air into her lungs, her seizure slowed—then stopped. I wasn't here sooner because I waited for her to stabilize before I left her side."

Dr. Nowiski looks at Gino with a question. "Mrs. Cavatelli's medical records don't reflect prior seizures. Are they accurate from what you know?"

"Yes. Julia's never had a seizure in the forty-one years I've known her. Nor has she ever mentioned seizures before."

Dr. Nowiski frowns and pauses. Careful with his words, he presents theories for Julia's seizure. He believes she had a rogue epi-sode without particular cause. He expects a brain scan to confirm his belief or pinpoint a specific cause.

"We need a CT scan to determine a few facts. First, we want clinical proof your wife's seizure ended. If not, we'll follow a different treatment protocol."

"You'll scan her tonight?"

"Yes. Your wife might be there as we speak."

"I'm sorry, I interrupted."

"No, you're fine. I want you to understand, so ask whatever questions you have."

"Thanks, Doctor."

"Sure. The scan also enables us to determine if Mrs. Cavatelli had prior seizures. If she has, it could explain this one, and it clarifies future medication needs to prevent another.

"Finally, I want to see if she suffered brain damage because of oxygen deprivation. If so, she'll undergo different treatment, and her overall recovery will take longer."

Gino stares trance-like.

Dr. Nowiski scans the group. "Questions?" Blank faces greet him.

"No matter the scan results, Mrs. Cavatelli will spend time in our intensive care unit (ICU) on a ventilator for at least the first night."

Julia's sister-in-law buries her face in a handkerchief. It fails to muffle her sobs.

"I know it's scary to see a loved one on this machine, but in our case, it enables us to monitor her without voluntary brain activity. We need this for accuracy. Anything else?" The doctor checks every-one eye to eye for reactions.

"Mr. Cavatelli, I'll see you when nurses settle your wife in the ICU."

Gino sits in a daze: *How did this happen? How did we go from thumbs-up all is well ninety minutes ago to double thumbs-down all is iffy now? From successful repair of her back to their need to check her brain? What if it's damaged? What will I do? What can I do?*

"Dad, did you hear the doctor?"

"I'm sorry. Yes, Dr. Nowiski said Mom goes to intensive care, and he'll see us again. Sorry, Dr. Nowiski."

"Don't be. This situation creates loads of uncertainty and stress."

The doctor rises from his knees, and Gino falls to his—emotionally. He gathers himself the best possible. "Thank you, Doctor. I appreciate all you're doing for us."

"I feel terrible we had post-op problems after the mechanical part of surgery went flawlessly."

"It's hard to fathom and accept, and we'll wait to see what comes next."

✝ ✝ ✝

Gino looks into his children's eyes. They scream, "Lead us, Pops." His world shattered, he needs resilience like his father had for him. Otherwise, he will disserve the man who modeled strength for over sixty years.

Despite best efforts, Gino's thoughts drift from Angela's and Dominic's needs. His hatred for the other driver overpowers his love for his children at their critical hour of need. While emotionally conflicted, there was little doubt this evening bodes crucial to their future.

✝ ✝ ✝

Visitors leave as afternoon turns to evening. To project an upbeat mood, they predict positive scan results and Julia's full recovery. Gino's embrace with each demonstrates how he appreciates their support. Although their comments were more duty driven than offered in belief, they comfort Gino. They did not neutralize his undercurrent of hatred for the other driver, however. He could not hide or escape this emotion.

His mind drifts to dark places again. *What are you up to right now, you scumbag? Maybe in a snuggle with your wife? Getting ready for your comfy bed? Whatever, it's better than here. No, this isn't right. I must move my plan from strategy to execution. But for now, my children and I must wait for what comes next. It's what we've done all day.*

CHAPTER 13

Alone

Sam Ellis laces his boots and steps out to the porch of his shared cabin in the Village of Lake Louise. The community sits nine and one-half miles from Moraine Lake. This turquoise beauty, Moraine, nestles in the Valley of the Ten Peaks, so named for the mountains that form the valley.

A fog curtain graces the valley, and nearby mountain peaks appear to float in the sky. Steam rises from Sam Ellis's coffee cup as he views the beauty in disbelief. Although he often travels here with friends to hike and for fellowship, each time offers astonishment as if a first-time visitor.

Today's view leaves Sam Ellis awestruck and breathless. The vista invites solitude and inspires deep thought. He finds this day perfect for a challenging hike.

Sam Ellis and his buddies respect the dangers of their sport. As seasoned hikers, they mostly trek as a group, or at least in pairs. A few cerebral types, however, venture solo for private time with nature.

Today, Sam Ellis plans to test the limit of his talents in the mountains. His pals fear for his safety but fail to convince him to scrap his high-risk hike. But Ellis's confidence borders on arrogance at times, a trait gained as a highway patrolman. This characteristic often clouds how he thinks and counteracts logic.

Inspired, he readies to freelance hike off regular trails at Moraine Lake. Potentially dangerous, Ellis trusts his ability to detect and react to dangers. Judgment errors on this outing, however, might put his life at risk.

† † †

Their coffee consumed, all men prepare to hike. As requested, Sam Ellis's best friend, Roberto Rozelle, talks with him again about his plans.

"All set for your hike, Sam?"

"Ready as ever."

"So no way to talk you out of this, huh?"

"Nope. Why?"

"Safety concerns. You misjudge the risks."

"Always a worrywart."

"No, realistic concern."

"I know."

"How do you plan to skirt the six people minimum rule at Moraine?"

Sam's smile suggests he has a plan. "I'll horn in on a group at the trailhead to Sentinel Pass. When the masses fork right to Sentinel, I'll go left to Eifel Lake Wenkchemna Pass. If members of my original group head my way, I'll hang with them, then slip away on my own."

"But the minimum exists to guard against bear attacks. Bears seldom bother groups but don't fear singles."

"Look, relax. You and I live with danger daily and survive. If I'm to die the meal of a grizzly bear, so be it—I accept my fate."

"I beg you, Sam, reconsider. We train others not to face unknown dangers alone."

"Chill, Roberto—honestly."

"Be real with yourself. Potential risks outweigh possible rewards, and you know it."

"Real with myself? You mean?"

"You know."

"No. I don't." Sam shows his first sign of anger. "But I look forward to my time alone even more."

"Hang out on the porch here if you want time alone. No need to traipse into the untamed wilderness. Heck, I find solitude on the toilet."

"I love your tenacity, but don't worry. You know I avoid undue risks."

"I know no danger exists that you consider excessive. And why are you so confident?"

"Listen to me, Rob. Despite John Glenn's fear of the unknown and risk, he still orbited the earth."

"True."

"Did fear stop Neil Armstrong from his venture out the Lunar Module to take man's first steps on the moon?"

"No."

Sam's right arm sweeps across the expanse. "I want different from these mountains today. To only do the routine fails to satisfy man's spirit of adventure."

"But—"

"Since our first trip here, I set a goal to hike off the beaten path into the Valley of the Ten Peaks."

"Why? What do you hope to find there different from trails here?"

"I remember Walter Wilcox's words from 1894."

"Who?"

"Walter Wilcox, the first person to see Moraine Lake and the Valley of the Ten Peaks."

"You heard him speak?"

"Funny."

"So what did he say?"

"I quote, *'No scene has ever given me an equal impression of inspiring solitude and rugged grandeur.'*

"I want to experience what Wilcox saw over a hundred years ago. Make sense?"

Roberto resigns to defeat. "At least let me join you?"

"Thanks, but, no, thanks. I want my own Walter Wilcox moment."

Sam cinches his gloves and moves to his rented ATV. He mounts and settles into its seat.

"Come on, join us for a hike here."

Friends chime in with supportive comments.

Sam fires up his ATV. "Guys, please relax. Enjoy your time with nature, and let me enjoy mine." He shifts into first gear, releases the clutch, and rolls from the cabin slowly. Sam yells as he pulls away. "Enjoy your hike, boys."

Within seconds, Sam Ellis disappears into the woods on his way to Moraine Lake. His date with destiny awaits.

The mountain rumbles.

† † †

Sam Ellis parks his ATV at Moraine Lake's Lodge. He stares across the lake with reverence. Winds whisper his name. The view consumes him.

He pops a piece of beef jerky and walks to the Sentinel hike trailhead. As other hikers assemble, he kneels and rubs a clump of driftwood worn smooth by years of lapping water. He inhales mountain freshness, which stimulates his senses. *Walter Wilcox was right.*

Every hiker makes last-minute adjustments to their gear. Sam Ellis cinches his backpack straps for comfort. At the designated leader's command, the group sets out for Sentinel Pass.

In forty minutes, the hikers reach the trail's fork, 1,200 feet above the trailhead. Sam Ellis's luck, everyone goes right. He follows them but slips away alone barely fifty yards after their turn. He heads off-trail into the woods on his way to the top of the tree line.

One hour later, Sam Ellis stops to appreciate the mountains, which create this incredible valley. Sheer cliffs reach skyward to staggering heights. He believes few before ever observed the valley from his vantage point. More rugged than most terrain, his course strikes him as unfit for hikers faint of heart or weak of leg.

His endurance tested, he needs rest.

Sam Ellis finds a suitable area and stops for water and renewal. At an additional eight-hundred-feet altitude, thin oxygen prompts longer rests. He has no idea, however, that he sits at the worst possible place at the most horrible possible time.

A flat rock beckons him. He opens his canteen. After a swish to cleanse his mouth, he gulps enough to satisfy his thirst but not sour his stomach. He bends his head back onto his shoulders and studies the sky. Large clouds look as if painted by a master artist. They dance with the wind and present a new scene every few seconds. Although alone, he deems his date with nature a spiritual success.

After several minutes of heavenly bliss, a deep rumble unnerves Sam Ellis. Fear grows. He looks up, unaware a sheet of shale readies to crash toward him in a matter of seconds.

† † †

Sam's buddies end their hike shortly after 2:00 p.m. They rest in the comforts of their cozy cabin. Sub sandwiches and worry head-lined their lunch menu. They decompress, unaware of Sam's location or status. Their hunger curbs the more they fret over Sam.

Roberto wishes he had confronted Sam harder about his hike. He shoulders responsibility for his friend's well-being. Hopeless and helpless, Roberto endures much stress. He calls Sam on his satellite phone. Someone answers, but he only hears static.

"Sam, this is Roberto. Do you read me? Come back, over. "Sam, this is Roberto at base camp. Do you read me?" Unintelligible garble mixes with static.

"I did not read your last transmission, over."
More noise.
"This is Roberto, Sam. Come back if you hear me."
Silence follows an odd clank.
"Sam!"

† † †

With a thunderous rumble, the shale plate breaks from the craggy rock face above Sam Ellis. It crumbles and builds momentum as the rubble slides downhill. The rocks gain momentum and will overwhelm him in seconds.

Sam Ellis springs up and sprints toward a potential haven from rock fragments. His satellite phone thumps against his thigh as arms pump to quicken his legs. The phone loosens from its case and bounces uninterrupted downhill until it clanks off a boulder.

Massive chunks of rock gouge the earth on their downhill path. The softer material above the tree line sloughs off to join the tonnage of rock headed toward Sam Ellis. He looks up. The slide gains force and energy with each downward foot. He prays he has time to lunge down and to his right toward the trees.

Before his desperate dive, a massive chunk of shale explodes into smaller pieces above his head. The energy blast hurls him several yards. Rock pieces whiz past him as he tumbles downslope. Miraculously, none hit him.

The mighty landslide shatters trees like toothpicks. One stately tree, however, survives the slide. Sam Ellis's left tibia strikes the tree's massive trunk. It snaps midway between his ankle and knee. He whips around the trunk, and momentum casts his body several feet.

The gruesome sound of cracked bone, intense pain, and immediate nausea signal he suffered serious injury—the extent unclear.

Now eerily quiet, Sam Ellis lays motionless as the dust settles. Only shifting rocks, branches, and dirt disturb the silence. He flinches and feels more at risk with each sound.

Sam Ellis's broken leg throbs in ways not meant for man to endure. His tibia, which protrudes through his skin, reveals the seriousness of his condition. Isolation and the vastness of his surroundings compound his problems. He considers what hurts more—his fractured leg or broken spirits.

Below him, endless yards of broken shale and shattered trees lie under a plume of ash and dust. He trembles in pain. Majesty turned into tragedy, but he might live if found soon enough. If not, he might die before day's end. Sam Ellis ignored his best friend's warnings and now lays alone, likely to bleed to death. Roberto's words echo in his head. *"I beg you, Sam, reconsider!"*

Sam Ellis's thoughts shift to survival. He rocks involuntary and thinks of his past. *Would Eagle Scout skills I criticized as geeky twenty years ago save my life today?*

Pain rips through his body and draws him back to the present. Answers to questions about his past mean little to his ability to survive today, which might be his last.

He squirms and struggles to find comfort—likely elusive until discovered or when the grim reaper takes him away. He cinches his belt around his leg to improve his odds. He bleeds only slightly less.

† † †

An hour since his tumble, Sam Ellis cannot reach his friends or do much to help himself. But in the open, he must move. The mountains' wild beasts would doubtless find his body tasty if found. He knows they can transform a human into a pile of picked-over bones in seconds.

He looks skyward and prays not to end up *their* prey if left to endure a painful night alone.

† † †

Roberto's heart aches. Although in the company of his buddies, he sits alone in despair. He failed to talk Sam out of his solo hike. And now his friend remains somewhere, perhaps lost, in beautiful yet rugged mountains.

Under Roberto's direction, searchers study area maps. His thoughts drift, which requires his buddies to draw him back to their task. Refocused, he shares what he knows of Sam's intentions.

Despite little to work with, they finalize a search strategy and set out to find their buddy. They pray against long odds to locate him soon and safe. They fear his fate alone in the forest if they fail. Time, their enemy, ticks on.

† † †

Sam Ellis's pain intensifies—now unbearable. Even alone, he fights the urge to cry. Others cannot know he showed normal human behavior and cried over pain. He finds weeping under any circumstance a weakness. When darkness protects him in his bedroom, however, he often weeps over those he harmed. Today, he reserves his tears for later. He looks for cover for the night, which he needs fast.

Dusk approaches.

He spots a small rockslide-created overhang above and to his right. *If I get there, this outcropping offers protection from the elements and predators.*

He faces one significant hurdle, however—how to move there. He only has one way.

Sam Ellis shifts his body onto his right side one inch at a time. Intense pain greets his slightest movement. With a grimace, he returns his tensed body to his original position. *I might not be up to the task.*

Minutes later, his laughter echoes around him. *As a grown man, I can't crawl—a skill learned as an infant.*

His hysteria short-lived, he concentrates on his need. With every ounce of strength and courage, Sam Ellis moves slightly more onto his right side. His temples pulsate with pain. He bites his lower lip, and with a lion's roar and a gutsy motion, he rocks onto his side. His broken left leg rests on his right. His tibia juts skyward.

In more intense pain than ever before, Sam Ellis lays ready to scoot to safety. He scours the area for other options but finds none. He must do whatever necessary to reach the overhang.

With renewed stamina and softer pain after biting down on a twig, Sam Ellis plans his route. Sadly, rocks eliminate a straight line to the overhang. He must make a small half loop around the barriers, but even a tiny increase in distance potentially creates significant problems.

He slithers time and again, with short pauses between to regain strength. He fights the urge to quit after each movement. He grits down on the twig and bellows a tearful grunt with his next thrust. And then the following over and over again. He drags his broken body inch by inch toward the overhang—his only chance for survival.

† † †

Searchers comb the Valley of the Ten Peaks, no one deep enough, however, to find Sam Ellis. Everyone carries a satellite phone, all of which remain silent due to a lack of clues. Their optimism wanes as sunlight fades.

"Sam, this is Roberto. Come in, please. Sam, come in if you hear me. Come in, buddy."

He receives no response.

As the sun lowers, Roberto directs searchers to return to their cabin. Each begins his long trek back.

†††

Sam Ellis slouches under the overhang. He looks around and still questions his safety. *This overhang protects me, but alone, is it enough? Is this ledge stable or destined to crash on me? Now here, how do I keep warm? Nightfall arrives soon.*

†††

Searchers debrief and finalize plans for the morning. Roberto, upbeat outwardly, labors inwardly because of the absence of clues today. Not a candy wrapper. Not a broken branch caused by man. Not even a human footprint. They found no reason for hope.

One searcher talks of an encounter with a hiker. Like Sam, the man wandered from the crowds alone. His physique and complex-ion made him look hardly fit enough to hike anywhere, let alone Canada's rugged Rockies. When asked if he saw other hikers, the man never responded. The searcher, who looked back several times, left the man without further interruption.

The exhausted searchers agree to regroup early the next morning to launch day two's search. They worry. They should.

†††

Julia lies in recovery. Nurses hover near to ensure her well-being. An endotracheal tube juts from her mouth. Tape secures the tube to its holder. Straps hold everything in place.

A ventilator huffs and puffs a cyclical flow of life-sustaining air. Nurses talk, hardened to the rhythmic drone.

Gino, Angela, and Dominic remain in the waiting room. They only break their silence with random questions. In the absence of answers, Gino cautions against speculation, a warning he fails to obey. So they sit and wait, although together, each one alone.

† † †

Sam Ellis's friends discuss the day as their late supper nears ready. Searchers rest tired bones and sore feet while others pace well-worn floors. Everyone processes next steps to find their friend.

Lit candles flicker rustic reminders of why they visit here each year. But their friend's empty chair at their table casts a pall on supper.

† † †

Stella Ellis sits alone on her sofa. Typical these days, sadness spills from her soul. She feels the same on Sam's workdays, when he pals around with buddies, or when home and isolated.

Tonight, she passes the time with a gorgeous photography book on Banff National Park. The book's descriptions and pictures enthrall her. *No wonder Sam goes there each year. The beautiful surroundings exceed spectacular.*

She thinks about her husband's activities today—where he hiked and the wonders he saw. She envisions her clean-shaven patrolman husband in uniform. Her image shifts to Sam as a rugged mountain man with a scruffy four-day beard. She imagines his mustiness, which she finds oddly sexy. She squirms with thoughts of Sam busting through the door to sweep her off to their bedroom. Dismissed quickly, she faces three more days before her sexy mountain man returns.

Back to her book, Stella Ellis enjoys each page's beauty. *I hope Sam remembered his camera.*

Most of all, Stella hopes Sam enjoys himself and unwinds from the rigors of his job. She prays renewal also helps resolve his night-mares. She has no idea he sits helplessly under an outcropping.

Sam Ellis, like the other people he affected, sits in a different part of the world miserably alone.

CHAPTER 14

Salvation

S tress smothers Sam Ellis as he prepares for the worst. He wrestles his backpack and removes some provisions. *A match. Fire protects and warms if I gather dried leaves, twigs, and small branches. But how—with my bone out of my leg. It throbs even when still.*

He wraps in his rain jacket. *Not as warm as a fire, but this beats no warmth at all. I might freeze overnight, but I'll warm up enough to fall asleep before I die.*

He looks at his tiny snack bags. *Not meat and potatoes, but trail mix and granola beat starvation. I must ration to survive. Then again, nutrients might not matter if I bleed to death because of this lousy tourniquet.*

He leans back, his eyes shut. Like those in a hospital waiting room, he has no option but to wait.

☦ ☦ ☦

As darkness covers the forest, Sam Ellis's eyes droop heavy with sleep. He fights to stay awake. *If eaten alive, I want to see the beast whose hunger I satisfy.*

He chuckles at the notion but understands the possibility.

Despite the sharp pain, he shifts to his opposite butt cheek for comfort. Usually comfortable in rugged environments, Sam Ellis longs for cushiness. *I'd give my left leg to lie on the foam mattress in the back of my SUV.*

A gentle breeze whistles through darkened trees. Atop a hammock, Sam Ellis might find the sound a serene source of calm. But little satisfies tonight, and his silent cries of pain destroy any chance for serenity. He nibbles the end of his right pinkie finger: *Perhaps meditation helps.*

Sam Ellis forms circles with both thumbs and index fingers. He raises his arms overhead.

"Om…"

After several minutes, he gives up. He shuts his eyes and creates images to mask his reality. *Ah, Tahiti.*

A sound interrupts his meditation. He squints and uses the full moon's light to identify the sound's source.

His spirits rise. "Who is it? Who's out there? If you seek a lost hiker, I'm here—Sam Ellis—under the overhang. Over here! Follow my voice."

The sound continues—louder, but still a mystery.

"I'm over here. Follow my voice. Please!"

A faint light bounces low among the trees. Sam Ellis scolds his heart as it beats out of control. He curses his eyes because they fail him more each year. He berates procrastination tendencies since he neglected to pick up his new glasses before he left. With new specks, he might better see who or what approaches.

The unusual sound continues, and the light shines brighter—as if nearer.

"I know you're out there. I see your light. Show yourself. I'm over here. I have a gun, so don't sneak up. I'll shoot."

He shakes his head. *Maybe my mind tricks me, and I'll go crazy before I die. Maybe I'm at the beginning of my end.*

He moves his pistol from backpack to under his healthy leg.

"Over here, I say again. Hurry! Continue this way. I'm here. Show yourself, or I'll shoot. I warn you, I'll shoot, and I have a killer aim. I earned medals for marksmanship, so don't test me. I'll pass."

The light dances between the trees and shines closer. Sam Ellis's emotions bounce between fear and joy. His rescue at hand, a man's image appears in the distance, silhouetted in fading light.

The man calls out from afar. "Sam Ellis."

He rocks on his butt. *Am I already dead?*

The voice sounds supernatural and calms Sam Ellis. Peace overpowers anxiety, which scares him more than his broken leg or the stranger's presence.

"Yes, over here. Are you here to rescue me?"

Sam Ellis grips his pistol under his thigh as the man approaches. Now only lit by moonlight, he presumes the man turned off his flashlight.

Now face-to-face, the stranger speaks again. "Sam Ellis, my name is I. M. Travis, but people call me Travis. You may do likewise."

Sam Ellis grimaces through a slight wiggle to sits more upright. "It's nice to meet you, Travis. You've made my night, man."

"Oh?"

"Yeah, I want to leave. I've laid up here several hours and feared a bear or mountain lion might devour me before searchers arrived."

Travis smiles. "And I am happy to see you, again, Sam Ellis."

"Again? What do you mean?"

"It is good I found you."

"Sure is. I worried."

"I know."

"What?"

"I am here now."

"Too bad you didn't find me sooner."

"It was not time."

"What?"

"All trials have a right time. Yours is now."

"What do you mean with all this mumbo-jumbo?"

"It is deep."

"I'm not into deep right now. I need relief."

"I will help."

"Thank God."

"Indeed."

"You better notify other searchers you found me?"

"Yes, when I leave you."

"Leave me? Give me a break. You found me only to leave me here?"

Travis looks at Sam Ellis's leg. "You seem to have a break already, Sam Ellis."

"Funny."

"Unintended."

"Do others still search for me?"

"They sleep now."

"I guess. It's late."

"Late, but never too late, Sam Ellis."

"What?"

"This area is hard to search in daylight, impossible at night."

Sam Ellis feels agitated. "I imagine so. You never answered why you said, 'Nice to see you again.'"

"You fell hard. Tell me your story?"

Sam Ellis lowers his head in reverence. "Yes, brutal, and, thank God, I survived. I heard like an explosion overhead while I rested above the tree line. I didn't know how or where to escape. I felt doomed."

Travis's eyes captive Sam Ellis and suggest he continue.

"After the loud crack, a large sheet of shale started a massive landslide. The huge rock disintegrated into pieces. Thank God, all smaller pieces flew over my head."

Travis nods.

"Sometimes I'm not too smart."

Travis's eyebrows arc on his light-colored face.

"I do crazy stuff I shouldn't, like this hike. But with you here, I'll apparently get away with it."

"To become old and wise, Sam Ellis, you must first overcome youthful stupidity."

"What?"

"Mistakes happen, whether or not a result of foolishness."

"Yeah, well, in this case, call me S-squared—Stupid Sam."

"Catchy and fitting."

"Well, I'm often my worst enemy. Today's one of those days."

"You say you got away with it. Do you believe people get away with their actions?"

The comment causes Sam Ellis to question *Do I get away with my actions? Did I do it again? Did I commit a stupid act and escape with my life? Maybe I shouldn't be here now. Have I been delivered again? Am I the beneficiary of earthly salvation?*

"I can't answer your question, but I've had two close calls. I believe this one penalized me for the first. And I survived both, at least so far."

"You were meant to survive, Sam Ellis?"

"You seem to imply I experienced both events for mystical reasons?"

"I do not imply, and reasons are not mystical, but they exist. You will learn yours in time."

The moonlight catches Travis's silvery-blue eyes. They eerily comfort Sam Ellis.

Sam Ellis adjusts his broken leg to ease his pain. "My leg kills me, man."

"Yes, you suffered a terrible injury, Sam Ellis."

"It hurts like the devil. You use my name a lot. How do you know my name?"

"Your words say more than you realize. The devil causes many to hurt."

Sam Ellis scowls. "You missed what I mean."

"Not at all."

"Whatever. All I know is I need help for my pain."

"The good news, Sam Ellis—your pain subsides soon, and a doctor repairs your leg tomorrow."

"Don't you have the sequence backward? Won't my leg be fixed before my pain improves?"

"Yes, for most."

"What do you mean?

"Have faith and trust, Sam Ellis."

"Trust is overrated."

"Only for those who lack knowledge."

"Will you take me from here tonight, or what? And what do you mean you're happy to see me again, and how do you know my name?"

"Sometimes one simply knows what he knows." Travis stares at Sam Ellis as if exceptionally knowledgeable.

"Huh. Yeah, like whatever that means."

"It means sometimes a person knows information that surprises others."

"Give me an example."

"I know you live in Phoenix, Arizona. You married Stella and have one child—Wendy. You graduated high school from Apollo in 1996. You studied criminal justice at Glendale Community College. You work for DPS as a highway patrolman. You possess great integrity, and you commit sincerely to your family and employer. You fear you failed both."

Sam Ellis withdraws slightly and moves his hand lower on his right thigh. Travis looks at Sam Ellis's hand, then back to his con-fused face. "You're not a nutjob ready to disembody me and eat my insides, are you? That was creepy, man."

"No, I am not. I am a servant here to help you."

"Servant of who?"

"I believe you mean whom, Sam Ellis—servant of whom."

"So I'm shaken with my English off a bit." Sam Ellis fails to appreciate the English lesson. "My words don't change the fact I'd like to know who you serve."

Travis nods toward Sam Ellis. "Right now, I serve you. I am here to help resolve this mess. By all accounts, you need assistance."

"That's great, but who are you, and how do you know so much about me? How'd you learn my location, and what do you want?"

"As I said, my name is Travis. You might not have seen me on November 8, 2011, but I saw you. You caused a mishap in your SUV. Many cars suffered damage, as did their drivers."

Sam Ellis leans away from Travis as far as possible. He grimaces. "You've taken this from creepy to scary. You—you freak me out. I don't know what you want."

"Our encounter is not about my wants, Sam Ellis, but about your needs."

"Like what? What do you think I need?"

"You need to know you will survive tonight uneaten by forest creatures. You need confidence searchers will find you soon enough to save your life and leg. And you need assurance your guilt ultimately passes."

"My guilt?"

"You cannot handle these weighty issues alone—thus I arrived to comfort and assure you, in time, matters resolve as you wish."

"And I should believe this because?"

Travis relaxes his face. Moonlight glistens off his eyes. "Because I commit to the truth. It is all I know—all I will ever say to you and others."

Sam Ellis grows cocky. "Oh, I get it. You're a religious whack job."

Travis's tone turns serious. "I am not as you say. No one ever suggested this of me. People express relief when I arrive to help. They offer respect. Perhaps they fear my departure as fast as my arrival if they do otherwise. But you, Sam Ellis, you choose mockery over gratitude—an unfortunate trait. Even so, I offer peace and comfort, if you allow."

"Allow?" Sam Ellis's voice echoes in the darkness. "What are my choices? I'm busted up and unable to move. You're fit as a fiddle, sort of, at least. Still, you can do whatever you want to me. I'm in no condition to stop you. Where's the comfort there?"

"One always has choices, Sam Ellis, like the night of your accident. Sometimes you choose right. Other times wrong. Tonight you opt for comfort or misery."

Sam Ellis lowers and scratches the back of his head with both hands, frustrated.

"I know you ache, troubled by your role in the crash. You bear guilt over your actions and suffer restless nights. You repent and desire forgiveness, although you do little to seek it. You fear how your boss and Stella will react when they learn details of the wreck. And I know your concerns alone in these mountains. Your choice tonight is to enable comfort and safety, or not. Say the word, and I leave, and you can join James Elder."

Sam Ellis freezes. *This guy knows about my friendship with James Elder and the fact he died.*

He plays dumb. "James Elder?"

"Yes, a recent person to reject my help."

"Yeah, and what happened to him?"

"He died."

"Died?"

"Yes, and your games over this inquiry does not flatter you."

Sam Ellis grows uncomfortable. "Will I die if I reject your help?"

"Yes."

"How do you know?"

"As I said, Sam Ellis, your choice."

Sam Ellis reels, more confused than ever. "How do you know about my accident? And how do you know what I did, or how I felt?"

"I was there."

"Where?"

"At your accident."

"Were you involved?"

"Not in a vehicle, but to comfort a lady, much like I desire for you."

"What lady?"

"A driver."

"Did you help in an official capacity?"

"Yes."

"For whom—that's proper English, right?"

Travis grins. "Yes, but my capacity remains a mystery to you."

"Did you see the accident?"

"Yes, and all that you did after."

"So you *were* there?"

"Upon impact."

"What do you mean? You make no sense."

"I am sure not, Sam Ellis. You cannot understand now. Believe I know."

"You might know what happened, but you couldn't have known how I felt then or how I feel now."

"Why not tell me about the accident."

"Why should I?"

Silent, Travis stares into Sam Ellis's eyes and smiles broadly.

As if compelled, Sam Ellis begins to summarize his accident. "I set out for San Diego. My wife and daughter went there earlier. I grabbed a burger and fries to go." Sam Ellis collects himself and considers his words.

"Continue, Sam Ellis."

"I got back on I-10 at 107th Avenue. Many cars exited at Avondale, which clogged the exit lane. Huh. I'd have merged left were I not busy with my burger. I knew not to eat until better settled on the freeway, but…I didn't. And lettuce and stuff spilled on my lap and who-knows-where-else. I lost concentration."

"Yes, one must concentrate while they drive, Sam Ellis?"

"Obviously—that's common sense."

"Might *sense* not be common at all?"

"What do you mean?"

"People would not need to remind others to use *sense* if it was common."

"A cool concept, I guess."

"More than a concept. It is the truth. Please continue."

"I knew mine was an exit only lane. Why wouldn't I know? I'm a highway patrolman." Sam swallows hard and shakes his head in sadness and disgust.

"When I lifted my eyes after I unwrapped my burger, I saw a line of cars, their brake lights aglow. Then I…then I made a sharp tug left on the steering wheel. Not able to stop, and with no room on the right, I took a chance and moved left."

Sam Ellis pauses; ugly accident details fill his memory.

"Please, continue."

"I failed to look left before I changed lanes. I sideswiped a sports car in my blind spot, which forced it left into another lane. I saw no other option."

He sighs in substantial pain.

"I first thought to stop, but that message never made it from my brain to right leg. Instead, I…ah, I floored my SUV. I checked my rearview mirror and saw residual smoke, a car in the air, and unimaginable chaos—a scene beyond horrible."

Travis's face shows compassion. "I know. Continue."

"I threw my burger on my passenger seat. Guess I didn't care this time about the mess I'd make. I slammed my fist on the steering wheel."

He looks down and raises his left hand to his mouth. His index finger rests across his lips, his thumb below his chin. His eyes hint of tears.

"I wish I broke the steering wheel. I'd have stopped if I had. If only—"

"But you did not."

"No. I did not."

"Continue."

"Once past the 303 freeway, I slowed so not to attract attention. I thought to stop and check my SUV but didn't. Nothing pulled or rubbed, so it seemed safe to drive."

He looks at Travis as if finished.

"You have more, don't you, Sam Ellis?"

"Sadly, yes."

"Please."

"I drove to Yuma and stopped. I stressed so much I'm surprised I made it that far. The tension shattered my soul, and knots gripped my gut."

Like a neurological tic, Sam Ellis's head jerks, his eyes more mournful.

"I phoned my wife, Stella and told her I stopped because I got tired. She acted surprised. I've made the coast trip often after work and never stopped before. I don't think she bought my story."

Travis nods affirmatively.

"Next morning, I found a body shop run by a guy named Bear. I'm sure it's a nickname."

"Likely."

"So I left my SUV there, got a rental car, and went to San Diego."

"Yes."

"Once there, I lied to Stella again about our SUV—that it broke down near Yuma. I told her my story the night before was to minimize worry. I wasn't about to tell her about the accident."

"And?"

"Those lies launched a series of lies I told Stella. She's...she's my wife." Disgust covers his face. "I lied to myself too. I convinced myself I had no choice in my actions during and after the collision—that everyone was okay despite the mangled cars. Inside, I knew better."

Sam Ellis's lips button inward. He rubs his fingers up and down his forehead. Travis touches his shoulder. Sam Ellis looks up and finds care and comfort in Travis's expression.

"I also told myself I didn't need to tell my boss. I knew better but simply didn't do what I should've."

"This ordeal wears on you, Sam Ellis."

"You mean my confession to you?"

"Yes. And the guilt you bear because of your actions."

"I always think about the people I hurt. I'm miserable and not proud of my actions. I even suffer recurring nightmares that I kill myself."

"I know."

"Huh?"

"I am aware of your torment."

"This bothered me so much I made a New Year's resolution to find and apologize to everyone I injured. I pray when I do, I assure my redemption."

"Redemption?"

"Yes, you know salvation from my mistakes, my sins."

"You seek salvation?"

"Yes, from those I harmed."

"Have you asked the great *I Am* for forgiveness?"

"No, why should I?"

"Don't confuse forgiveness given by someone you wronged with forgiveness of sins from God. The first provides satisfaction on earth—the second eternal life."

"You sound knowledgeable."

"You might say, Sam Ellis, but our encounter centers on you, not me. Please continue."

"I don't know, some weeks later, Bear finished my SUV. He found it odd I paid cash for repairs since I have insurance, but I avoided questions triggered by an insurance claim at all costs."

Travis nods aware.

"So here I sit, broken in many ways. The sharp ache in my leg pales compared to my intense heart pain. Man, you can't imagine how I hurt."

"Wrong, Sam Ellis. As I said, I am here to comfort and help relieve your pains. I know your heart aches as much as your leg. Both improve soon. As for yearly declarations, understand a daily devotion beats annual resolutions. The latter helps one do right when inclined to do wrong. With devotions, you have little need for resolutions."

Sam Ellis looks at Travis in awe and disbelief. "You're too much. I don't know you or how you know so much about me. I guess you just do."

"Yes, as I said, Sam Ellis—at times you just know what you know."

"Yeah, I guess."

"See, I said you would get it."

"I get it, okay. But I don't know what I get or what to do with it."

"You will."

"Are you only here to encourage my apology?"

"Let me answer two ways. First, I already stated my purpose. Beyond, and more importantly, I seek to share concepts to guide your life."

"I can't wait."

"I will tell you despite your sarcasm, but learn this: wisdom shows when one without knowledge stays silent."

"I'm sorry. You didn't deserve my comment."

"I sometimes receive undeserved thoughts and remarks, Sam Ellis. But I love despite, as I do you."

"What were you going to say, Travis?"

"Think about this once alone again. The first to apologize is bravest. The first to forgive is strongest. And the first to forget is happiest."

"Yeah, another great adage, but so what?"

"Apologize to everyone you hurt and tell your wife and employer. Next, forgive yourself for your wrongs. You are human. Finally, forget you made those errors. If God forgives and forgets, surely you can likewise. He knows your heart and desire for forgiveness."

Sam Ellis looks uncommitted. "You're inspirational and all, but for now, my leg needs to be healed, not my soul. Can you help my leg?"

"Two points, Sam Ellis. First, blisters on the feet of the shoe-less reveal their commitment to move forward. You, fully shod, sadly appear disinterested in my ability to help you advance. Second, I am not a medical doctor. I am a comforter and healer of hearts."

"But you said my leg would be okay."

"Move it."

"I can't—the pain's too great."

"Move it, Sam Ellis."

He wiggles his leg and beams at Travis. "It feels better." He lifts and moves his leg freely. "Unreal—my pain is tolerable."

"Your leg will be fine, Sam Ellis."

"Will my other pain resolve too?"

"All matters about both accidents turn out fine. You will heal from both."

"But I wasn't hurt in the crash."

"Oh, you were, Sam Ellis. The fact you caused the accident breaks your heart. Fear you hurt others weights heavy on your spirit. And those outcomes shatter your belief you are a proper and valued patrolman."

"How do you know?"

"How matters less than the fact I know. Believe in my help and receive your wishes. And let our time together produce wisdom that changes your life forever."

"Can you tell me precisely how I come out of this accident?"

"Yes, Sam Ellis. You survive tonight. As your leg pain eases further, you gain comfort and rest." He points around Sam Ellis. "These rocks retained heat absorbed throughout the day. You become no colder than now. Hungry animals leave you alone, and rescuers find you early tomorrow morning. Your friends ensure you get medical care for your leg. Together, others fulfill your needs."

Sam Ellis teeters between belief and doubt. "Yeah, well you tell a good story, but I'm screwed if you missed on only one detail."

Travis stares intently. "You must believe, Sam Ellis. Believing is not new to you."

"What do you mean?"

"You believed your union with Stella would enrich your life. It has."

Sam Ellis remembers his wedding day. "Yeah."

"You believed you possessed skills needed of a professional patrolman. You do."

Sam Ellis pictures himself in his uniform. "True."

"And when you left the accident you knew your actions would haunt you. They have."

Sam Ellis silently shudders with visions of his nightmare.

"You see, you previously believed much, so trust what I say now. Uncertainty surrounded your other beliefs. You lack reasons to doubt my words."

Sam Ellis leans his upper body left to peer over Travis's right shoulder. His jaw drops and eyes widen with fear. He leans back to upright.

"What bothers you, Sam Ellis?"

Frozen with terror, he squints and nods upward slightly.

"Don't be alarmed. You face no danger."

Both hear a large animal's guttural growl from behind Travis. Sam Ellis mouths, "There's a mountain lion behind you."

Travis responds aloud, "And he troubles you, Sam Ellis?"

Sam Ellis peeks again to see if played by his imagination. The lion licks his chops and exposes large, sharp teeth. The beast moves two steps toward Travis and stops. Another lick suggests the hungry lion anticipates a meal.

Sam Ellis whispers, "We'll both die if I don't act fast."

The lion continues to assess his prey.

"We need not worry, Sam Ellis. And do not remove your pistol from under your right thigh."

Sam Ellis slowly reaches under his leg. He whispers, "It's our only hope for survival." He grips his .45 caliber pistol. "How'd you know about my gun?"

"Put it away. We do not need weapons. Besides, yours will not fire."

Travis takes two steps to his left. The lion now faces Sam Ellis directly. He pants heavily and bares his teeth with a mighty roar. Sam Ellis tightens his grip on his pistol.

With a sudden leap, the mountain lion lunges toward him. Sam Ellis lifts his weapon and pulls the trigger. His gun misfires.

Midair, the lion nears his target—Sam Ellis's throat. Sam Ellis squeezes his eyes tightly, his face contorts. He senses his death. He braces and awaits the lion's fangs to pierce his neck.

Travis raises his right hand, and with a blinding flash, the lion vanishes—gone, as if never there.

After a few seconds, Sam Ellis peeks out of his right eye. He clutches his chest over his heart, which kettle-drum thumps in his body. Calm consumes his anxiety moments after his eyes meet Travis's.

He sits confused. "What just happened?"

"You needed proof to accept what I told you. Like many, you disbelieve until you see. People who believe without such need experience inexplicable joy. Allow yourself this privilege, Sam Ellis. Do what you must to free yourself. I need not say more for you to comprehend."

Sam Ellis sits in a quiet stupor. At peace, his eyes rapidly blink as if to review this encounter mentally.

"Do not let how you feel scare you, Sam Ellis. The lion was real. So too the sheet of shale I disintegrated above your head. But neither posed a real threat. And your current sensations are typical after such miracles. You witnessed events inconceivable to others."

"How do you again know what I feel?"

"You survive tonight, Sam Ellis. And you heal in the future."

Sam Ellis looks up at Travis. "You know what, I believe you."

"You should. I am committed to truth."

"I'm lucky you shared your wisdom."

"Consider our encounter and all I said a gift, one you cannot repay. The good news, no one will ever seek recovery. Like salvation, today's gifts are free."

Sam Ellis wonders and waits for more. *Why has this happened?*

"Allow another point before I go, Sam Ellis."

"Yeah?"

"Prepare for future events to challenge your calm and peace. In one case, you will face emotional destruction or worse if you lose faith. I urge you—trust, and never doubt again."

"God bless you, Travis."

"I must go now, and help your friends help you. Be courageous, and follow my words."

Sam Ellis reaches his right hand outward. "Please, take me from here—now. I'm not sure it's safe to stay here alone."

"You still disbelieve, Sam Ellis. I am disappointed but understand."

"I wouldn't want an overnight stay here if healthy. Since I'm lame, the thought scares me."

"Sam Ellis, consider these words carefully."

"Yes, of course."

"Courage is not the absence of fear. It is to do what you must in spite of fright. My purpose is not to take you from here. You must stay until others find you. It must be this way."

"Mission accomplished, I guess. Before you leave, may I ask a favor?"

"I do not have a flashlight, Sam Ellis."

"How in heaven's name did you know I'd ask about a flashlight?"

"You chose interesting words."

"But I saw a light bounce among the trees and grow brighter as you neared me. The beam faded once you appeared."

Travis smiles, turns, and walks away. The light reappears.

Sam Ellis yells, "Travis!"

His voice echoes.

In an instant, Travis disappears.

CHAPTER 15

Setup

The call thrills Mark Lyle. As Southwest Scientific's CEO, he under-stands a high-profile project like this strengthens a firm's credibility, helps ensure long-term viability, and provides employee job security. With a contract in hand, he ponders how to ensure project results back up his bravado used to seal the deal.

His client the *Phoenix Evening Herald* hopes to prove or disprove scientifically that I. M. Travis exists. Presently, he only does so anecdotally. The paper intends to publish photos and scientific data on the world-famous enigma. And if he is real, executives expect to establish if he exists a mystery man or, in fact, a miracle maker.

† † †

Mark Lyle endlessly stirs his coffee. His project orientation notes must thoroughly convey the significance of the company's next assignment, the most crucial in Southwest Scientific's history. Success assures worldwide recognition and future high-visibility projects, so he commits to whatever expense needed to ace the job.

Lyle's staff expresses enthusiasm when told of the project. Their *setup* involves the full array of Southwest Scientific's technical tools and most skilled technicians. Never before has the company commit-ted so many resources to a single contract.

Project Manager Shirley Smythe assigns roles and covers logistics. She and Mark Lyle secured a location for this setup off Forest Road 141 on the Mogollon Rim, a summertime playground where Phoenicians and others escape Arizona's summer heat.

The ideal site sits in a secluded clearing with geographic features that naturally limit access. A sheer drop exists to the west. A fall of a hundred feet there means certain death. Almost 90 percent of the remaining perimeter faces steep crescent-shaped cliff faces. Nature's restrictions, therefore, limit entry to the clearing from the east to about twenty-seven feet.

With staff briefed, the company prepares to move from plan preparation to execution.

Travis waits.

† † †

Anticipation mounts.

Shirley Smythe makes eye contact with each person. Her excited staff awaits direction. "All right, gang, it's *go time.* Everyone clear on their assignment?"

Nods follow team member glances at each other. Smythe has never seen employees this giddy.

Her all-business approach earned Shirley Smythe's role as Southwest Scientific's lead project manager. Often direct, her employees always know their position and what she expects on a project. Today proves no exception.

The plan calls for a plant, Adam, to appear severely injured, stranded, and unable to help himself. If believable and I. M. Travis shows, they stand to accomplish a first—capture critical, scientific documentation on Travis's existence. The world awaits.

† † †

Travis leaves for a series of encounters—some deadly and others less so. When expected, he never disappoints. Relative to the setup, many people put much effort into this effort to leave it unfulfilled. Moreover, those who seek to trap him work unaware of dangers they created for one of their own. Travis will use their setup to fulfill his purpose.

† † †

Employees scurry to their stations. After time enough for every-one to reach their destination, Shirley Smythe conducts final tech checks.

"Let's start with Adam. Give me a mic check."

"Testing three, two, one." Adam's voice is loud and static-free through a radio mic, which tucks hidden in his flannel shirt. He slumps against a fake boulder. A sizeable artificial branch rests on his torso. He simulates an injured and helpless camper stranded outside his tent.

Smythe's control technician responds, "Copy. I read you loud and clear."

The EVP recorder operator follows. "Testing one, two, three."

"Adjust your mic, EVP."

He fiddles with the mic on its tripod to ensure optimal clarity.

"Testing, testing. Any better?"

"Ten-four, EVP, loud and clear."

High atop a camera blind built by coworkers, Amanda, a full-spectrum thermal camera operator replies, "Testing one, two, three. Testing. Testing."

"Solid, Amanda."

The EMF meter and Zoom H1 Recorder operator tests next. "Setup test: five, four, three, two, one."

"Creative H1. Read you well."

"Everyone sounds good." Shirley's broadcast mic off, she turns to her control technician. "You ready?"

"Ten-four, our gear registers correctly."

Shirley nods approval. Adam seeks clarity. "Alert when I *go dark*."

"Ten-four, we go live shortly."

Shirley Smythe announces over her loudspeaker, "All nonessential personnel return to the command post. We begin to monitor in five minutes on my count, which starts…now."

People scramble like ants after crumbs at a picnic. Within minutes, the sounds of their ATVs fade in the distance. The quiet of a secluded forest location at dusk surprises Adam and other technicians. The area feels eerie.

Shirley Smythe gives final instructions in a whisper. "All right, team, heads up and be ready. Let's do this. We go dark in ten, nine, eight, seven, six, five, four, three, two, and one."

Silence.

CHAPTER 16

Foiled

After midnight, only whispers and nature's sounds spoil total silence. Control center audio monitors barely flicker. Motion-sensor video cameras likewise record no action. Boredom challenges each technician's professionalism and dedication.

More hours pass. Yawns test attention and alertness. Team members suggest Travis might be too smart for their set-up. They wait.

† † †

At 7:33 a.m., the EVP technician crashes the airwaves excitedly. "I hear movement behind me—source unknown. Rhythmic, its orientation sounds human—not animal."

His report confuses Shirley Smythe and her control technician. All monitor needles rest unchanged. No sound. No motion. Similarly, the technician's screen records no activity. Southwest Scientific employees never encountered such an anomaly—noise without registered results.

Shirley Smythe cautions everyone to stay sharp and on task.

At least for the moment, yawns stop.

The EVP technician's hand cups around his radio mic. "Control, the sound seems close now. I'm stumped. Still no blip on my monitor, but I hear it loud enough I should—"

The zoom technician breaks their transmission. "Heads up, everyone, my—"

Adam interrupts both peers. "Everyone, a silhouetted image stands in the distance. I'm not sure if male or female. The image moves toward me. What do—wait, I now confirm a male figure approaches. What do monitors show?"

The control technician shakes his head, confused. "Flat, Adam."

"Amanda here, I hear sound also."

"Do you have visual, Amanda?"

"Negative. Only sound, which passes me…now!"

"Amanda, Smythe here. The sound passed you?"

"Ten-four."

"Your camera trigger?"

"Negative."

"Who or what made the sound?"

"Unknown. I saw no visual but heard plenty. It fades now in front me. Impossible to understand—neither my naked eye nor Full Spectrum recorded an image, over."

Adam breaks in. "Do you guys get this? Fully in the clearing now, the man continues toward me."

"This is Control. Earphone and monitors still negative for activity."

Adam grits his teeth in anger. "Impossible—the man approaches maybe twenty seconds from me."

"Amanda here, I feel odd."

"Odd?"

"Yes, Shirley. I became anxious when the sound passed."

"To be expected, over."

"No. I anticipate something unexpected."

"You okay? You scare me."

"Yes, but I stir and worry about an incident, but not its outcome. Weird."

"Ten-four. Sit tight. Breathe deep."

"I'm okay."

"Control here—I retested monitors while you guys talked. Still, blanks on all screens. Adam, I'm not sure what you see, but zip registers."

The audio technician responds, "No movement on my monitor either."

"Ten-four." The control technician defends his preparation. "We set up all equipment correctly, and it should work well."

Adam's anger boils over. "Then your gear sucks. I see the guy plain as day. He must've walked right past Amanda."

Amanda fears her peers might question her credibility. "I swear I heard someone pass me. I felt funny but confirm no image."

The EVP technician interjects. "Same here. Not the funny part, but no recorded audio signal."

Shirley Smythe needs to restore order and find answers. "All right, everyone. Calm yourselves. Stay on your gear and quiet, please."

The control technician looks at Shirley Smythe.

"I register nothing, boss."

"I noticed. I don't understand it, either."

† † †

Shirley Smythe calls to update Mark Lyle about her team's situation. Although he trusts Smythe's capabilities, he questions how well they set up their trap. Convinced his equipment works well and staff remained attentive, his tone shifts.

"Shirley, don't let me down. If you have Travis, you must capture electronic evidence. You *must!*"

"I understand. Perhaps when I loop back, the situation will have changed. I wanted to brief you now in case not, given how you hate surprises."

"I need not remind you, our professional lives rely on your success."

"Yes, sir, I understand. I assure you if we fail, it won't be due to inadequate preparation or execution."

"If we fail, *why* won't matter." Lyle's tone reflects sternness Shirley Smythe never heard before.

"I understand. Let me get back to the team."

"Keep me posted."

"Yes, sir."

"Shirley!"
"Yes?"
"Get this done."

† † †

Adam moans as if in agony. "Thank God you found me. Please help. This log crushed my leg, and I've been lying here helpless all night."

The silent man stares. After uncomfortable seconds, from Adam's perspective, the man responds. "Yes. You have been lying here—in more ways than one."

"What?"

"If hurt, call for help on your communication system. Many people wait to hear from you."

Adam, deep in his role, moans louder. "Yeah, my leg's pretty messed up. Here I sit in love with nature, then, *bam*—this branch snaps and crashes on my—Wait a second."

"Yes?"

"What do you mean my communication system? Do you mean I should holler? Who would hear me?"

"You might damage eardrums if you holler."

"Eardrums?"

"Your leg looks a mess."

"Yeah, and…and I hurt a lot."

"I see."

"What do you see?" Adam comes off smart-alecky.

"I see what you think I cannot and know what you think I do not. I am displeased with what I see and know."

"I have no idea what you mean and couldn't care less. What I wonder is if you can help me?"

"You should care more—not less. To care less helps no one, not even you. To show care comforts and inspires. Remember, sweetness from a man's lips flows from the honey in his heart. Sadly, you lack honey."

Adam shakes his head, confused and angry with the man's life lesson. "Forgive my tone, but will you help or not?"

"I am here to assist one with a legitimate need."

Adam furrows his brow and feels smarter than his visitor. "I didn't get your name. I'm Benjamin, and I beg for your help."

Not to be outsmarted by a fool, the man said, "My name is I. M. Travis, Adam. But you may call me Travis."

Adam freezes as if trapped. "Ah...you misheard me. I'm Benjamin."

"I heard you well. And I see you well. I know you, and your associates from Southwest Scientific set this trap for me."

"Trap?"

"Yes, and I dislike your actions, Adam. No one sets traps for noble purposes."

"You confuse me."

"Trappers set snares for financial gain at the expense of innocent animals. Your company set this trap to use me for the mutual benefit of your employer and client."

"I don't get what you mean."

"You expect your employer and the *Phoenix Evening Herald* to gain in many ways once you trap me like an animal. But neither company cares about who I am, what I do, or what I stand for beyond their chance for gain. No one earns honor through traps, Adam. And now your ploy is foiled."

The zoom technician questions if control is capturing this back and forth. "Shirley, you on this conversation? The guy says he's thwarted our setup. He might be right."

"Ten-four, we hear the convo through headphones, but negative on the monitors. Silence—please!"

"I can't make sense of your words." Adam acts artificially coy.

"I am sure Ms. Smythe, who listens in, knows what I mean."

Shirley Smythe looks at the control technician. "How does he know my name?" Bewildered, the technician shrugs and returns attention to his monitors.

"Ms. Smythe now knows I know her name and plan. Neither you nor she has secrets. Not even about the foam branch on your leg or other fake items."

"Foam branch?"

"You introduced items here ill-suited for the forest. When finished, dispose of all properly. I do not want animals, which belong here, harmed by creatures that do not. They should not be affected because of your trap for me."

"If you thought this a scam, or trap as you say, why'd you show up?"

"Not for you Adam, nor to participate in your folly, but one per- son here needs my help. And she needs it now. I came to serve her."

"What? Who?"

"If I did not appear, the tragedy portrayed in your trap would happen, only not to you."

"What do you mean someone—"

Smythe bursts into the transmission. "Adam, find out what he means. Who needs help? Follow up—who's in trouble?"

"What did Shirley Smythe say, Adam?"

Adam ignores Travis's question. "As I asked, who else needs help?"

"I passed your associate, Amanda."

The control technician pulls his headset off and looks at Shirley Smythe. "My God, he knows Amanda's name too."

"She stands on the blind your associates built for her camera. In precisely forty-two seconds, a real tree branch will fall, unlike your representation here. Enormous and dense, the branch will crush her to death if she fails to leave the blind now. I know she hears me."

Travis raises his right hand. "Amanda, move now—*fast!*"

His eyes focus like lasers on Adam. "Do you believe what I said about Amanda?"

"I don't know what to think. I'm just—"

Travis raises his other hand and signals Adam to stop talking. "Listen!"

A loud crash fills the forest and causes other technicians to race to Amanda's camera blind.

Terror fills Shirley Smythe's eyes.

Technicians gasp. A large ponderosa pine branch lies splayed atop the demolished camera stand. They fear Amanda's fate. Closer, they fail to see her among the rubble.

They hear Amanda's trembling voice. "Over here. I'm over here."

Technicians find Amanda many yards away under another tree. Dazed, she shakes and sobs.

"Thank God you're okay."

Tears stream down Amanda's face. "Thank God for being."

Travis snaps his attention toward Adam. "I support scientific study formulated for noble intent. But, Adam, I do not condone data gathered under pretense."

"How'd you know this would happen?"

"How is unimportant, but realize I used your setup to achieve my objectives—not yours. Amanda has not fulfilled her purpose yet."

"You did?"

"Yes, and you may report what you want. You proved I exist and help people in need. Mine is a higher purpose, however. I used your setup to show I know all, see all, and help all who accept my offer. So a truthful story reports I. M. Travis helps people in need, even when recipients are unaware their need exists. Beyond truth, you have no story."

Adam sits stunned. Travis leaves—within seconds—out of sight.

Adam asks, "Control, did you capture this exchange?"

"Not a blip, Adam. Not a single blip."

Shirley Smyth removes her headset and slumps into her chair, exhausted. *We failed. Travis foiled us, just as he said.*

CHAPTER 17

Empty

Waiting alters one's concept of time. A clock watched turns minutes into forever. Minutes ignored fly like seconds. But, today, the cruel-est day ever, time stands still. CT scan results might change Gino's and his children's lives forever. So they wait—their emotional tanks empty.

Angela responds to her dad's edginess. "Relax, Dad. CT scans take time. Remember how long we waited at West Valley Hospital?"

His eyes bounce between fear and affection. "Yes, of course. It took forever, but forever felt shorter then."

Dominic adds, "This delay bugs me too. Guess I don't understand."

In the midst of their discussion, Dr. Nowiski approaches. His step shows the day's weightiness. He manages a tired smile. "We found no signs of brain damage or evidence her seizure continues."

"Which means what?"

"While not one hundred percent, Mr. Cavatelli, these results suggest an unlikelihood for future seizures."

Dominic leaps from his seat. "Fantastic!" He smiles back and forth between his father and sister.

"Yes, but I'm still unclear why she seized today. We might never know, but as I said earlier, we prefer rogue episodes over a predisposition for seizures."

Exhaustion coats Dr. Nowiski's face as he answers their questions. Once finished, he urges everyone to leave and get rest.

Gino nods. "I agree. Why not head home, kids? I'll stay until Mom settles in the ICU."

"You also need a break, Mr. Cavatelli. Your wife will be out all night, so you can't help her here."

"I know."

"She will need your help once home. To best help her, you need strength now. You can't risk exhaustion or illness. You must recharge after long days that tax your system."

"Yeah."

After more coaxing, the doctor departs—spent. Despite his encouragement, Gino, and his children worry and await Julia's arrival in the ICU. They continue to mark time.

† † †

Another hour passes without updates. Frustrated, Gino rises. "I'm off to find out when Mom's due in the ICU."

He finds a central station, where a nurse's smile greets him. "May I help you, sir?"

"Yes. When do you expect my wife, Julia Cavatelli?"

"She's here in room three."

"Why wasn't I notified?"

"I'm sorry. We weren't aware family waited."

He bites his lower lip and exhales through his nose loudly. "I'd like to see my wife."

"Yes, of course, but she's asleep."

He imagines Julia. *How can she help but sleep? She's in a coma.*

"We'll take good care of her tonight, Mr. Cavatelli. I'm sure she'll be happy to see you in the morning, so please go get some rest."

"I will, but I first want to get my children and peek in on Julia."

"She won't know you're there or acknowledge you."

"But we'll know we tried, which is important to us."

"By all means, go ahead."

Gino gets his children. He wants to see Julia for the first time together. They enter the ICU.

Julia's room sits at the end of a short aisle after turning left at the nurses' station. Dark and quiet, nurses enter electronic patient data at workstations. Then they see her.

Gino blinks back tears for his children's sake, a trait learned from his Italian father, but at which he often fails. His children understand his human frailty.

Misty eyed, Gino stares—numb. *There she lies, my wife of over forty years—my love, in a coma.*

Tubes run everywhere. Annoying machines buzz and beep, the only sounds to disturb the quiet.

Julia's nurse, Maria, smiles warmly. Her summary of Julia's status fails to comfort Gino. Her empty words seem straight from a *How to Ease Family Member Worries* instruction manual. Their inter-action validates Gino's belief. *People believe more what they see than what others tell them.* What he sees scares him.

Gino leans to Julia's right ear and speaks sweet words for naught. She lays motionless—his wish for a sign of hope unfulfilled. She looks lifeless. But to expect more from someone comatose is like waiting for the Stone People of Pompeii to come alive. Both Julia and the Pompeiians exist rigid and incapable of movement.

Each child cradles one of Julia's hands for contact and closeness. Gino shares Angela's caress of Julia's left hand. *I'm here to comfort you, Julia. I don't know how this horror story ends, but until then, I'm here to comfort you.*

After several empty minutes, Gino urges they leave. He wants to stay but knows better.

Maria enters. "Mr. Cavatelli, I have your cell phone number, so I'll call if necessary. Please go rest."

"Yes. I won't help Julia if I stare at her all night, but it'll tear me apart."

"Correct, and you need rest, not anguish."

"Will you be here when I return tomorrow?"

"I leave at 7:00 sharp. The day nurse and I review patient charts just before I leave, so I can't talk then. I'll update you if you arrive early enough, however."

"I see."

"Mrs. Cavatelli won't change much between early and mid-morning, so no need to rush back."

Gino nods agreement, covering a yawn with the back of his hand.

The Cavatellis kiss Julia's forehead. Gino prays from his heart of hearts for the slightest response. He sees none, which confirms a fear in his brain of brains. They find it hard to walk away.

The trio leaves the ICU arm in arm for the parking lot. After heartfelt hugs, Gino slips into his van. Alone with his thoughts, he feels empty, spent, and troubled.

Gino's anger and obsession with the other driver again interfere with thoughts of Julia and adds weight to an already heavy day. Still spiritually wart-laden, his thoughts ring inconsistent with his wishes and core beliefs. Since Julia's accident, however, he travels a men-tally dark road filled with hatred, which intensifies daily. *I'll find and punish you. Remember, an eye for an eye.* He deems the biblical adage beautiful justification.

† † †

After a late-night snack, Gino slides under the sheet. The time nears midnight. Lonely and unsure about changes ahead, he looks at Julia's pillow. Misery fills the room and blocks sleep.

Gino watches the news, which helps little. One story catches his attention, however. The piece involves a Phoenix-area highway patrol officer and his woes on a hike in the Canadian Rockies. A stranger named I. M. Travis helped him survive a potentially deadly situation.

Gino rejoices for the patrolman. If true, the story marks another time Travis saved someone from high anxiety and apparent death. The feel-good story also provides a peaceful transition to a restful night. He chuckles. *Even stories of Travis comfort.*

Exhaustion overtakes Gino in minutes after the hiker story. Exhausted, he fails to finish his prayers for Julia, the hiker, and others who need spiritual intervention, himself included. Short-circuited prayers happen far too often.

†††

Maria's monitor glows on her face. She glances up only long enough to observe her two patients. Eyes back on her screen, she notices strange changes in Julia's and other patients' monitor readings. Puzzled, she speaks to others at the nurses' station.

"Hey, has anyone heard of system problems? My patients' vitals improved at the same time my monitor acted up. I don't know if they're accurate."

Another nurse walks up. "I have the same issue. My equipment went haywire seconds ago."

A third nurse approaches. "What's the deal? My patient readings seem messed up. No way possible both patients' numbers improved so much so fast."

The lead nurse looks toward Julia's room. "Maria, who's the man with your patient?"

"What man?" She looks toward Julia's bed. Concern covers Maria's face. "I have no idea."

"Where'd he come from?"

"I don't know." Maria scratches her temple. "Nobody passed us." She nibbles her lower lip. "I'll check."

Maria approaches the stranger and whispers, "Excuse me, sir. May I help you?"

The visitor turns, and his eyes stun her. He speaks softly. "No. Thank you, though. I am here for Julia. I care for her when necessary."

"Are you a doctor?"

"No. I am more to Julia than a doctor—our bond stronger. She needs me, and I must help her. We band together in her times of need like now."

"How'd you get here? I stepped away, and seconds later, here you stand."

As she speaks, Maria notices his unique appearance.

"You must not have seen me in the corner. Darkness fools many."

Maria considers calling security. *He couldn't have been there. In the corner or not, I would've seen him. I'm in and out of her room often. And here he stands—not there one moment, but here the next.*

"Are you related? We limit nighttime visitation to immediate family."

The mysterious man's silvery-blue eyes seem to glow and mesmerize. "What is a family?"

"What do you mean?"

"Is family those who live and die for others?"

"Yes."

"And do members place needs of others above their own and deem sacrifice a privilege?"

"I suppose."

"And their support knows no limits?"

"I'd say yes."

"And they share love and joy, dreams and disappointments, and successes and failures?"

"Yes, of course."

"They nurture each other and grow together?"

"Yes, that's what family members do."

"And they defend one another against all enemies and odds?"

"Yeah."

"And, finally, their blood seals their unconditional bond?"

"For sure."

"Then I am family."

Maria looks away unable to comprehend the man's complicated answer to her simple question. She looks back at the visitor—awestruck. "I don't know what to say."

"Then do not speak."

"Yes, but—"

"Then do not ask."

"But I must. May—"

"I. M. Travis"

Maria's jaw drops. "How'd you know I'd ask your name?"

"Logic."

"Huh?"

"I never said my name, and you never asked. My assumption about your question seemed logical."

Maria grows confused. "It did?"

"Yes. How else would I know how to answer?"

"I'm not sure, but you talk like someone who knows much about a lot."

"You observe well, Maria."

"You know my name? How? I never said my name."

Travis points toward Maria's upper torso. "Your identification lanyard."

"Oh—how silly, of course."

Travis smiles and sits in the chair next to Julia's bed. "I await Julia's awakening."

CHAPTER 18

Awakening

Gino awakens at 3:00 a.m., in need of more sleep. Like much in life, though, unfulfilled expectations drive one to press on. So he tosses and tries to nod off. At 4:30 a.m., he surrenders to first hints of day-break. He rises, showers, and departs for the hospital by 5:00.

Ahead of rush hour traffic, Gino enjoys his drive. Stop lights allow time to relax and think. He needs the relaxation. His thoughts bother him.

He enters the hospital at 6:02 a.m., surprised by the buzz of activity. The ICU, however, appears darker and quieter than the prior night. *Maybe some patients moved to regular rooms. Perhaps some died.*

Whatever the cause, Gino notices several empty rooms.

Nurses prep for shift change at workstations. Maria—stumped by her visit with I. M. Travis—smiles at Gino. He nods good morning. His heart throbs as he nears Julia—then sinks to his stomach. Julia *still lays* comatose.

Maria approaches. "Mrs. Cavatelli rested well last night."

She finds Gino unresponsive. *How could she have done otherwise?*

"She'll awaken from her coma soon. It takes considerable time to do so safely."

Gino concentrates on Julia.

"Since the process could take a few hours, why not catch some winks in our waiting room? The day nurse will get you upon your wife's awakening."

Against his heart's desires, Gino abides.

Some people sleep in the half-empty waiting room. A few yawn and fight to stay awake. Others whisper back and forth. They all notice Gino's entry. He smiles and heads for the refreshment room, in which volunteers stock coffee. Too early for helpers, he turns to a seat with his crossword puzzle.

Within minutes, Gino folds closed his puzzle page. Words elude him like sleep. His focus centers on his forty years with Julia. A question nags. *How many more years do we have together?*

He scans his newspaper. A story with local interest catches his eye. The headline reads "Foiled Trap Yields Lifesaving Action." Gino enjoys the article about Travis. Thoughts of Julia and love, however, and evil thoughts of the other driver consume him.

Gino marks more time and fights urges to return to the ICU. He weakens in time and enters to check on Julia. She lies asleep, so Gino heads back to the waiting room—a pattern he repeats several times with growing anxiety. All he wants is to talk to precious Julia. More importantly, he longs to hear her voice.

Finally, Gino settles for a cup of coffee. He even tries his cross-word again without luck. He focuses on one, no two thoughts—Julia and the man who harmed her.

† † †

Gino reenters the ICU and notices lots of motion in Julia's room. Two nurses stand by Julia, their backs toward his approach. Their arms flail over her. His eyes dart everywhere, and his mind stirs. *Is Julia okay and awakening from her coma, or is she in trouble?*

He continues carefully to avoid disruption. He inches past the nurse on Julia's left. Her eyes meet Gino's with a look of urgency.

Julia lays distressed. A tube still protrudes from her trachea. She thrashes to expel the invasive device. One nurse adjusts Julia's straps in one place, and then another. She strains to see who entered as the nurses finish their work. Julia cranes her neck to face Gino. Her wide eyes convey confusion and terror. She jerks her head around as if an attempt to speak. She looks and acts imbalanced, and Gino feels helplessly unsure of what to do.

Gino stands at a loss for what to say—if anything. "Do you want to speak? Do you have a question?"

He immediately recognizes his stupidity. Julia cannot respond, although she tries, which frustrates her. Glances from the nurses confirm his foolishness.

Julia tosses her head side to side. Her eyes, large as half dollars, look crazed.

Attempts to raise her arms fail since they remain strapped to her bed. She kicks her legs, which does not to free her arms. Cinched, Julia suffers high anxiety and demonstrates unruly behavior.

Gino nears tears. "Are you in pain?" *Stupid question number three*, he decides.

Julia thrusts her head again, wiggles her chin, and moves her mouth over the endotracheal tube. Despite intense efforts, she only mutters unintelligible sounds.

Helpless, Gino looks around, for what, he does not know. Julia's struggle increases. "Do you have to go the bathroom?" *Another question—idiot!*

Gino startles from a nurse's hand on his forearm. Her look shows sympathy over his hopelessness. "Mr. Cavatelli, why not go back to the waiting room. Mrs. Cavatelli might calm down if you're not here."

"But why does she thrash so much and look so wild?"

"It's normal because of her medical coma. Patients often experience delusion and uncertainty over their location and events around them when fresh out of a coma. This confusion resolves in time."

"But I hate to leave her this way." Pain blankets Gino's face and pours from his words. "She needs me."

The nurse searches for sensitivity. "Your wife *needs* less of what-ever confuses her. You should go back to the waiting room. It'll be good for you too."

"Okay, but you'll get me the minute Julia relaxes, right?"

"Of course."

Gino's prior experience causes questions about the unit's notification protocols. He lacks other options, however. "Fine, I'll go for coffee. Please get me soon as possible."

"Indeed."

Gino glances back on his way out. Like daggers, Julia's eyes follow him. Her look shreds Gino's heart.

Back in the waiting room, Gino settles in an all-too-familiar seat. With a tired sigh, he thinks of the other driver. His gut tightens. He grits his teeth and unconsciously says aloud, "I'll make you pay."

A lady opposite him lifts her eyes from her magazine. Gino notices her troubled look. "Ma'am, I'm sorry I blurted that line from a movie. My thoughts moved from my mind to my mouth without thinking."

"You startled me. More than your words, your tone frightened me."

"I'm sorry."

"I heard real hatred."

"No."

"Yes. I've never heard the likes of it before. And your eyes—laser focused."

"Guess my frustrated actor behavior surfaced. So sorry I unsettled you."

"It's okay. I'm glad you're not angry, or someone would be in big trouble."

"Yeah, he would, wouldn't he?"

"I expect so. Please forgive my nosiness."

"Sorry I distracted you from your magazine."

"It's a snoozer."

"Regardless."

Gino forces a smile. She returns to her magazine, while he alternates between thoughts of Julia and the other driver.

† † †

Gino heads for Julia's room an hour later. She sits in bed awake but dazed—tube removed. She fails to acknowledge him. He walks to her side and lays his hand on her arm. Seemingly unaware, she sits still. Her eyes draw closed.

Julia's nurse notices pain spread over Gino's face. "It's good to see her awake, isn't it?"

"Yes and no." He feels worse than earlier when Julia at least seemed to know him.

"I'm sorry you saw her struggle earlier. I can explain."

Gino grows angry. "A job well done requires no explanation. But in your case, you'd better try, and your clarification better make sense!"

Taken aback, Maria swallows hard and speaks softly. Her justification angers Gino more. While patients with spine surgeries typically go on a pain pump right away, doctors kept Julia off because of her seizure. They monitored her brain to detect further seizure activity. The nurse said pain medication would have altered Julia's *normal* state. Gino gnaws his index finger's big knuckle. *As if a comma is natural.*

Incensed, Gino swallows hard and speaks loudly. "Respectfully, I can't buy disorientation and anxiety caused Julia's terror and anguish."

Maria listens. No one ever challenged her this way.

"To my mind, pain drove her behavior, and your med transition procedures suck. I can't believe you didn't increase her pain medication proportionate to her comma medication's decrease. Then again, what do I know? I'm only a husband who cares and prays for a miracle."

"I understand, Mr. Cavatelli." Maria knows more words likely won't satisfy Gino. She tries anyway. "Thankfully the worst is behind us."

"Thankfully? I question if she'll ever be the same."

"I understand."

"Do you?" Gino shows disdain for the nurse's patronizing response. Maria looks away.

Gino leaves the ICU, ready to explode if anyone else says *I understand.* They do not. They cannot unless they had a similar experience from a patient's perspective. Aside from a comparable experience, empty words reveal false empathy, and Gino loathes fakeness.

Back in the waiting room, Gino thumbs through a magazine he found on the seat next to him. After a minute, he senses a person hovering over him. He lifts his eyes to see a middle-aged man with a serious scowl.

"I was reading that magazine."

Gino motions to an empty seat. "I found it here."

"I placed it there when I went to the restroom."

"I'm sorry. I didn't know."

"Look, I don't mean to be rude, but I'd like to finish my article."

Gino extends the magazine to the man. "Sure. I understand." He realizes what he said and fights back laughter, which the other man does not comprehend.

The man resumes reading the article. Gino closes his eyes and wonders where his life is heading.

CHAPTER 19

Miracle

His eyes blur. Faint sounds disorient him. Sam Ellis lies loopy and confused. He turns his head. As if in slow motion, he slips back into a fog. His recovery nurse shakes his arm lightly. "Mr. Ellis. Mr. Ellis, can you hear me?"

Sam Ellis nods slightly and moans.

"Mr. Ellis, you're in surgical recovery."

He drifts in and out of minimal consciousness.

"You'll go to your room soon, okay?"

Silence.

† † †

Sam's friends fidget in the waiting room. His surgeon arrives to report on his surgery. "Is anyone here for Sam Ellis?"

Six guys in outdoor gear signal the doctor.

After introductions, the doctor reports on Sam's surgery. He tells the hikers how he stabilized Sam Ellis's break with a titanium rod and screws. He predicts a full recovery barring unexpected complications.

Each hiker checks the others' reactions.

"Given the hour, we won't get him up today. But I want him to walk early tomorrow. He might push back, but he needs to rebuild strength and become comfortable on his feet again. Mr. Ellis's walks up and down his floor will provide first steps back to normal. Your encouragement will spur him along and help his recovery."

Group members remain silent.

"Did you all travel from Arizona?"

Roberto Rozelle speaks as the group's spokesperson. "No, we're from across the country, but I'm from Arizona. I work with Sam, and we're scheduled to fly home day after tomorrow."

The doctor orders sternly. "No travel for several days. Do what you must to make notifications and reservation changes. You plan to stay with him, right, Roberto?"

"Yes, and our boss knows what happened and our need to stay longer."

"Good. I'll not release Mr. Ellis to fly any sooner than Friday, even better—Saturday. This time frame contemplates he progresses as I expect. His preinjury condition is sure to help."

"Makes sense."

"I'll start Mr. Ellis on inpatient rehab here. I'll order two weeks of outpatient rehab upon discharge. His local doctor controls treatment once home, however."

"Yes, sir."

"Now back to travel. I doubt you fly first-class but upgrade if you can. Mr. Ellis needs extra legroom. A bulkhead seat works if you can't swing first-class, or if it's unavailable."

Roberto jots a note to himself. "Sure. I'll call today."

The men talk longer, after which the doctor asks for questions.

Roberto looks at his buddies. "No, Doctor. We appreciate your summary."

"Of course, and if I don't see you later, safe travels."

"Yes, sir, and thank you. Sam means a lot to us. I'd do anything for him."

With goodbye salutations and a nod, the doctor leaves. After a few steps, he turns. His index finger rests across his lips, then points to Roberto. "Say, I have a question. How did Mr. Ellis keep his break protected? I heard he injured himself on a hike."

Group members point to Roberto for a response. "Yes. Sam went by himself and had a fall. Even though we're all experienced, careful hikers, we worry when someone goes alone, especially in remote locations."

As a hiker himself, the doctor understands. "But how did he protect his leg?"

"We're not sure, but here's what we know. Sam stopped to rest. A landslide started, and a sheet of shale exploded over his head, He tumbled down the mountain until his leg struck a tree trunk."

Roberto finds the doctor's grimace odd, his comment less so.

"I'm sure pain sent him into shock."

"I assume so. How else could Sam have slithered to an overhang for protection if not for shock?"

The doctor still awaits an answer to his question.

"Soon after, a stranger supposedly appeared to comfort and keep Sam safe."

"A stranger?"

"Yes. Sam said he didn't know the guy."

"Was the man medically trained?"

"I don't think so. In any event, the guy didn't mess with Sam's leg. I'm pretty sure he didn't even touch Sam."

A head shake accompanies the doctor's perplexed look. "Did the stranger transport Mr. Ellis to you guys or elsewhere for treatment?"

"No, he calmed Sam and assured his safety. Sam called this encounter weird, like a miracle. He sensed an *'odd peace of mind'* and felt he'd be okay. Somehow, his pain eased."

The doctor tilts his head with a quizzical look. "Do you mean to say his pain decreased solely because of what the stranger said?"

"I guess. Understand, this information comes directly from Sam."

"But those facts are illogical and against medical probabilities."

"I know, and Sam said the stranger shared ideas about life and left soon after. The man returned to the forest."

"I can't make sense of this story."

"Yeah, I know, nor any of us.

"But if Mr. Ellis waited isolated and the stranger walked away, how did you find him?"

"Okay. So here's the rest of the story. A bunch of us gathered in our cabin at four thirty the morning after to finalize search plans. We got an unexpected knock on our cabin door. This guy named Travis stood there, and he—"

"Pardon my interruption, but did any of you know this guy? Was he part of your search party?"

"No. No one knows the guy."

"A stranger, he showed up unexpected? Didn't you find that odd?"

"Yes. Wait. Travis told us his name, where to find Sam, and he gave us spot-on directions."

"Did he take you there?"

"No. Travis told us Sam was safe and where to find him. Then he split, exactly as he did with Sam."

"Then you guys went to get Mr. Ellis?"

"Yes, we found him right where Travis said."

"This fascinates me." The doctor exhibits childlike excitement. "Did you ask, by chance, why Sam felt he'd be okay?"

"Well, one of the other guys asked the same question."

"What'd he say?"

Roberto turns to his buddy. "Tell the doctor what Sam said."

"He said something weird. He said, *'Sometimes you simply know what you know.'*"

"Huh?"

"Yeah, my reaction exactly. That makes no sense, but it's what Sam said."

"Odd."

"I'll say. Now, may I ask you a question, Doctor?"

"Yes, of course."

"Why so much interest in Sam's situation?"

"ER staff documented Mr. Ellis's leg looked freshly broken when he arrived. They disbelieved the break was old. They said his tissue erosion was inconsistent with an untreated wound of such severity and alleged duration. Nothing made sense."

"Huh?"

"Travis must have a medical background."

"Even if he does, he never touched Sam. He merely talked to him for several minutes."

"Did anyone ask Travis what he did with or to Sam? "No. But Sam said Travis spoke with him, then left."

The doctor squints and furrows his brow. "You know, a similar strange incident happened some time ago with a girl in California.

Others occurred elsewhere too. I wonder if Travis and the guy in those situations is the same person."

"I don't know, but Travis saved Sam's life. Without his directions, Sam would've bled to death before we found him."

The doctor shakes his head affirmatively. "Yes, another peculiar detail."

"How so?"

"Emergency room staff said Sam cinched his belt around his thigh above his knee."

"Yes, he had a tourniquet when we found him."

"But his belt wasn't tight enough to serve as a functional tourniquet. But upon arrival, Mr. Ellis hadn't lost blood."

The hikers' expressions range from surprise to disbelief. "Every fact in this case defies logic. Mr. Ellis and Travis's encounter stands as a modern-day miracle."

CHAPTER 20

Despair

Julia slumps motionless, emotionless, and bewildered. Acts of affection or conversation fail to penetrate her lack of awareness. She smiles randomly without purpose, which casts Gino into despair.

Dr. Nowiski, there to check his patient, shows less concern. "Mrs. Cavatelli, can you tell me what month it is?"

Julia turns halfway toward the doctor's voice. She answers in a garbled voice. "Twenty-twelve."

Gino's heart drops. *She responded correctly to a different question.*

"What's the president's name?"

Julia bristles. Not a fan of the president, she refuses to answer, but her look says plenty.

"What's in my hand?"

"A pen." Julia's childlike tone agrees with her impish grin.

Dr. Nowiski looks toward Gino. "I'm optimistic. She hears, understands, and answers questions well. I believe she'll recover fully from this temporary loss of memory. I'm not worried one bit."

Angela nears as the men talk. Julia peers past everyone to anywhere.

"Good morning."

"Hello, Doctor."

"I just quizzed your mother. She answered questions well. As I told your father, I predict her memory issue will resolve fully in a few weeks."

"May I ask a question?"

"Of course."

Angela looks back and forth from the doctor to her mother. "Does a seizure affect memory differently? Mom may answer questions well, but she doesn't seem to know me."

"Let me answer this way. If she were my mom, I wouldn't worry yet. I suggest we monitor her today and tomorrow before we conclude anything."

Angela appears only slightly relieved. "Still, I hate to see Mom this way." She looks at Julia again, who watches blankly with another hint of a smile meant for no one.

Dr. Nowiski also looks at Julia, then Angela. "I understand your concerns, but let's see what happens today, okay?"

Gino agrees. "We have no choice. Besides, after yesterday, we wait well, right, Angela."

"Unfortunately, yes. We got plenty of practice."

Gino hugs her. "So let's follow doctor's orders and avoid premature conclusions. We should save our worry for if and when needed most."

The doctor nods. He looks at Julia, Gino, and Angela, all of whom remain silent. "Good. Then we follow this plan. We'll monitor Mrs. Cavatelli's progress today and tomorrow before we buckle to worry."

Gino supports the doctor. "Right."

"Good. I'll check on Mrs. Cavatelli periodically today."

"Thanks, Doctor. I'm happy you continue to follow Julia."

"As my surgical patient, I'm interested in her total recovery, not just from her surgery. I want to ensure she's well overall."

Dr. Nowiski wiggles Julia's big toe on her right foot through the sheets. "Mrs. Cavatelli. I'll see you later, okay?"

Julia sits unresponsive, her expression bland and fixed. Angela dashes several feet away. She hunches over and buries her face in cupped hands.

Gino follows. "What's wrong, honey?"

Angela teary eyes narrow.

"Sorry for my stupid question. I have a knack for stupidity today."

Angela glances back at her mother. "I heard Dr. Nowiski, but look at her. Just look at her."

Gino clutches her tightly. "I know this is hard, Ang, but I value Dr. Nowiski's opinion. We can't expect Mom's recovery to occur based on our desires. She needs time and rest, so let's sit in the wait-ing room so she gets both."

"I know you're right. I'll be okay."

Gino and Angela move back to Julia's side. He cradles Julia's right hand. Angela holds her other. Julia's smile widens slightly, then returns flat.

"Julia, we'll be in the waiting room, so please rest, okay? We'll check on you later."

She turns toward Gino, her head tilted and expression hollow.

Her eyes convey nothing.

Angela cannot understand her father's raised voice. *Mom's had a seizure. She's not deaf.*

Gino turns from Julia and struggles to hide from Angela how overwhelmed he feels.

† † †

Dominic arrives while Gino and Angela discuss family matters. His tie hangs loosely, his neck button undone—a typical summer look in Phoenix for people who wear ties. His face reflects a miserable night's sleep. His firm hug offers support.

"How's Ma?"

Gino summarizes Dr. Nowiski assessment. He tries to maintain the doctor's positive vibe but fails.

"Will she be okay?"

"I wish I knew. As Dr. Nowiski suggests, let's monitor Mom's progress today before we worry too much. She's off, for sure, but I look for improvement today."

"Can I see her?"

Gino fears his son's reaction. "Of course, she's in the same room as yesterday. Please remember, Dominic, Mom remains in recovery."

"I understand. I don't expect grins and giggles."

"Let's visit together. Come on, Ang."

Gino's pep talk continues as they walk to the ICU. He wants Dominic to see the glass half full, a view Angela misses. She doubts her dad even believes his enthusiastic banter.

"Hi, Mom." Dominic slumps with a needy child-to-mom tone. His voice lacks the high spirits Gino hoped to instill. He turns toward his pops. "This kills me."

The left corner of Julia's mouth twitches like an involuntary tic when she hears Dominic's voice. Beyond, she offers family members sporadic smiles without recognition of anyone.

Dominic dries his eyes. Angela places clasped hands over her cracked heart. Gino buries his pain and still tries to act positively. But a phony exposes himself in time, and Dominic knows his *pops* well.

Silence follows, which troubles everyone except Julia, who sits oblivious.

Gino and his children return to the waiting room. More at peace there, they need not watch Julia struggle. Her daze appears too real and too permanent. They suffer degrees of despair.

† † †

Gino keeps up positive talk for two hours. No one buys his bull, and his task grows harder the longer Julia fails to improve. Pain plays a sad tune on Gino's heartstrings.

Gino checks the time on his phone, which reads mid-afternoon. "I'm off to see Mom again. I'd like to see her alone."

Angela and Dominic stay with family and friends. These well-wishers arrived to support their family. Italian *paisanos* support one another well in crises.

As Gino nears Julia's room, a young lady in a lab coat stops him. "Excuse me. Are you on your way to Mrs. Cavatelli?"

"Yes."

"I didn't mean to startle you."

"Guess thoughts of my last forty years distract me."

"Are you her husband?"

"Yes."

"May I speak with you?"

Skepticism fills Gino. "Sure, if you don't take too long."

"I'll be brief."

The lady introduces herself as a hospital speech and occupational therapist. Moments ago, she completed her initial assessment of Julia.

"I observed how your wife handled two simple tasks."

"Oh?"

"Yes, we gave her a cup of applesauce and a spoon. She struggled to load the spoon without help."

Gino's face sags with sadness and his Adam's apple bobs.

"Once in her hand, she missed her mouth and hit her left eye-brow. So she knew what to do with the spoon but couldn't execute."

Gino's stomach sours. The lady's perspective and input differ from Dr. Nowiski's.

"Mrs. Cavatelli also failed to use a straw properly."

"You're serious?"

"Yes. The nurse gave her a half-filled water glass and a straw. After she had moved the straw a bit, she lifted the glass toward her head and tried to put the straw up her nose. Repeated efforts produced similar results."

Gino fights back tears. "I'm glad I missed this."

"In both cases, Mrs. Cavatelli tried to use utensils correctly but fell short."

His voice cracks. "So what does it mean?"

"I fear she lost brain function because of her seizure. A damaged brain explains her difficulty with simple tasks."

Gino weighs the therapist's words. *She acts confident but lacks Dr. Nowiski's impeccable credentials. One is right, the other wrong. I bank on the doctor.*

"Do you expect she'll improve?"

"I'm afraid she presents with cerebral hypoxia."

Her jargon agitates Gino, who barks, "I'm not a doctor. What does hapax—"

"It's hypoxia—cerebral hypoxia. And I apologize for the tech talk. I often forget to simplify. The term means her brain suffered a lack of oxygen when she seized."

Gino wants to blast her since she used *tech talk* to apologize for using technical talk. He composes before he speaks. "But her dam-age—you find it permanent?"

"I don't know, but I felt it necessary to alert you to the possibility."

Gino wishes he could alter history and end this brutal night-mare. For now, he needs this therapist out of his face. "Thank you, I guess." Gino's mind buzzes with conflicted thoughts. "Wish I had better news, Mr. Cavatelli."

"Yeah, me too."

As the therapist departs, Gino considers serious issues. *I'm distraught and can't hide my concern from my children. What do I tell them? They'll find me out if silent. But if I share the therapist's comments, I might unduly cause alarm. I'm in an uncomfortable state of confusion.*

† † †

More relatives await Gino's return. He greets each with customary hugs and kisses. An obligatory smile disguises his despair. By all indications, he fools everyone but his children, who see through him.

After several minutes of chitchat, which twists Gino's insides, he asks his children to join him in a consultation room. Angela notices heightened angst. Once away from others, she questions his demeanor. "Everything okay, Dad?"

Gino waits to enter the room before he answers. He shuts the door and pauses to gather his thoughts. "I'm not sure, Ang. When I last checked Mom, a therapist stopped me and said Mom likely suffered permanent brain damage. The therapist used a medical term related to oxygen and her brain."

"Cerebral hypoxia."

"Yes, Angela, exactly. This therapist watched Mom incorrectly use a spoon and straw."

Their conversation deepens their dejection. Julia, once vibrantly alive, might now lack the ability to function, communicate, or feel and express emotions. Gino's faithful wife and loving mother of their children might have brain damage.

Dominic breaks his deep thoughts. "I want to see her before I go back to the waiting room."

In a sign of unity, Angela grabs her brother's arm. "Me too."

"Fine, we'll all go. But let's not stay long. Your mom needs rest, and I don't want to disrespect our friends in the waiting room."

The Cavatellis walk into the ICU, slumped shouldered with grief. Their roller coaster ride continues to cause fear and nausea. Now, after they endured multiple loop-de-loops, the family twists in a corkscrew of emotions. Julia looks the same, and each Cavatelli prays for a calmer coast to this ride's finish line.

Gino's mind roams. *Where's Travis to give us comfort? Why hasn't he appeared and showed us love?*

His thoughts shift to the other driver. *If our lives are destined to change, so is yours, you two-legged snake.*

Back in the waiting room, visitors ask to see Julia. Gino approves with stipulations. "Sure, but don't stay long. Julia's awake, but she's often unable to recognize people. Please understand if you experience this behavior."

Visitors appreciate Gino's caution. And after visiting Julia, each person shows shock at her condition. Although she smiled, she did so for no apparent reason at unusual times. Her behavior left visitors distraught.

As for Julia, she remains unchanged—in a state of incoherence incapable of despair.

† † †

Travis embarks on another Phoenix hospital encounter. Many need his help, to include Julia Cavatelli.

Some patients rest near death and await their light of transition. Others, like Julia, whose time has not come, work through recovery. For each, fulfillment rests around the corner.

While Travis's intervention causes skeptics' confusion, Gino prays for Julia's health and relief from his hopelessness. Travis prepares to satisfy both outcomes.

† † †

Elsewhere, the leg of a man already spared continues to heal. Sam Ellis nears ready to return to work, his future defined but hidden from knowledge. His role, integral for many people he never met, resumes soon.

But, at this moment, a man who feels lost needs confirmation and inspiration. He fears if he fails his children, he leaves them vulnerable to more significant pain. Gino Cavatelli requires strength to cut through despair, and he needs it now.

CHAPTER 21

Lost

The clock reads 7:30 p.m. Gino relives the past two days. He also projects the most difficult aspects of those days into the future. Foreseeable outcomes frighten him. He must escape this hospital to free his mind.

"I want to check on Mom one more time before I leave. It's late. You guys should also go home."

Angela yawns. "Yeah, I'm beat, and it hurts to watch her." Dominic agrees.

Gino feels lost. His knees are weak, he needs food and rest, and his look undermines his upbeat words. "Let's hope for a miracle, and Mom recognizes us. I need a positive send-off."

They enter Julia's room. She still sits half slumped in a bedside chair, her position unchanged from mid-afternoon. Angela covers her eyes. Dominic looks away.

When he gains enough strength to talk, Dominic breaks the silence. "I'll see you tomorrow, Mom. I wanted to say good night, and I love you."

Julia lifts her head slightly toward Dominic. Her sliver smile lacks warmth. Her empty eyes meet his without recognition. Broken by her silence, Dominic moves to the foot of Julia's bed. Her eyes follow, although delayed.

Angela embraces her brother, a sign of affection rarely shown. Her look says, "I understand how you suffer. I do too."

Dominic seldom acts so emotional and lost.

Angela turns toward her mother. "Do you know who I am, Mom?" Julia's blank expression confirms Angela's fears. Her presence confuses her mom.

Desperate, Angela probes further. "Do you know your oldest granddaughter's name?" This question also fails to cut through Julia's bewilderment.

Angela blinks back tears. She swallows grief. "Good night, Mom. I love you. I'll see you tomorrow."

Julia sits silently unfazed.

Angela buries her face in her hands. She leaves Julia's room to release a flood of tears. Dominic follows and returns Angela's earlier affection.

Now alone, Gino looks longingly at Julia. *What if I kiss you? Will you be startled? But what if I kiss you and you don't react? In either case, can I handle the heartache?*

Gino fears the latter and foregoes a kiss. Instead, he caresses her hand, much like he expects Travis did nearly two years ago.

Julia retracts slightly, so Gino tightens his grip. She looks at him, to their clutched hands, then back. Neither speaks. Her stagnant smile remains pointless. Her distance destroys him.

Gino releases Julia's hand and weighs what to say. "Good night, love. I'll see you tomorrow." Julia's left eye twitches. Her smile turns up slightly. Unsure if he imagined her movements, Gino accepts this as the day's first sign of promise.

† † †

Gino's children wait for him at the visitor elevators. Angela sobs against Dominic's chest. Gino touches her shoulder. She bellows. "Mom doesn't know me." Grief fills the elevator lobby. "The therapist must be right. Mom will never recognize my children or me again."

Gino's heart sinks to the pit of his stomach. With Angela's loss of hope and calm, he looks to build her spirits. "I'm not sure about the therapist, Angela. Why not wait and see what happens tomorrow?"

Angry, Angela hollers, "Dad! She didn't know my daughter's name."

Gino's jaw quivers. He struggles for a response but understands the moment requires one. "Sometimes, we must accept we lack control over every aspect of life. It's hard, I know. But to show faith in our faith, we must accept God's will in every situation. This critical time requires we trust and behave based on our beliefs."

His comments meet deaf ears. Despair etches Angela's face. She saw what she saw and experienced what she experienced. More words, no matter how eloquent, fade, lost in her despair.

"We should go." They leave arm in arm.

Outside, Gino bids his children good night. Their group hug, which drips with affection, makes each feel closer than ever.

A slender man walks toward the hospital's entrance. He stops to admire the Cavatelli's embrace. Gino's eyes meet his. The man nods and smiles his approval. Gino squeezes his children with a surge of calm and sense of hope.

He glances over his shoulder. *I've seen this man before.*

† † †

Gino waits in his car for Angela to leave. They live five houses apart, so he will ensure she gets home safely.

Soon after he turns west on Dunlap Road, Gino calls Angela to reinforce his confidence in Dr. Nowiski, the bright and talented neurosurgeon. Based on age alone, the therapist lacks experience in her field compared to Dr. Nowiski in his. He prays this fact restores Angela's faith her mother will improve.

"Hello."

"Ang, it's me, Dad. You okay?"

She suppresses her sobs. "I'll be *all right*."

"I know you *will*, but how about now?"

"No." Angela's response reflects tears and exhaustion. "But I'm well enough to drive home."

"Good. Please think about this on your drive. Dr. No— "Please! I'm not sure I can think anymore today."

"Try."

Angela's silence causes him to wonder if he pressed too hard and direct. "Fine."

"Dr. Nowiski possesses incredible credentials. I'm not sure you know, but he did his residency at Barrow Neurological Institute."

"Yeah."

"The young therapist, although friendly, maybe spoke beyond her experience."

"What do you mean?"

"She based her opinion on two three-minute assessments—"

"Yeah."

"Please let me make my point."

"Sorry, Dad."

"Dr. Nowiski based his judgment on clinical results and association tests. Besides, he's known Mom for two years. The therapist interacted with her, what, ten minutes max?"

"True."

"I've got my money on in-depth medical knowledge, experience, and clinical tests over youthful observations."

"You make good points."

"Maybe you'll feel better if you trust his judgment too."

"Dad, you saw her." Angela sharp response suggests, *cut the bull.*

"She didn't recognize me and couldn't remember Adriana's name. What am I to think?"

"I can't tell you how or what to think, Angela. I don't claim this type of influence. But if we trust what we profess to believe, we'll survive this with inner peace. We can hope for no better. No, we must pray for no less."

Angela pauses and slumps resigned. "I know you're right, and I'll feel better after some sleep. We've had a long, hard two days, and I have little left in my tank."

"Yes, but the sun rises again tomorrow, I promise. And we do too, God willing. For now, please know how much your mom and I love you. She'll tell you herself tomorrow."

With resignation, Angela says, "Thanks, Dad. I'm glad you called. I feel better than before."

"Do you? You still sound down."

"My emotions aren't on a switch. I need time, but I'm as good as can be expected. I'll feel better tomorrow."

"Good. You said what I needed to hear."

"Okay, and thanks again, Dad. I love you."

"I love you too, Angela, and thanks for your support the past two days. You and Dom gave me the strength I needed to survive. I'd have felt lost without you."

Pleased with his conversation, Gino turns to Dominic. Before he autodials, Gino checks his side-view mirror. His shoulders scrunch, his jaw juts, and he witnesses the unthinkable—a near-miss accident. Gino and Angela passed through the same intersection seconds ago. He exhales loudly as one car whizzes past another. Both vehicles continue unscathed.

This example of a careless driver, who escaped consequences of his actions, outrages Gino. One driver ran a red light but thankfully missed the other car. *Oh, if Julia had such luck in November 2011.*

Gino bangs his fist against his thigh. He mentally summarizes his harsh feeling toward reckless drivers. *Criminals!*

Gino's conversation with Dominic runs less emotional than Angela's. Dom, with concerns of his own, displays greater optimism than his sister. He speaks of how his faith gives him peace, which comforts Gino. He hangs up, satisfied. *I did my parental duty, but what about me? Do I believe what I told my children about how I feel? Will it help me through the night as I expect it might them? Is it time for me to redirect some energy to the other driver? He can't stay lost to me forever. I must find him—soon.*

With an extended blink, an image invades Gino's mind. *Who was that odd thin man at the hospital?*

CHAPTER 22

Recovery

Exhausted, Gino retires for bed without news updates or snacks. Tonight, sleep for emotional recovery tops informational and nutritional needs. But he stares at his ceiling tired and unsettled. A movie—*Away from Her*, a gut-wrenching story about a woman with Alzheimer's disease—haunts him. The film portrays a husband's pain and guilt as his wife falls further into forgetfulness.

Over time, she turns her affections toward a male nursing home patient. After her friend's family removes him from the facility, she deteriorates faster. Through a kind act by her husband, his wife and her companion reunite one last time.

In a touching final scene, the wife momentarily remembers her husband and thanks him for his kindness—for her visit with her friend, which he arranged. His selfless act taken for her and her brief remembrance of him creates a significant impact.

Gino's fear mirrors the husband's. *Will Julia remember me—our family—again? Or am I like the movie husband—lost to her memory? Can the therapist be right and the doctor's optimism only offered to pump up loved ones' spirits? Will I grow away from her during her recovery, or has Julia already fallen away from me?*

As usual, time holds all answers.

Sleepiness grips Gino shortly after midnight, so he turns off his lamp. He tosses some then settles on his back. A voice shakes him.

"Gino, do not be afraid. Julia and your family survive this ordeal. Trust." He flicks on the lamp and scans his room nervously. No surprise, he finds no one. *The voice, so close, so real, came from my mind.*

If not, where? Have I succumbed to stress and border on insanity?

One of the girls licks his cheek as he douses the light again. The mysterious voice rings out again. *"Trust."*

More relaxed by the moment, Gino rolls over and falls asleep unaware of what lies ahead shortly.

† † †

The clock reads 2:42 a.m. Gino awakens to dampness against his face. A tear trickles from the corner of his left eye and falls to meet others as if in slow motion. It moistens his pillowcase with a splash of a glacier calving into the sea.

The experience confuses Gino, but soon reality grips him. He has been crying in his sleep. No moans or sobs, just tears, which leak from his eyes. A tear forms with each heartbeat. Once large enough, it spills from its tear duct to well in his eye socket. When sufficiently large, the droplet dribbles out and rolls down his cheek as another forms. *Damn that movie—a film I both love and hate. Tonight, like when Julia and I saw it in a theater, the movie weakens me beyond imagination.*

Gino tosses more. *Where's the sleep I need? Robbed by a sad movie? I'm up now, so I may as well head to the hospital.*

He rises and showers by 4:45. Before he leaves, he calls the hospital to check Julia's status. To his joy, she improved considerably.

He rushes to see Julia and enters the hospital deep in thought near 6:00. A man on his way out smiles warmly, and Gino barely lifts his eyes and bids good morning. Two steps further, he remembers the man from the prior night outside the hospital. He feels an odd bond and turns to talk with him.

With the lobby empty, Gino races outside to find no one. *It's impossible. He can't be out of sight already. I saw him there one second. Then he's gone.*

An eerie sensation overtakes Gino. A wisp of wind fluffs his hair and piques his wonder. He turns an ear to the breeze. *I swear I heard someone say, "Trust."*

Gino hears nothing else and sees no one, so he reenters the hospital and moves to the ICU. Staff mill at the nurses' station. He nods to Maria, who stops him before he reaches Julia.

"Mr. Cavatelli."

Gino turns, and he and Maria exchange smiles.

"May I speak with you?"

"Sure."

"I'd like to discuss your wife's night."

"Me too."

She points to an area clear of others. "Let's walk here out of the way."

"Sure."

"She did great, Mr. Cavatelli."

"I heard. I called earlier."

"Yes, her memory improved a lot, and she mastered our battery of questions. She even did her ABCs accurately. You'll be happy with her progress."

Stress leaves his body. "Thank you. I'm stoked."

"I know. Joy covers your face."

Gino looks toward Julia, who lies asleep. He looks back at Maria. She beams.

"May I ask a question?"

"Of course, Maria."

"Travis?"

"Travis?" Gino questions.

"Yes, the man who stays with your wife at night."

"Mr. Cavatelli, you okay?"

Gino squirms while his mind searches for a response. "Yes— fine. Um, he's a *brother*." He nods to affirm. "Yeah, he's a brother we don't often see."

Gino's story gains momentum as he guards against lying. He scratches his chin. "He's not from here, and we never know when to expect him. He always knows when to show up, though. Why do you ask?"

"He's unique."

"Oh, for sure." *You have no idea.*

"He's a special guy. No doubt there."

"Yeah, he visited your wife both nights, and odd events happen when he arrives."

"Oh?" Gino knows he's about to hear an unbelievable story.

"Yes. Patients often perk up when family visits. So I'm not surprised your wife improves when Travis arrives."

"I'm sure." Gino struggles with how anyone in a coma knows of another's presence.

"Here's what's odd, though."

"Yeah?"

"Nurses say *their* patients also improve during Travis's visits."

"Really?"

"Yes, and this defies logic. Unlike Mrs. Cavatelli, however, these patients return to their prior condition after Travis leaves."

"What do you make of this?"

"We attribute those improvements to Travis's presence, as nutty as that sounds. His impact is hard to comprehend, but impossible to deny."

"I'm not surprised. You're probably stirred too. Travis lifts everyone's spirits. His aura reaches far."

"You know he just left, right?"

Gino wipes his brow. "Uh, yeah, I saw him when I arrived. He knows my schedule and looks over Julia when I'm away."

Maria suspects Gino doubts her comments. "We document changes when Travis arrives and leaves. The whole vibe is different— if an ICU has a vibe."

"I'm speechless." Questions fill Gino's mind.

"Mrs. Cavatelli might go to a regular room later today. So please tell Mr. Travis how much I enjoyed his visits."

"Sure."

"I lack an explanation, but I talked with Travis only minutes, and I feel like I know him as a friend."

"I'll bet."

"Strange. I've never felt like this before and doubt if I ever will again. As I said, I can't explain my experience."

"You owe no explanation. I know how you feel. Travis impacts everyone he meets. He makes people feel good—in a better place. It's just him."

"He's remarkable."

"I'll tell him how you feel."

"And one more comment, if I may." Maria raises her right index finger to the corner of her mouth. "When I asked his name, he said it's *I. M. Travis.*"

"Right, for ease, Travis goes by his last name."

"Yes, but he chillingly emphasized the *I. M.*"

"Hum?"

"Right."

"Travis—he's mysterious."

"I'll say." Maria's tone suggests Gino masters the obvious.

"He'll never change, I'm sure."

Maria beams. "I hope you're right. I find him a good man, and his calm and gentleness encourage me to live more like him. I've never met a more peaceful person. I need peacefulness, and whatever else he has, in my life."

"Don't we all?"

"Yes. And I believe Travis changed my life with little more than saying his name."

Gino's cat-bird smile intrigues Maria. "I'm sorry. I said too much."

"Don't be silly. I enjoy comments about Travis."

"You sure?"

"Yes, and he'll be glad to hear how you feel, but I expect he already knows."

Maria melts, pleased.

Gino heads for Julia's room. He wants to wake her but chuckles at his reason. *I want sixty-year-old Julia to do what most three-year-olds can do—recite the ABCs. Based on yesterday, that would be a significant accomplishment.*

He watches Julia breathe, overjoyed. He laughs. *Neither Officer Rozelle nor I found the other driver, but Julia encounters elusive Travis twice in as many days.*

After a short time, Gino returns to his usual seat in the waiting room. He expects he might be the only person there without the weight of surgical uncertainty.

A man, whom Gino spoke with earlier, asks, "When your wife went into surgery the other day, did someone sit with and encourage you?"

"A volunteer, I suppose. Why do you ask?"

"This guy, not a hospital employee, came to me and others and encouraged and ensured us our loved ones would be okay."

Gino's thinks of Travis. "Did he use *comfort* while talking with you?"

"Yes, how'd you know?"

"I guess sometimes you simply know what you know."

"I'll say this, my confidence in my wife's recovery soared after he left."

"I'll bet." Gino smiles full-faced.

Hope rises for both.

CHAPTER 23

Beaming

Gino returns to the ICU within an hour. He hopes to find Julia awake but accepts if not. Sleep helps to heal, and Julia needs both.

He rounds the corner at the nurses' station and sees Julia seated next to her bed. His heart leaps; she looks more herself.

"Well, good morning." Gino wears a smile absent past days. Julia beams ear to ear. "I wondered when you'd get here." Gino closes his eyes; his heart fills with joy. *Thank you, God.* "What's wrong, Gino?"

He tilts his head and softens his eyes. "Tired, that's all. But let's focus on you. You're awake and better. That's what matters."

Julia stretches her arms outward, and she and Gino embrace. He pulls a chair near Julia's and considers a question he must ask but fears.

"Come on, what's on your mind?"

"I have a question."

"Ask."

"Do you know who I am?"

"Of course." Julia's voice is cheery and bright. "You're Gino. You're my husband."

Gino melts inside over Julia's return. He wondered if this day would ever come.

He shares details about her hospital stay: the surgery, seizure, memory loss, her reactions the previous night, or lack thereof. She only remembers up to her goodbye with Gino outside the surgical suite.

Julia regrets the emotional hardship she caused. "I can't believe I couldn't recognize anyone. It seems impossible."

"It broke my heart."

"Could you have dreamt or imagined it?" she asks, hopeful.

"I wish, but no."

"I'm sorry I caused such pain."

"It's not your fault. You know how I feel about this. The other driver's at fault, not you, and he'll get payback in time."

"What do you mean?"

"You always speak of karma. The other driver's hardship begins when what's gone around comes around—to him."

"Gino, let your bitterness go."

"Oh, I'm not bitter. I'm enraged."

"Please stop."

"In time."

"No, now—for me."

"I can't."

"You must."

"We'll take it up later. Here comes Dr. Nowiski."

The doctor smiles, happy seeing Gino and Julia converse. "Well, what a pleasant sight. How are we today?"

Gino rises to shake the doctor's hand. "Both better than yesterday."

"I'd say so." He smiles at Julia. "Ready for some questions?"

Julia grins and shakes her head *no* in wonder. *What's with all the questions?*

Seconds later, she shrugs. "Okay, ready." She responds correctly, albeit agitated. "Dr. Nowiski, are you testing me?"

"Yes, and you passed. We ask questions to assess your brain function. And I have one more. Do you know who I am?"

Julia smiles wide. "You're my doctor."

Dr. Nowiski nods satisfied.

After more discussion, Gino relates his experiences over the past eighteen hours. The doctor's disappointment with Gino's run-in with the therapist shows. "She shouldn't have given her opinion. She lacked clinical evidence to support her observations."

"She confused me, and I'm embarrassed to say I questioned your certainty about Julia's recovery."

Dr. Nowiski nods toward Julia. "Let me put a bow on this present you see here. Even though your wife's memory might still be sketchy on occasion, I'm 99.9 percent sure she'll fully recover. Temporary loss happens with a seizure, and I find her progression rational."

Julia reacts. "I didn't know any of this, but I trust Dr. Nowiski's opinion."

"Please understand, I don't mean to knock the therapist or imply incompetence. I expect she's young?"

"Yes."

"Yep, she's too inexperienced to withhold her initial impression until confirmed. She'll recognize and regret her error once she learns how Mrs. Cavatelli's progressed."

Gino affirms his confidence in the doctor. "I only care you continue to be right. I'll take 99.9 percent every day."

† † †

Gino recognizes Angela's and Dominic's voices down the hall. He motions thumbs-up, which quickens their pace. They display relief and join Gino's and Dr. Nowiski's high spirits. They cry joyfully when their mother stretches out her arms for a hug.

This family's reintroduction pleases Dr. Nowiski.

Gino hugs his children and sings Dr. Nowiski's praises. The doctor deflects. "I'm glad my certainty comforted you."

The Cavatellis look at each other and smile at the doctor's word choice. Dr. Nowiski leaves stumped by their reactions.

† † †

By mid-afternoon, Julia transfers to an orthopedic floor for continued recovery. Angela and Dominic rest at home. At Julia's request, Gino moves a recliner closer to her bed. She sleeps on and off through late afternoon and early evening.

At 8:00 p.m., she and Gino ready for bed. They share exhaustion and need sleep.

Gino butts the recliner against Julia's bed. She flinches; her expression questions his actions. Worse, her appearance seems to ask, *who are you?*

"Are you okay, Julia?"

"Yes, why?"

"No reason, just a question before I turn out the lights."

"Yes, I'm fine. I'm tired but otherwise okay."

"I'm sure you're pooped." Gino feels equally spent. "Good night, love."

"Good night, Gino."

Julia's eyelids shut tight. She sleeps soundly until her intrusive nurse wakes her to administer meds.

Gino wonders if Julia's confusion continues over his identity and their relationship. Exhaustion rules his worry, however, and sleep consumes him minutes after he grasps Julia's hand.

† † †

Julia's doctors release her after five hellish days. While happy to leave, Julia fears recovery at home and questions her return to the life she has known. Rough roads lie ahead.

While Gino gets his van, Julia waits in a wheelchair. She marvels at how a breath of a hot August breeze beats cold, stagnant hospital air. Her attendant's small talk interrupts her thoughts of freedom and about what lies ahead for her and Gino.

Minutes later, Gino pulls up. The attendant helps Julia from wheelchair to car seat. He notices paper on the ground, picks it up, and hands it to Julia. "I think this fell from your van, ma'am."

Julia takes the paper and thanks the attendant for his kindness. With a smile, he wishes her a speedy recovery and shuts her door. She rests her eyes for a while, then looks at the paper. One side blank, a single word scrolls across the other.

Julia holds up the paper. "Gino, the attendant gave me this note." Gino shrugs.

"He said it fell from the van."

"Yeah."

"Is this yours?"

Gino's eyes flash back and forth from the road to Julia and back. "I don't know. Besides, it's blank."

Julia's eyes widen. "Huh? There's only one word on the other side."

"And?"

"*Trust*. The note reads trust."

Gino stares ahead, silent. Julia notices his distant reaction. "Are you okay?"

"Yes, beautiful."

"Is the note yours, and what does it mean?"

"No, not mine, and I expect it's for encouragement."

"Encouragement?"

"Yeah, you know, *trust*."

"Trust what?"

"How do I know?" Gino is anxious to change the subject. "It's not mine. Look, let's not play twenty questions over a random one-word note."

"I find this good advice for most situations, to include mine."

Gino looks at her. Julia smiles affectionately. Both sit silently the rest of the way home.

† † †

The girls yelp madly when they hear the chirp once Gino locks his van. While he unloads Julia's walker, he marvels at their intuitiveness. *Oh, that everyone possessed such awareness.*

Barks, yips, and leaps greet Julia when she enters the house. The girls rejoice over her return. Once seated, they cover her with kisses faster and more affectionate than ever.

Gino slumps onto a recliner and looks for a televised preseason football game. One of the girls jumps up and nestles beside him. Eyes closed, he reflects on the last five days. *I pray the worst is behind us.*

Her energy sapped by their trip home, Julia chooses to nap before supper, so Gino moves her from sofa to bedroom. He lowers her gingerly. She sighs; the comfort of her bed ranks high among items most missed while hospitalized. Gino lifts the girls to nap with her. Once snuggly, he turns out the light on the sleepy trio.

Gino must do much while Julia rests, not the least of which is to prepare supper. Julia cautioned her first meal home had best be amazing. After days of hospital food, she craves Gino's home-cooked meals.

He scrubs his hands and splashes water on his face to refresh. He retrieves vegetables needed for supper. His chef knife feels oddly comfortable as he envisions a face-to-face confrontation with the other driver. An odd time for this thought, the blade seems decidedly more useful than for solely chopping veggies.

He sets the knife down and retrieves the accident folder from his office. He lays it open on the kitchen counter, Rozelle's document visible. His eyes drift back and forth from the butcher block cutting board to the folder. With a final look at the report, his eyes narrow, his nostrils flare. *It's time I search for you, whoever you are.*

With a snarl and grunt, he embeds the blade into the cutting board. *No time beats now!*

CHAPTER 24

Discovery

Gino stares at his telephone. Tattered pages of phone numbers lay to its right. After three more calls, his road to discovery dead-ends. Discouraged, he dials the next number.

The phone rings endlessly. After no answer, Gino waits a few minutes and calls again. He taps his pencil harder against his knee. *Come on—answer.*

A gruff voice greets him. "Bear's."

"Hi, my name is Gino Cavatelli."

"Persistent, aren't you?"

"I thought a second call might give someone time to reach the phone."

"Yeah, what do you need now that I'm here?"

"I hope you can help me."

"Yeah?"

"Do you have a—"

"I'm busy. Do you need an estimate?"

"If you let me—"

"If not, I'm not your guy."

"No. I—"

"Then why'd you call?"

"May I speak?"

"Don't be a wise guy?"

"Not my intention, but a few seconds to share my needs might help."

"Go ahead."

"On November 8, 2011, my wife..." Gino summarizes accident details. The man on the phone acts disinterested.

"Nice story, pal, but it relates to me how?"

"I need to find who repaired the SUV."

"Yeah."

"I've checked far and wide with no luck."

"You work for an insurance company?"

"No. I'm a husband on a mission."

"Look, I don't give information over the phone. I don't know you, and no offense, man, I don't give a rip about your *mission*. If you drive here, we'll talk face-to-face, or maybe not."

"Yuma's too far a drive for iffy chances."

"Look, I'm careful about my business."

"I understand."

"Hello, you there, Bear?"

"Yeah, I'm here. Let me help you out, pal. Make the trip."

"So you did repair the SUV?"

"Since you called, I guess you know my shop's location?"

"Yes. Yes, of course. Can you assure me you have information I need?"

"I'm here Monday through Friday, 6:00 a.m. until 6:00 p.m."

"You'll give me the name and such?"

"No need for an appointment. I'm here half days on Saturdays."

"What's your name? Who do I ask for?"

"I'm the only one here. I'm Bear."

"Bear?"

"You'll understand when you see me."

"Thank you, Bear. Thank you big-time."

"Sure."

The phone buzzing in Gino's ear leaves him eager to go to Yuma. *Why toy with me, Bear? You either made the repairs or like to mess with me. But you gain squat if you force me to drive there for no reason. You evidently fixed the SUV? I'll talk with Julia and head there tomorrow.*

† † †

Gino and Julia exchange morning greetings. Like most days, he acts preoccupied, so she allows him to direct their conversation when it suits his fancy. After casual small talk, Gino mentions Yuma. He sells his trip under the guise of business, which Julia struggles to understand. She suspects his journey involves the other driver—indication he still intends to find him and do who-knows-what. She values accountability like Gino but does not hate the guilty driver.

Gino fears he might slip and reveal his real reason for this trip. He wishes she could understand his obsession with the other driver and back him.

"So what business do you have there?"

"A guy has information I need. We agreed to meet today."

"What information?"

Gino proceeds with caution. "You remember the lady I helped with her business plan?"

"For the charter school—sure."

"Yes."

"You buried yourself in your office."

"True. Well, I need more information from this guy in Yuma. Call this another discovery expedition."

"Why not get what you need over the phone?"

Turning edgy, Gino says, "I tried."

"No need for tension—I want to help save you a trip."

"I know and appreciate your consideration."

Julia's recollection of Gino's charter school deal eases her suspicion. "Will you return today?"

"Yes, late afternoon or shortly after."

"Remember, I have a dinner meeting tonight."

"Okay. I'll eat out, perhaps before I leave Yuma."

Julia still questions Gino's story. "I ask you straight out, does your trip in any way involve the other driver?"

"I always think about him."

"But this trip?"

"As I said, I need to meet a guy. You honestly think I'd find information on the other driver in *Yuma*?"

"You're right. That doesn't make sense."

Enjoy your day and meeting." Gino grabs a small notebook and folder. "I expect I'll beat you home."

"Okay, but be careful."

"Of course."

† † †

Gino dreads his Yuma trip, an unbearable drive with endless desert boredom. The only plus this time—he stands to learn about the other driver.

Soon after Gino enters I-10 westbound, a car speeds past him. A common occurrence on this interstate, this driver exceeds norms for most speeders. Gino peeks at his speedometer and estimates the vehicle approaches ninety to one hundred miles per hour.

He checks his rearview mirror and spots a car with emergency lights on. A highway patrol cruiser fills his mirror within a minute, with the speeder now out of sight. Seconds later, Cruiser No. 40733 whizzes past and disappears into the horizon.

Several miles further, the patrol car rests on the westbound shoulder. Gino moves left to create a space cushion between his and the stopped vehicles—the speeder and Cruiser No. 40733. He smiles because of justice served.

† † †

Gino exists at Sixteenth Street in Yuma. Familiar with the city, he finds the body shop with ease. From afar, the yard looks ghastly, even worse close-up.

Parked, Gino looks around and questions what lies ahead. He scrunches his face. *No right-minded SUV owner would stop here.*

Out of his car, he stretches. His creaky bones and stiff muscles enjoy their freedom. He scans the yard and looks for signs of life in the pigsty named *Bear's Paint and Body Shop*. He yells for Bear several times, but no one stirs.

After a bit, Bear lumbers toward the gate. Gino watches negatively awestruck.

"I'm Bear," the behemoth man says, his voice loud and raspy.

"I'm the guy who called yesterday about the SUV."

He laughs. "So you came after all."

"May I ask why you said *'after all?'*"

"You *may ask* whatever you want, mister." His gruff response fits his unpolished appearance. "I may not answer, but ask away."

Gino sighs perplexed. He drove 180 miles and cannot under-stand Bear's hard-guy attitude. This crapshoot trip suddenly stinks, even though Gino just met Bear. Apparently, Bear gets his kicks when he busts people's chops.

"Bear, I drove far to get information important to me. I'll leave without another question if you say I wasted a trip."

"I'm sorry Carrarich—"

"Cavatelli."

"Right—whatever. I bet a lot of people screw up your name."

"You might say."

Bear points toward a shanty. "Follow this way."

Gino follows Bear to a small run-down shack. He chooses caution over trust and scans for a guard dog. Bear opens the hut's door, which creaks eerily. Gino tries to peek around Bear to see inside. Once there, Gino's anxiety about the dog decreases, but concern for his health increases.

The *office* interior, the filthiest room Gino has ever seen, justifies his worry. Afraid to breathe, Bondo powder, or everyday south-west dust cover every square inch of every surface.

A stench of a salami sandwich left unrefrigerated too long fouls the air.

Bear's appearance fits his office well. His teeth sport various shades of yellow—some approach green. They are as disheveled as the papers on his desk.

His matted hair looks slicker than the tip of a lube shop's grease gun. Wiry ear hair sticks out long enough to braid, and he smells rancid. The gunk on his soiled clothes exceeds the junk under his fingernails. On every level, Bear disgusts Gino.

Car components lay everywhere, which make it impossible to avoid bumpers, fenders, or other parts. Bear directs Gino to a chair—a metal saddle seat affixed to an axle connected to a wheel. Ready to topple, the contraption awaits a victim.

"So how can I help you?" Bear asks as he lowers to a worn yet ordinary padded chair. Gino prays the resultant hiss emanates from Bear's seat cushion rather than elsewhere. He holds his breath through a smirk and breathes through his mouth. Seat cushion con-firmed, the salami smell still challenges Gino's gag reflexes.

Teetering atop the seat, Gino says, "The driver of the dark SUV caused a serious four-vehicle accident and fled. My wife, one of the drivers, suffered severe injuries, which resulted in multiple spine surgeries."

"I'm sorry. How's your wife now?"

"Not well—lives with daily pain and other problems, which have changed our lives radically."

"What a shame."

"Yes, horrible. DPS conducted an investigation but failed to find who if anyone repaired the SUV. Soon after, I pledged to locate the vehicle and its driver on my own."

"Yeah, DPS sucks. What'll you do if you get the driver's information?"

Gino crafts his response to avoid a lie. "I'll give his information to my insurance company."

"I'm not sure how much I should say."

"What stops you?"

"A promise."

Gino carefully pries. "Such as?"

"I don't know, man."

"Look—"

"Dude paid me extra to keep his deal hush-hush, okay."

"He what?"

'Yeah, he paid an extra two large to keep me quiet."

"I'm sure his need for secrecy related to the law and insurance companies."

"Huh? Maybe."

"I'm sure."

"You know someone else poked around about a dark-blue SUV, right?"

"No. How would I?"

"Yeah, I guess."

"Who inquired?"

"You might be surprised."

"At this point, little would surprise me."

"I'm not sure with what I know."

"Tell me."

"I'm not sure I should."

"Then why bring it up?"

"It's related."

"How, Bear?"

"Guess I'll tell you. Remember I said DPS sucks?" Gino stifles a sneeze. "Yes, your words hang in the air."

"They suck because an officer snooped around here and asked tons of questions. He forced me to come clean."

"Do you remember his name?"

"Let me see." Bear opens the center drawer of his desk, which looks littered with—well, litter. He rifles through crumpled nasty stuff and removes a mangled card. "Here we go. Let's see. Officer Roberto Rozelle. Yep, that's him."

Gino's brow furrows. "I'm sorry, you said Rozelle?"

"Look, you heard me. The officer's name is Rozelle. Roberto Rozelle. Why?"

"I need to ensure I got the name right." Gino's heart races.

"Yep, Roberto Rozelle." Bear hands Gino the card.

"So you gave Officer Rozelle information on the SUV?"

"Hey, what's with the shakes?"

"Tension from a long trip, I expect."

"Yeah, I gave name, address, and phone number. You know— all the stuff from the work order."

"Then you repaired the SUV."

"Yes, the driver dropped off his SUV November 9. The owner, a highway patrolman, was headed to San Diego to visit family."

"I see." Gino muses. *Hum…a highway patrolman.*

He jots some of what he has heard in his notebook.

"Dude said he damaged his vehicle in a wreck in Phoenix, but he kept on the road since his SUV drove okay. He stopped here because of the late hour and found me the next day."

"I understand." Gino looks up from his notebook. "Did he mention how the accident happened?"

"No, and I didn't much care."

"What else?"

"I don't know, man. If the guy wanted insurance companies to know his business, he'd have reported the wreck. Instead, he paid with cash. Look, I don't want to get tangled up in some legal mess."

"What if I promise you won't?"

Bear rakes his hand over his sand papery chin. He comments through his awful smile. "Okay, but listen. If you mess me up with some insurance company or the law, I'll come for you."

Gino hopes his closed-mouth grin encourages Bear to keep his germ-ridden pit closed.

Bear shuffles papers in a desk drawer. He finds an invoice.

"Dude's name is Sam Ellis. I'll write it down with his address and phone number."

Gino watches Bear write on a grease-stained pad. His skills with a pen match his oral hygiene. Both need help. Bear labors to print; his tongue hangs like an English bulldog's, which might be an insult to bulldogs.

"I appreciate this, Bear. I hope someone repays your good deed when you need help."

"Yeah, okay. Just don't do me dirty."

Bear's word choice amuses Gino. He grips an unsoiled corner of Bear's note. He avoids contact with Bear's paws at all costs.

"You have my word."

"Yeah, well, you'll have to worry about one of my size eighteen feet halfway up your backside if you sucker punch me."

Gino offers a final button-lipped smile. "My word is my bond. You don't need to worry."

"Good."

With the needed information in hand, Gino and Bear move toward the gate. Gino extends and retracts his right hand quickly. Bear looks at his hand and understands Gino's avoidance.

Safe on the other side of the fence, Gino settles into his van. Bear stares and hollers, "Remember, no funny stuff," as he raises his right dungaree leg to reveal his anchor-sized boot.

Gino backs away and waves goodbye through his open window. Bear stands still. Gino imagines he grunted or made some other foul noise.

Discovery accomplished, Gino expects a better trip home. *This greasy note provides details I need to begin the next phase of my plan, but what a bear-of-a-time getting the information.*

CHAPTER 25

Encounters

Gino drives home from Yuma, preoccupied. He glances at Bear's note. *Sam Ellis—a DPS Office. Honor binds you, so what caused you to run after the accident? You know the consequences of your actions. Little adds up.*

Officer Rozelle seemed kind—sincere. But also corrupt, you omitted crucial information and filed a fraudulent report because of coworker implications. You commit to peers more than the public through your cowardly actions.

After he merges onto I-10 eastbound, Gino's speed reaches eighty-seven in a seventy-five-mile-per-hour zone, drawing the attention of a DPS officer. Within seconds, a cruiser appears in his rearview mirror. The patrol car tucks behind and follows Gino onto the shoulder.

In his side-view mirror, Gino watches a tall officer approach. He limps slightly, and his hand rests over his revolver. Gino rolls down his window without a defense.

"Good afternoon. My name's Officer Ellis. I need your driver's license, registration, and insurance card."

Gino reaches for his glove box. Officer Ellis trains his eyes on Gino while he retrieves and hands over requested documents.

"In a hurry today, Mr. …is it Cavatelli?"

Shocked and silent, Gino's eyes lock onto the officer's name-plate. *Here I sit on my return from discovering the name of the other driver—the monster who caused Julia's accident. Bear identified him as DPS Officer Sam Ellis. Might this man be him?*

"Sir, are you okay?"

Gino snaps alert. "Sorry. Yes. I'm all right." His heart swells, and his blood boils because of disdain for the name Ellis.

"Did I pronounce your name correctly?"

"Yes, Cavatelli. Guess I daydreamed, which caused my speed to creep up."

"So it appears."

For the first time, Gino hopes for a ticket to learn Officer Ellis's first name. *This must be him. How many patrolmen named Ellis work on the force?*

"My radar captured your speed at eighty-seven. You know the speed limit on this stretch of I-10?"

"Yes, sir—seventy-five." *Give me the ticket already!*

"I'd only warn you at ten over, but at twelve, I must cite you."

"I offer no excuse and accept responsibility. I broke the law. You must ticket me."

Officer Ellis stares into infinity undecided. *What's with this guy? He takes responsibility for his actions unlike me after my accident. I shunned my duty to stop, and I pay for my inaction daily. Now this guy responds like I wish I had. Will I ever escape guilt?*

The officer bends over to check for passengers in Gino's car. "I have second thoughts about the citation because of your honesty. I'm inclined to let you slide."

Gino strains for an angle to ensure he gets cited. Stress draws sweat to his brow. "Sir, I'd prefer not to get a ticket, but I can't escape the truth."

Sam Ellis's inner voice confirms. *Neither can I.*

"You got me speeding, which increased danger around me. You must ticket me."

Sam Ellis's internal dialogue continues. *I sense this encounter holds a message for me. If I expect those I injured to accept my plea for forgiveness, must I show forgiveness first? Is this the initial step on my road to recovery? Why does this stop feel so different from all others?*

Officer Ellis continues to reconsider. "Every driver's day-dreamed and lost track of their speed. Heck, I've done it. So I struggle to fault you."

Gino's inner voice confirms. *Yeah, you've daydreamed before, haven't you, Officer Ellis?*

After many uncomfortable seconds, Officer Ellis determines to end this traffic stop and resume his patrol. He stares at the ground and considers his next step. "On second thought, you're right. I'm bound under the law and owe a duty to do what's right—to issue a citation."

While he waits for his ticket, Gino harnesses his emotions. *He must be Sam Ellis. And, sure, he wants to obey the law—this time! Go ahead and show me mercy. What's your motive—to earn sympathy when called to account for your actions? No, Sam Ellis, our encounter is not about tolerance but to help seal your fate for how you impacted others.*

"Here you go, Mr. Cavatelli. Please sign below." Officer Ellis hands Gino the ticket and returns his identifications.

"I suggest you pay close attention and watch your speed. It's dangerous to daydream and often causes an accident."

Gino stares at the officer's signature. *Sam Ellis, cruiser No. 40733.* He signs the citation with a shaky hand.

Sam Ellis slips his pen into his lapel pocket. "You have a good rest of your day, Mr. Cavatelli. And be careful on the roads."

"Oh, I will. You too."

"Say, Officer Ellis, I noticed your limp. Service related?"

"Ah…yeah."

"Oh?"

"Why do you ask?"

"Curiosity." Gino hates the officer's bold-faced lie.

Sam Ellis wonders about Gino's interest in his limp. Few ever ask about his affliction.

After final comments, Officer Ellis returns to his cruiser with-out a clue about the significance of this encounter.

Gino merges into traffic and slams his fist on the center console. *I should've jammed my van in reverse, gunned it, and run you over when I had the chance. I could've left you mangled on the same interstate you left Julia injured. Sam Ellis, you'll get yours. It's a matter of time.*

† † †

Hunger pangs plague Gino. With Julia away, he opts to eat out in Buckeye. A meal at Cracker Barrel will fulfill two objectives: to satisfy his hunger and to get Julia Chicken n' Dumplings to go. He expects his kind gesture to please Julia at a time little else can and to help her forget his Yuma trip.

A pleasant hostess seats Gino. His server approaches seconds later. "Good evening. My name is Amanda, and I'll be your server. Can I start you with a drink: coffee, tea, or soda?"

Predisposed, Gino fails to acknowledge her. "Excuse me, sir? Would you like me to come back?"

Gino startles. He glares at Amanda. She shifts her weight, uncomfortable, and waits for him to speak.

"Guess you caught me in a daydream, an odd pattern today."

"No problem. Can I get you a drink?"

"Black coffee, please."

"Are you ready to order, or do you need more time?"

"Give me a minute or two, will you!"

Apologetically, Amanda says, "Of course. I'll be back with your coffee."

Gino scans the restaurant and fights inner turmoil. His out-of-character bark at his server troubles him.

Amanda returns with two coffeepots in hand. She asks timidly, "That was regular coffee, right?"

"Yes. Regular."

"Here you go."

"You said your name is Amanda?"

She responds cautiously. "Yes."

"I snapped at you, Amanda, and I'm sorry."

"No apology needed. Most travelers need time to settle once off the highway. Perhaps I approached too abruptly."

"No. I got a ticket earlier and mismanaged my emotions."

"Ouch."

"Yeah, but you shouldn't pay for my problem. I acted rudely, and I regret my actions."

A lady at a nearby table watches this encounter with interest.

"You came off troubled but far from rude."

"Fair enough, but I behaved in ways I dislike, so I apologize."

"I accept if it helps you feel better."

"It does."

Amanda's smile and moxie suggest she enjoys and excels at human interactions. "Are you ready to order?"

Gino orders a hearty supper and Julia's to-go entrée. As Amanda walks to the kitchen, he rubs his temples in a circular motion. He moves to his eyes, followed by a rake of his hair with both hands. *I can't believe the other driver's in law enforcement.*

He shakes his head, still amazed. *And...another officer covered for him. Sam Ellis—the guy who caused so much physical pain in Julia's life, and misery in mine.*

Gino's mouth turns down, and his eyes narrow to thin slits. His changed expression reveals deep thought. A slurp of coffee satisfies. The curious lady nearby, one of three chatty women seated when he arrived, feels his angst.

After supper, Gino lingers over another coffee. He stalls to allow Julia to beat him home. The thought of another arrival to an empty house sickens him.

Bibles open, the three ladies talk, one of whom leads the group. Gino catches the inquisitive woman's stare. She redirects her eyes when Gino notices. So not to gawk, Gino shifts attention to his table. Still in thought, he stares at his empty plate. He shakes his head and mumbles and again rubs his now tired eyes. His neck cracks with a stretch right. He rubs where a nerve pinched.

The nearby woman notices and asks her friends if she might appear forward if she talks with the nearby man. She fears for his soul. They encourage her.

Gino's server returns. He raises his head; his road-weary eyes meet hers. "Would you like more coffee?"

With strained voice, Gino said, "Yes, thank you."

"You sure you're all right? While none of my business, you still seem troubled. Do you need help?"

Gino stares into openness.

"Can I call someone for you?"

The nearby lady leans toward Gino to hear his answer. Her interest intensifies.

Gino offers another manufactured smile. "No. I'm fine. Thanks for your concern."

"I'm worried. People seldom dine here alone in such a dark state. You're this depressed over your ticket?"

"No. I face a huge decision. I near a fork-in-the-road and waver, undecided over which way to turn. Inaction might lead to lifelong strife. I risk a lifetime of separation from those I love if I act." He shakes his head and exhales loudly. "I've said too much."

Both remain silent until Amanda speaks. "You know, some forks-in-the-road lead to happy outcomes."

"I know."

"May I share a story with you?"

"Sure. It only seems fair after all I've spilled."

"I once worked for a scientific company and experienced a traumatic event. The situation placed me at a fork-in-the-road, and I chose to leave the business for a simpler career—to serve nice people like you."

"Did you ever regret your move?"

"No, I believe once you consider all pros and cons of a situation you act and never look back.'

"You seem wise."

"No. I'm only happier with my decision than you appear to be with your choice."

"You're right, but I'm wrong to burden you or anyone else with my problems."

"I hope the rest of your night turns out better than your afternoon."

"Thanks. I fret a lot over my dirty laundry, but I had no right to dump it on your table."

Amanda, with a warm smile and her eyes filled with sympathy, asks, "Can I get you anything else?"

"No, I'm fine for now."

Amanda sets Gino's bill on the table. "You pay up front. Please wave if I can help you further."

"Thanks. I will. You're kind, and your fork-in-the-road story will help me process my choices."

"It was my pleasure to serve you."

Gino notices nearby movement. The lady, who on and off spied on him, inches close. *You're kidding. Who is this woman, and what does she want? I don't need another encounter. I don't want another. I can't let this, whatever it is, happen.*

The lady raises her hand as if to ask for permission. "Excuse me, sir. I don't know how to do this, so I hope you don't find me forward or odd."

Not sure of her needs, he finds her intrusion strange. "What can I do for you, ma'am?"

The pleasant lady has soft features. "I'd like to talk with you."

"About what?" Confusion covers Gino's face.

"My friends and I meet here weekly for Bible study. It's not my practice to snoop into other people's business in public, but I noticed you're distraught. You worried your server."

"Oh?"

"Yes, and I share her concerns. My friends and I, as ladies of faith, seek to help forlorn people in our community with offers of encouragement."

Gino's face tightens. *And I had to stop in your community. In a metro area of four and one-half million people, I stopped at this Cracker Barrel, on this day, when this lady happened to be here. How much luck must one unlucky guy endure in a day?*

"Lady, I've had a bad day. I drove three hundred and fifty miles on a lark and got a ticket for my troubles. I hate a person I never met until today and didn't even know his name until earlier. Other than that, I've had a beautiful day."

"According to the Bible, we all sin and allow evil like hatred to enter our minds. We even act on those thoughts on occasion, don't we?"

Gino braces himself. *She's a mind reader too?*

"Yeah, I guess."

"Yes, we do. We do it when wronged and want to get even. But our troubles worsen when we act on bad intentions. We sink deeper into a pit of despair by actions we thought would lift us. Revenge seldom produces expected results."

Gino views himself a man of faith, but he never expected or wanted a personal Bible study when he stopped for supper. "Listen, lady—you don't need to hear about my problems. I expect you have enough of your own."

"You're right on your second point, but I turn them over to God, and you should too. As to your first point, burdens often ease when you discuss them. I wish to encourage you, so you have a better rest of your day."

"Ma'am, you're exceptionally kind. And you provide an excel-lent service to your community. But I'm not ready to talk with a stranger about my problems, how I think, or what I feel. I've already said too much to my server and you. Please understand, I appreciate your concern but ask you let me work this out for myself."

"But if you allow I'll hear your story, offer encouragement, and provide comfort."

Her companions smile, pleased.

Gino sees no way to shake this Bible thumper until he *shares* his troubles. People of faith don't talk—they share.

"I'm sorry and didn't mean to be rude. Please sit down. By the way, I'm Gino."

"I'm Phyllis."

"It's a pleasure to meet you."

"And you as well. So tell me, why so troubled?"

† † †

Julia's meeting fails to meet her professional needs. But it allows her to catch up with her friend, Diane. As usual, their conversation centers on their husbands.

"So how have you been, Diane?"

She instantly turns mopey. "No change in my life. Geoffrey believes his job is the only significant work in the world. And I still defend the value of my activities."

"I'm sorry."

"And why must I justify?"

Julia shrugs, her hands flipped upward. "Men. We might never understand them, nor they us."

"Is Gino still angry with the other driver?"

"Yeah, he claims not, but his actions suggest otherwise. I'm worried. Some days I think he'd kill the other driver if he could. It's scary?"

"You honestly think he'd hurt him?"

"Look, Gino blows hard at times, but he *rages* over the other driver. So, yes, I believe he intends to get even. Gino hates that I suffer and seethes over his inconveniences."

"*Inconveniences?* You survived a near-deadly crash. To help you hardly seems a high price for survival."

"I agree."

"Is he still nasty with you?"

"His actions vary. One day he's calm and pleasant. The next he's outraged by any mention of my back or pain."

"That's unfair."

"Yes. So I never know how to act. Gino prefers I pretend the accident never happened."

"He's unkind, dear friend."

"Most talks end in a fight, and I go to my room teary. Gino broods alone elsewhere. He loves me, but his insensitivity to my condition makes it hard to care for him."

"Can he change?"

Julia looks away with a slight headshake. After several seconds, she said, "Yes. Gino accomplishes what he commits to."

"More importantly, *will* he?"

Julia thinks a moment. "He must, or our marriage might end soon."

†††

Gino gulps his coffee and rubs his right cheek. "I'll give you a summary."

"I'll listen to as much or little detail as you feel appropriate."

"I'm sorry. How about a cup of coffee or other drink?"

"Thank you, but no. I'm saturated."

"Fair enough, but let me know if you change your mind."

"Thank you. Now, Gino, tell me about you."

Gino's brow raises, and he half snickers. "Tell me about you? What an invitation to an abyss."

"Oh?"

"Yeah. I'll spare you and only focus on items on my plate now. Let me know when you're full."

"I'm not worried. Go ahead."

Gino cranes his neck and gathers his thoughts. He returns full attention to Phyllis. "Over a year ago, my wife had a bad four-vehicle accident on Interstate 10."

Phyllis squirms. Her smile fades. "How horrible."

"Yes, and reminders haunt us every day. My wife was in our van…"

Phyllis misses what follows. Instead, as Gino's words trail off, she hears in her mind tires squeal and metal crunch, feels the rear-end impact, and remembers her nose-up launch skyward.

The kind lady fights an urge to tell Gino about her similar experience. She fears Gino might perceive it as phony empathy. Besides, she wants the emphasis on him—not her.

"One of the cars flew through the air and landed on our van."

Phyllis remembers how her car cut through the night sky. In some ways, it resembles a theme park ride until a jolt rocks her senseless. The bumper and trunk of her car crumple the front of a van.

"The car that hit our van flipped down the freeway."

Phyllis cringes with her memory of how her car rolls side over side, down the freeway until it settles on its roof.

Her face sags like a bloodhound's with the realization she shares reality with Gino's wife on November 8, 2011. "May I ask a question?"

"Yes, ask whatever you want?" Gino inches to the edge of his chair to near Phyllis.

She squints with intensity, unsure she wants to know the answer. "Did the driver who caused your wife's accident flee after he sideswiped someone?"

Her question confounds Gino. *How can she know? I found no news of the wreck. Did she hear about this crash from friends? Her knowledge unsettles me. Why her? Why here? Why now? How have so many factors converged at this time—with this encounter?*

Gino responds after collecting his composure. "Yes, the driver left. How'd you know?"

"May I ask another question?"

"Yes, of course."

"You said your name is Gino."

"Correct."

"Is your last name Cavatelli?"

Gino freezes with astonishment. He answers after a quick thaw. "Yes."

"I'm Phyllis Waddell. My car hit your van. Do you remember we talked over the phone?"

Gino's jaw drops. "What do you mean you're Phyllis Waddell?"

"I drove the car that smashed your van."

Gino's eyes grow big as saucers. "Unreal. Encounters like ours only happen in movies."

"I can't explain and also find it strange. But I think our connection happened for a reason—this night—here and now."

"So it seems."

Gino and Phyllis discuss her many challenges after she lost her baby. She credits faith in God as all that held her and her husband's life together while they mourned.

They also discuss Julia's multiple surgeries and how she struggles since the accident. Phyllis's look reflects profound compassion. Gino offers his handkerchief for her eyes. *Thank goodness it's fresh.*

Standing to leave, Gino notices movement to his right. He turns and sees the back of a lean fair-skinned man moving from another dining room to the country store. He looks back toward Gino and Phyllis and smiles as he nears the hostess stand. Elegant, the man looks familiar to Gino.

"Yes, Phillis. There's a reason for our encounter, indeed."

CHAPTER 26

Seeking

Sam Ellis parks in his usual spot at St. Gregory's. He stops here each Tuesday for private prayer and penitence. A smell of purity permeates the church, which deepens his guilt. As usual, his sense of unworthiness grows when his fingers find the holy water.

He crosses himself and stands in the center aisle. Sunlight splashes through stained-glass windows to cast a rainbow of color on the altar and walls. Their brilliant hues lure Sam Ellis and captivate his soul whenever he enters.

Officer Ellis walks to the third pew from the front on the right. He genuflects and crosses again, closer to the splendor from the front. With three paces right, he sits in silent adoration. Worn pews bear witness to this church's service to God's seekers.

He lowers the kneeler and his body in one motion. His knees meet familiar indentations in the padding. He follows this ritual for consistency and comfort and has since November 15, 2011.

Emotions smother Sam Ellis. He speaks in a faint voice. "Heavenly Father, I'm here for our weekly visit—just you and me, so bless me, Lord."

His words echo in the empty church.

"You know I'm sorry for the accident I caused, Lord. I lack peace of heart, mind, and soul despite my sincere remorse and how hard I repent. So hear me now, Lord. Forgive me."

Some of his police gear jingles as he repositions on the kneeler.

"I know I can't revise history. I can only atone but lack the backbone. So strengthen me, Father, and provide opportunities and courage to make amends.

"I realize you hear me, Father. And I know you'll provide needed peace and forgiveness when you find me worthy. But, Lord, if it's your will, I'll bear this burden for a lifetime. If my pain must equal that I caused others, I accept this penalty as just. But I'll continue my plea for mercy and a place at your table of forgiveness.

"You know my heart, Father. I repent for my actions. I earned your wrath but seek and pray for grace. Father, I leave my fate in your hands. Amen."

† † †

Tuesday morning finds Gino restless. Last night's evil thoughts spill into his day, as usual.

Still asleep, Julia rolls over with a pained moan.

Gino stares at the ceiling. He visualizes actions he intends to take for Julia, for Phyllis and her unborn baby, for the other lady driver, and for everyone else affected by the wreck. Fear threatens his resolve, however. *Can I do this? Should I? Are my reasons valid or artificial ammo to justify evil intent? In truth, I lose if I succeed or fail. But why doubt now? I need strength over weakness to block all attempts to stop me. Sam Ellis must pay—and his time is now!*

Julia stretches, yawns, and rolls to face Gino. He looks too awake to have just stirred, likely the result of another sleepless night.

"Good morning, Gino." She wipes her eyes of sleep and reaches for her low back.

Gino lays distant and disinterested. Julia knows not to speak again.

He responds as if a delayed reaction. "Good morning. Did you sleep well?"

"Not bad—only suffered five or six spasms. None lasted long. Once my tizanidine kicked in, I kicked out until around 3:00 a.m. Perhaps I'll have a good day."

Gino purses his lips. *Drugs—where would Julia be without her mind-numbing drugs?*

"Great." He lacks her optimism.

"Yes, not bad at all. How about you?"

"Lousy. I've got much on my mind."

Gino refuses to forgive Sam Ellis as Phyllis Waddell urged weeks ago at Cracker Barrel. The other driver remains a dragon Gino must slay.

"You still obsessing over the wreck."

"I suppose he's always in the back of my mind."

"He?"

"You know what I mean—the wreck."

"You must let go, Gino. The accident happened. So be it. We can't change history, so to worry about how or why it happened or affects us wastes energy. How many times must we go over this—a million?"

Gino despises exaggeration. He sneers disrespectfully. "You know how I feel."

"But you lecture *me* to put the wreck behind us only to fret and fidget over the other driver until you can't sleep. It's like I told Diane. I can't wait until your actions match your words."

Gino faces Julia beet red with anger. "You told Diane?"

"You know we discuss life issues. We support one another. She relates situations about her husband, and I discuss ours. Best friends share this way."

"Yeah, well, keep our business in our home. Don't air what hap-pens in our lives."

"I hardly broadcasted, Gino. And, after sixty-plus years on earth, I don't need your approval. Besides, where else can I vent? Certainly not here."

"Great. Turn this on me. You always make your problems mine."

"That's how marriage works. One's challenges and cares become the other person's as well."

"Relax, will ya, Julia? It'll all be over soon."

"What'll be over?"

"My obsession with the wreck."

"And this miracle happens how?"

"Show faith and patience. You realize my resentment stems from how the accident destroyed your life?"

"Of course, I understand, but come on. The incident occurred two years ago. Let it go. You care and hate to see people harmed, which I admire. But *I* endured the surgeries, not you. And I accept my lot and reasons for it. Why can't you?"

Gino smirks. "I'm happy for you."

Julia touches his arm. He pulls away. "Look, I don't presume to know why God allowed the accident. But he wanted me involved for a reason."

"Stop, already."

"No. This time, you listen to me."

Gino shifts to relax his body.

"I stopped to use the restroom on the way out of work? I never stop there, but I did on November 8, 2011. If I hadn't, I'd have missed the wreck. Don't ask why, but God allowed me to be in this accident. Good must come from this."

Gino grasps her hand. "You amaze me. Sadly, my faith fails yours. But here's my promise. After today, Gino Cavatelli never consciously thinks of the accident again."

"Promise?"

"Yes." He moves closer to snuggle.

"Know what?"

"No, what?"

"I believe you."

Gino tightens his embrace. "Then kiss me."

With Julia in his clutches, Gino marvels at how the worm has turned. *I once counseled her about negative thoughts and behavior over the accident. Now she advises me—an unusual reversal. Thank goodness her patience and understanding exceeds mine.*

"This madness ends soon, I promise."

"Good."

"By the way, I hope you remember I need to go out a little tonight."

"Remember? I don't recall discussing this."

Gino is again careful not to lie. "Guess I forgot to tell you. But no biggie, I'll only be out a few hours."

Julia insists on more from Gino about his outing. Unlike most times in their lives together, he offers generalities, which fails to please. She lowers back in their bed and turns away. "You apparently need to hide your reasons."

Gino is exasperated and grows more nervous. "No. I'm saving you from details of no interest."

"You're my husband—"

"And you're my wife."

"And what you do affects me."

"Yes, but you're not interested in everything I do, right?"

She rolls back to face Gino. "I suppose."

"And I'm not interested in everything you do."

"You're right there."

"And this is one of those times. I'll be gone an hour or so."

"Fine, I'll shut up."

"Good."

Julia bristles at Gino's sharp tone, but for the sake of argument, she buttons her lip.

† † †

Sam Ellis struggles to leave the church. He feels he might discover better words to express his heart if he stays longer. But prayed for pearls of wisdom elude him, and he leaves each week inadequate. His Heavenly Father, however, knows Sam Ellis's heart without the need for words.

He stares at the crucifix, which hangs at the front of the sanctuary below the softening colors. He pleads for leniency and clarity. *Is the absence of hope genuine hopelessness?*

Creaks of a door hinge interrupt his thought. A shrouded priest approaches. His face barely visible, Sam Ellis determines the man is not a parish priest. The man's eyes, however, rivet the officer where he stands.

"Pardon, my child."

"Father, yours is never an interruption."

The priest takes Sam Ellis's left hand in both of his for an extended shake. He softly rubs the top of the officer's hand.

"Sit."

"As you wish, Father."

The priest joins him on the pew. "I commend your faithfulness. You pray here weekly and while away, which demonstrates devotion. What is your name, my son?"

"I'm Sam Ellis."

"Sam Ellis, your presence pleases your Heavenly Father."

"Thank you, Father. But I come with selfish desires. Rather than to thank God for his blessings, I selfishly seek more. I come each week and beg for forgiveness for my actions."

"The Father bestows mercy upon those seeking it and who repent."

"But it takes so long."

"Delay tests sincerity."

"But I am sincere."

"We believe you."

"It's true. I'm abundantly sincere."

"I do not judge words. I measure hearts."

"Well, my heart aches."

"Tell me your troubles, Sam Ellis, while I comfort you."

Officer Ellis relates accident and following details to the priest, who listens intently. Compassion pours from the priest's silvery-blue eyes, which are all Sam Ellis see of the man's face. He remains silent until Sam Ellis finishes his story.

"Believe this assurance, Sam Ellis: the absence of hope on earth does not render one eternally hopeless."

"Father, you know how I feel?"

"Yes, your tears are the language of your soul, whether spoken or not."

"You see into my heart?"

"Yes, and hear me now: Guilt cannot alter the past and misery cannot change your future. What God intends will be in time."

Gino considers the priest's words carefully. "Thanks for your insights, Father."

"Bless you, my child, Sam Ellis. Have you confessed your act of omission to the parish priest?"

"No, I never find the time when he hears confessions."

"Danger often accompanies delay. God guarantees no one later today, let alone tomorrow. You must rid yourself of guilt before it's too late."

"I'll do my best, Father."

"Do not let your best be inadequate, Sam Ellis. Continue seeking a Christlike existence."

"Yes, Father. And thank you. Your words comfort me."

The priest smiles, and his aura spills from under his hood, or so it seems to Sam Ellis.

"I will be with you, my son, as you do what you must."

"Thank you, Father. I'm confident with God's help my issues will work out."

"As you do God's will, do not let events derail you, Sam Ellis. Stay repentant and rejoice when your anguish disappears."

"Events?"

"They will become evident."

Intrigued, Sam Ellis recalls a similar warning a few years ago. He looks at his hand, which the priest still rubs. "Okay. Thank you again, Father, and bless you."

"God bless you, my son."

The ethereal priest walks to the door through which he entered. Sam Ellis waits for the hinge to creak, but he never hears a door open or close. The priest just vanishes, or so it seems.

Sam Ellis's mind races. *I've seen this man before.*

† † †

Back home later, Sam Ellis feels an unusual warmth on the top of his hand the priest held earlier. He rubs it softly.

"Stella, come here—fast."

"What is it?" She enters the room briskly.

"My hand."

"What about it?"

She looks at the top of his left hand. "How did this happen?" Sam tells Stella of his encounter with the priest.

"So you think this mark is the result of him rubbing your hand?"

"I have no other explanation."

"It sounds far-fetched to me."

"Far-fetched or not, there's no other way I could've gotten this mark."

"Does it hurt? It looks like a burn."

"Not at all."

"I'm curious to see how long it lasts."

"Me too."

Stella returns to her activities in the other room. Sam walks to the kitchen sink. He runs hot water and lathers his hands. The mark remains.

He slouches onto their sofa in deep contemplation. He stares endlessly at the faint red mark on his left hand. Unmistakably the shape of a cross, he seeks clarity on its meaning. *The priest—this cross—both signs to move forward?*

Sam vows to tell his employer about the accident. He prays for a suspension over termination but commits to accept whatever his boss deems just. He worries about his buddy. *I put Roberto at risk if I come clean. There's no place for unlawful, dishonest lawmen on the force. But we have been both. I know, however, to attain the spiritual and emotional freedom I'm seeking, I must tell my employer the truth and accept the consequences for doing so.*

Sam picks up his cell phone to warn his friend.

† † †

Gino prepares for his date with destiny. He slips into his bed-room, cautious to cover his actions from Julia.

He reaches for the shelf above his pants and finds his target. The small metal box hides behind boxes of baseball cards he and Dominic collected years ago. Gino remembers with a smile. *Will we ever share such experiences again?*

Contents clank as he pulls the box from the shelf. He searches his key ring for the smallest key, the one about which Julia often asks. She is unaware he has this box; its contents would horrify her.

Gino opens the small tin container to reveal a Berretta 9 mm pistol, which lays wrapped next to a box of ammo. Both unused, Gino purchased the gun for this time and purpose.

He unwraps the weapon with care and loads the clip. Shaky hands make the task harder than it should be. He rushes to complete the process before busted by Julia.

Once filled, Gino inserts the clip into the gun and places it in his right pocket. His tremors worsen as he returns the box to its safe spot. He feels he might explode and settles a while on the sofa. Julia attributes his flush complexion and anxious behavior to his meeting. Gino marvels at her insight.

Gino kisses Julia and jumps in and starts his van. Each time he drives this vehicle, he wishes Julia's biomechanical repairs equaled his van's mechanical fixes. Sadly, his van is good as new, and his wife remains a wreck.

The bulge in Gino's pocket feels uncomfortable, so he stows his pistol under the seat. He must ensure nothing foils his plan should he be pulled over for some reason.

With a toot of his horn, Gino pulls away from home, seeking his nemesis.

CHAPTER 27

Fulfilled

Sam Ellis's supervisor detects odd behavior. The usually steady officer fidgets, stutters, and stammers through casual talk about life on the freeways. His peculiar actions worsen as he nears his confession.

After Ellis fesses up, his boss reserves comment and judgment. He phones dispatch to summons Rozelle off his beat to immediately join them. He dismisses Ellis until Rozelle arrives and advises their lieutenant of the situation.

Once Rozelle appears, the men sort out his and Ellis's role in the accident and subsequent investigation. Based on protocol, the supervisor places both officers on paid administrative leave until after an internal investigation. Sam Ellis considers paid leave heaven-sent; it eliminates the potential for financial hardship, the likes of which he caused the Cavatellis and others.

With their department's decision, both officers turn in their gear and call their respective wives for rides home. Embarrassed, they walk to a break room near the exit to wait. Coworkers offer encouragement, which Sam Ellis acknowledges with a head-down nod and hint of a smile, a fraction of the man he was hours ago.

Officer Rozelle's wife arrives before Stella, which leaves Sam Ellis alone to stew over his failures and to concoct a story for Stella. Already trapped in a web of lies, he struggles for another. His closed eyes flinch with each heartbeat. He waits for the overstressed organ to burst.

After several breaths to calm himself, Sam Ellis envisions the front of St. Gregory's Church. The priest's words in his mind cause sweat beads, which he wipes with the back of his hand. His neck squarely on Stella's chopping block, Sam Ellis settles on a story and focuses on how to prevent the drop of her ax—at least for now.

Livid but composed, Stella enters the parking lot. She taps acrylic nails against the steering wheel and alerts Sam of her arrival. She walks around to the passenger seat and tempers her impending tantrum.

Sam Ellis enters his dark-blue Dodge Durango and leans to kiss Stella. She stares out her passenger-window—silent. She concludes the cold shoulder treatment is better than a full eruption.

Sam Ellis secures his seat belt, and they head for home like total strangers. He expects a quiet ride.

Stella speaks after twenty minutes of silence. "So what did you do to earn administrative leave?"

Sam answers carefully. "I didn't know you wanted to talk."

"I don't, but I want to know what happened?"

"I'm embarrassed to say."

"Yeah, well, swallow your pride."

"You remember I complained about departmental nitpicking over paperwork?"

"Yeah?"

"Well, I cut corners and got a verbal reprimand a month ago."

"You never mentioned this."

"I know, and I'm sorry. I messed up."

"And?"

"Weeks later, an accident happened on Interstate 10, and the person who caused it fled. I investigated the wreck and didn't find the responsible driver. Because of—"

"That warrants a suspension?"

"No. Here's the offensive part. My paperwork omitted my efforts to locate the vehicle, so my supervisor inquired. I admitted I took shortcuts."

"Shortcuts? That's unlike you."

"I thought it impossible to find the other driver, and I already had a heavy workload, so I cut my search short."

"But your job requires you abide by and enforce laws and con-duct investigations based on truth and facts."

"It does, but I didn't."

Stella shakes her head in disbelief. "What prompted you, especially after already warned?"

"I'm not sure. I goofed up."

"Then you earned this leave."

"Yes, and likely more."

†††

Gino rounds the curve and turns off his headlights. He positions his van on the curb for the best view of Sam Ellis's house. Satisfied, he shuts off his van.

He removes the pistol from under his seat and leans back. His shirt rhythmically pulsates to his heartbeat. Energy buzzes through his nervous system like a swarm of bees. With sweaty hand, he tucks the pistol under his leg.

His throat dry from nerves, Gino grabs a bottle from a cup-holder. His hand shakes as he raises it to his lips. Gino gulps hard and spills water down his front. Panic-stricken, he checks his pistol, thankfully still dry.

Gino settles down after a few minutes. Too excited to notice details before, he finds Sam Ellis's driveway empty at the end of the street. *Of all days for him to be late. On second thought, this enables me to accomplish my task outside—much cleaner—than to drop him in his house.*

For now, Gino watches for the officer to arrive, jumpy as an expectant father.

He checks the time. Fourteen minutes elapsed since last checked, and Sam Ellis remains a no-show. More calm and calculated, Gino feels emboldened, more like all assassins before they pull the trigger. Now, if his actions match his convictions, Gino stands to fulfill his objective and to secure his place in history.

Headlights shine on the street perpendicular to Sam Ellis's. Tension grips Gino again. *The lights grow brighter every second. It must be him.*

Gino reaches for his ignition switch.

A vehicle turns right onto Sam Ellis's street and not into his driveway. Light beams fill Gino's car. He slumps slightly.

Streetlights reveal a city of Phoenix police car. Gino chooses not to duck in case the patrolman spotted him already. He lowers his pistol to the floorboard and kicks it under his seat. He panics for an excuse for parking there. It might be his turn to lie.

The patrol car slows as it nears Gino. Once next to Gino's car, the officer glances at him and almost stops. He continues down the street, however, and Gino wipes his brow, safe for the moment. He watches the policeman disappear around the corner at the opposite end of the street.

On a night Gino intends to use his pistol for the first time, he dodges the evening's first bullet. He closes his eyes and drops his chin to his chest with a shaky sigh.

† † †

Gino startles from a knock on his window. He turns his ignition to *Accessories* and lowers his window a few inches. An average-looking man stands there. "Yeah, what do you want?"

"My visit concerns you, not me, Gino Cavatelli—about your wants."

"About what I want?"

"Yes, what you want tonight is wrong."

"How do you know my name?"

"Focus on your intentions, Gino Cavatelli."

"What are you, nuts?"

"You know, Gino Cavatelli. You intend an action, not yours to take."

"I don't know what you mean. Move along, and leave me alone, buddy. If a beggar, I've got nothing for you."

"You spend much time alone, Gino Cavatelli, even when with others. Those times lead to illogical decisions and a plan unworthy of humanity. And, no, I do not beg but come with wisdom for you."

Gino's eyes narrow, and fine hairs rise on the nape of his neck. He moves his right hand to the side of his leg, forgetting he relocated his pistol. "What do you mean?"

"Your facade does not hide your heart, Gino Cavatelli. The action you intend tonight cannot instill accountability here or any-where. No, worse, you plan to take from Sam Ellis what he did not take from Julia Cavatelli. Your wife lives, so he may likewise."

"You make no sense."

"I do not *make* anything. I speak the truth."

"Go lecture elsewhere."

"No. You need me tonight."

"I told you, get out of here."

"Only after I fulfill my mission."

"Yeah, well, don't make your mission mine. Go away."

"Oh, but my mission is yours, Gino Cavatelli. The person who spared your wife and looks after her since sent me to save Sam Ellis."

"How do you know what you say?"

"Sometimes you simply know what you know."

"Yeah, and that means?"

"It means every second of every day, my friend, and I stand by Julia, you, and others involved in your wife's accident. We know what happened, Gino Cavatelli, and how everyone fares today. We witnessed pain and recovery and remorse and rage. Neither you nor they possess secrets. All is known."

Gino gestures the man go away. "You're nuts, man."

"No, men and women who believe they control matters over which they have none are misguided ones. I seek no rule but warn you against the life-altering mistake you intend tonight."

"What mistake? You say crazy stuff."

"I say nothing on my own, Gino Cavatelli. The person who sent me says all things in all situations. My friend knows your dark heart and how you let evil rule your life. He chooses to spare you like he saved Julia the night of her accident."

"Is that right? And your friend accomplished that, how?"

"He exerted a force on a car, so it hit her hood—not the roof. He fulfilled his purpose—assuring Julia's survival instead of demise. She has much to accomplish."

Gino's insides twist like a pretzel. *This stranger knows so much about Julia and me. How, and who is he?*

"And my friend, who accomplishes many miracles, tells you now, *'Do not commit your evil act tonight.'* Evil acts never rectify evil acts, Gino Cavatelli. They compound to create a horrible world."

Gino's tone turns sarcastic. "And what's your friend's name?"

"He is I. M. Travis."

"Travis?"

"Yes."

"Why are you here instead of him? Why doesn't he tend to his own business?"

"Travis mostly comforts and encourages after unfortunates encounter unexpected trouble. We identify, and I discourage people on the verge of terrible acts. Thus, I stand here, and Travis serves elsewhere."

Gino raises his cupped right hand to his mouth and closes his eyes in disbelief. He shakes his head repeatedly.

"Yes. Travis comforted Julia the night of her accident, Gino Cavatelli. And he stayed with her nights in the hospital. His presences calmed all patients there."

Gino weeps.

"Gino Cavatelli, you must heed his words. Do not fail. The rest of your earthly life rests at stake."

With eyes closed, Gino thrusts his head back and shakes it side to side. "No...!"

Gino opens his eyes. No one stands outside his rolled-up window. Frantic, he looks up and down the street. He sees no one and turns on his headlights to no avail, even though they shine brighter than ever. Though alone, he hears a stranger's voice in his mind.

Follow the light. Let it lead you from the darkness of evil.

Follow it to a haven from wickedness.

Follow it to Julia, who awaits you.

Follow it now, so the light of virtue leads you into eternity at life's end.

Gino sits, as if unconscious, emotionally wrung. His mind stirs, his stomach aches, and his hand trembles while he reaches for the shift lever.

A weak heartfelt message fades. *Stay and fulfill the task.*

A powerful brain-driven message grows. *Go and obey.*

Gino rests his hand on his lap and inhales to settle his nerves. He grasps the gear shift and pauses. *I let evil rule my life and nearly devastate my final years.*

He sheds tears of gratitude over this encounter, which blur his vision. Gino wipes his eyes with his palms, shifts into drive, and pulls from the curb. He glances at Sam Ellis's house as he passes and bellows in anguish over the act he nearly committed. He feels like the monster he previously deemed Sam Ellis.

Gino signals a left turn at the subdivision's exit. He must wait. A vehicle with the right of way approaches from his right. The dark-blue Dodge Durango also signals a left turn. The SUV slows and turns in front of Gino. The drivers' eyes—those of Gino Cavatelli and Sam Ellis—meet as the Durango passes. Sam Ellis searches his memory and remembers the other driver's face, unaware how close he came to a formal reintroduction.

† † †

After Sam Ellis parks their Durango, he opens their house door for Stella. They talk about how life might change if DPS terminates him. They pray for mercy and his job.

He opens two beers and returns to Stella on their sofa. She snuggles and looks at him lovingly and longingly. Sam leans to kiss her. He whispers, "I love you."

Stella closes her eyes, "I love you too, Sam. We'll be all right, won't we?"

"I've screwed up so much. I hope so."

† † †

The chirp of the door lock announces Gino's return home. His dogs bark and dance.

"So you took care of what you were seeking tonight, right?"

"Yes, much better than expected or imagined."

"You achieve an acceptable outcome?"

"You have no idea."

"You intend to discuss your evening, or must I remain in the dark?"

"Not tonight, Julia. One day, though. For now, rest assured I resolved the situation."

"Wonderful."

"Yes. Yes, indeed."

Gino moves toward Julia, arms extended. "Hey, I'm tired. Let me put the dogs up, and we'll hit the sack. Can I kiss you?"

She turns from him playfully. "If you tell me what you're up to."

"Bribes aren't allowed and won't work." He hugs her from behind and turns her. "Now where's my kiss?"

"I love you, Mr. Cavatelli."

"And I love you, Mrs. Cavatelli. Come on, let's get some sleep. The past twenty-plus months have drained me."

"What do you mean twenty-plus months?"

"Did I say *months*?"

"Yes."

"Obviously, I meant hours—the past twenty-plus hours after a sleepless night. Here, let me turn off this light."

"Good night, Gino. I hope you sleep better tonight."

"Without a doubt. I hope the same for you, Julia."

†††

Travis turns to his companion. "Tell me of your evening."

"It is well."

"You save much misery."

"I achieve what you inspire and enable."

"Then I am fulfilled."

CHAPTER 28

Wonder

It has been several months since Gino's encounter on a Phoenix street. After curbing his obsession over Sam Ellis, he no longer seeks retribution. He uses meditation daily to prevent regression. Although Julia wonders if Gino will maintain his new attitude, she accepts it as valid.

His life with Julia remains unchanged, however. He still handles every task in and out of their home and chauffeurs her on jaunts over fifteen minutes from home. Pain still controls Julia's life, and her enslavement binds Gino by extension.

Julia continues to decline since a third spine surgery in July 2013. With more titanium rods and screws in her back, Julia has less physical and emotional flexibility, and Dr. Nowiski calls other levels of her spine "ticking time bombs." She fights discouragement daily.

Unable to stand, to walk, or to lie down longer than ten minutes without position changes, Julia no longer works. Pain and exhaustion govern her life, which limits and stresses her.

Sam Ellis and Officer Rozelle continue to work for Arizona's DPS as highway patrolmen. With his reprimand behind him, Officer Ellis again serves as a model officer. Personal regret haunts him still, but his confession provided professional and legal relief. He remains committed to seeking forgiveness from those he harmed.

I. M. TRAVIS MYSTERY MAN OR MIRACLE MAKER

Stories of Travis find headlines around the world. People with personal experience follow him in wonder—others unaware observe with disbelief.

Recent headlines include:

Reno Gazette-Journal headline: "Mystery Man Helps Injured Skier"

Cronkite News headline: "Man from Nowhere Saves a Woman from a Suicide Attempt"

USA Today headline: "Elderly Lady in Deadly California Mudslide Rescued by a Stranger"

Religion News Service headline: "Pope Calls a Lifesaving Stranger a Man of God"

Associated Press headline: "Investigative Reporter Validates Events Across the World"

Fox News headline: "Man in Philippines's Tsunami Spared Certain Death"

CNN headline: "Hoax Label Removed from a Mysterious Event in Nepal"

As avid Travis fans, Gino and Julia enjoy each story about the enigmatic man. Each news account causes them to dissect Julia's encounter with him. His good deeds move her heart. Despite continued pain and limitations, she desires to model Travis in every way possible. She believes doing so might provide on earth rewards previously considered reserved for heaven. Moved to act, she intends to share her thoughts with Gino soon. Her time has arrived.

† † †

Gino and Julia read in bed. He flies through a plot-twisting page turner oblivious to Julia's presence. She waits for the right time to read him an unbelievable story. Minutes later, she interrupts his concentration. "Gino, may I read you a story about Travis?"

"Sure, but let me finish this paragraph."

"Okay, but you might not believe this. On second thought, you might."

Gino marks and closes his book. "All right, what's your buddy up to now?"

"Let me read the article. It's not too long."

Gino's anticipation grows. He enjoys Julia's excitement. She perks up when she talks about Travis.

"I'm all ears."

"Fox News broke this story earlier today. Here it is."

It seems the mystery man named I. M. Travis—or Travis for short—recently confirmed his affinity for the out-doors. Many beneficiaries of his help worldwide encountered Travis outside and in crisis. This most recent sighting also confirmed his bent for high adventure.

According to Nepal National, the country's primary news organization, Travis recently worked his magic in this tiny nation known for majestic mountains, Sherpas, yaks, and yetis. Nestled between the Himalaya Mountains and western planes of India, Nepal serves climbers who challenge Mr. Everest via the mountain's South Summit.

Travis allegedly appeared at Base Camp IV, located 27,001 feet on the mountain's south column. From here, climbers launch their assaults on the mountain known as the Top of the World.

First reported as a hoax perpetrated by a climber seeking notoriety, Nepal National verified a Sherpa also saw Travis on the mountain.

Climbers believed Pierre Lemieux of France made up his story about Travis. His motive—to shift attention from other climbers to himself. Lemieux, unable to complete his assault on the mountain, sought to steal attention from those who succeeded.

Lemieux suffered from high-altitude cerebral edema, known as HACE. People with this condition experience several symptoms—cerebral edema or swell-ing of the brain the most severe. Left unchecked,

HACE often results in painful death. The best remedy for HACE is quick removal to lower altitudes.

Lemieux, delusional with fever when Travis appeared, said this in his native French, "I lied fever-filled on my cot, covers pulled to my neck. Off and on, I saw images unclear to me if real or imagined. My muddled mind moved me from calm to panic. I've never been closer to death."

It was then a pale-skinned stranger opened Lemieux's tent unannounced and unexpected. Lemieux did not recognize him as part of the Everest expedition.

Lemieux said, "The mountain's bitter winds whirled and howled with fury—typical this time of year. Our tents withstood the bluster—a tribute to the care used to setup these camps."

Lemieux called the visitor's apparel abnormal. He lacked arctic clothing needed to survive on the slope. Instead, he wore jeans and a button-down shirt. Awed and in wonder, Lemieux said, "I've never witnessed the likes of this before on this or any other mountain."

Usual temperatures in May at Base Camp IV range from ten to twenty degree Fahrenheit without the wind chill factor. Lemieux said the stranger never acted cold.

"He amazed me," Lemieux said. "I shivered even though covered with inches of blankets. He walked in insensitive to the cold without a hair out of place despite the tempestuous winds outside my tent. He sat down without a word. I asked his name, and he said, 'I. M. Travis.'"

Lemieux said Travis looked different—his skin whiter than flesh tone. He questioned if the stranger's appearance was real or a product of hallucinations.

Mr. Lemieux said, "I asked Travis what he wanted. He said he came to comfort and assure me I'd be okay. I wondered how Travis knew I'd survive, but I didn't understand his answer. He claimed to know all things all the time.

"I asked where he came from or lived. Again, Travis confused me. He said, 'I am from all corners and heights and depths of the earth.' He made no sense, and I felt in a dream or delusional."

Travis's message to Lemieux matched assurances given others he's helped throughout the world. Travis comforts and calms and, in Lemieux's case, guaranteed survival without permanent effects from HACE. Despite the presence of deep tissue damage, Travis also predicted Lemieux's frostbitten nose and fingers would heal.

Lemieux added, "After Travis had made those comments, he stood, smiled, released my hand he rubbed, and asked me to believe his words. He said significant rewards await me if I do. After those insights, he left my tent without so much as a shiver, and my health improved."

Nepal National reported a Sherpa witnessed a man who matched Lemieux's description of Travis. He saw the stranger on the date, and at the time, Lemieux said he encountered the mystery visitor.

The news service also verified Pierre Lemieux's sta-tus as somewhat of a medical miracle. In spite of HACE and frostbite, Lemieux reached Mt. Everest's summit with his group on May 10, just days after his near death with altitude sickness. And before his return to Base Camp IV, tissue on his nose and fingers improved to where doctors predicted his full recovery without noticeable damage. After two weeks, Lemieux showed no signs he ever suffered frostbite.

When asked his reaction to Lemieux's experience, the base camp manager expressed happiness and called his encounter a miracle. Beyond, he intends to spread the word of Lemieux's incident to anyone who cares to listen.

Herein lies the lesson from Pierre Lemieux's encoun-ter. Pay attention if you meet Travis. Your life just might miraculously improve if you do.

Julia, eyes wide, looks at Gino. "Well?"

Gino pauses in awe before speaking. "What a fantastic article. Can you imagine? Wait, I guess you can."

"Without a doubt, I can."

"But the guy had frostbite, Julia, which improved with even more exposure to the cold. How does that make sense? Then again, when does anything related to Travis make sense?"

"I'm not sure anyone on earth can explain a miracle like Lemieux's."

Gino is out of bed, pacing. "I still struggle with one issue."

"What?"

"It's obvious Travis was your guardian angel at your accident."

"Yes, of course."

"He saved you from death, but why didn't he simply spare you from the wreck, the surgeries, and lifelong pain in the first place?"

"As I said before, I believe my involvement happened for a reason."

"It had to."

"It's obvious."

"But what reason?"

"We'll know in time." Julia appears more at peace than usual.

"It's God's work."

Julia's expression fills with wonder. "No doubt."

"There is no question. Consider these facts."

"Facts?"

"Yes. So many factors harmonized to place you on the freeway when the accident happened."

"I said the same already."

"Yes, related to the restroom. But consider others details."

"Others?"

"Yes."

"Okay."

"Your problem-solving with your coworker took long enough for you to be in the wrong, or maybe right, place at the right time. Why? What if you finished sooner or took longer to complete your task?"

"Good point."

"Why did your conversation with your social coworkers last as long as it did versus shorter or longer?"

"Huh?"

"Why did you only let the van warm up as long or little as you did?"

"I never thought about it."

"Exactly, but you warmed it long enough to place you in the wreck."

"Huh?"

"I know. Why did traffic flow as slow or as fast as it did, which in combination with other factors, put you at the accident site at the precise moment impact happened?"

"I drove as fast as traffic allowed."

"I'm sure."

"This interests me."

"Yes. And why didn't *you* drive faster or slower once traffic eased? Why? Why? Why? Change one variable, and you miss the accident."

"What a mystery."

"Right now we only have questions and no answers. We'll solve this one day, Julia, and I pray we're astute enough to know when it happens."

"I know. But you forgot another variable—how long I waited to exit the parking garage. I sat until a kind driver let me join traffic. If a driver before or after him let me out, I'd have also missed the accident—all other things being equal."

"Right on. See what I mean?"

Julia stares into emptiness and comments softly. "I've thought about this a thousand times. With so many factors, some of which I controlled, others not, how'd I arrive at Mile Marker 133 when I did? There must be a reason, which gives me hope."

"Hope's desirable."

"Yes. Before I die, I wish to learn why God made me suffer all this pain. I believe the reason relates to my purpose on earth."

"Purpose gives hope."

"But I wonder what?"

Gino reaches for Julia's arm. "We must keep our minds open and seek those reasons. But the chance we'll find answers tonight rates zero. For now, I'm sleepy. How about you?"

"Yeah, me too. I'll get the lamp."

"Julia."

"Yes?"

"Thanks for the article."

"You're welcome. It was magnificent, wasn't it?"

"Yes. The message inspires me to do what the guide manager said—to tell everyone you witnessed Travis's power."

Julia, eyes droop shut.

"We should, but not tonight. I'm bushed. Good night, Gino."

"Yes, you too, Julia."

CHAPTER 29

Rebound

Julia and Gino talk about Pierre Lemieux's experience often. They reflect on the mystery of Julia's accident, Gino's hatred, and other unexplained encounters. They want to understand the whys of these events and to rebound from this calamity. Only time will tell if they are successful.

† † †

One of the girls flaps her ears, which announces movement in the bedroom. Julia yawns long and loud. "Good morning, Gino." She wipes the sleep from her eyes.

Glued to his iPad, Gino asks how she slept.

Julia presses her palms against the small of her back at the waistline. Sharp pain interrupts her stretch. After it eases, Julia relates her night to Gino, which by all accounts proved better than most. Gino's indecipherable mumble and disinterest hurt Julia. With more to share, she continues despite his indifference.

"Honestly, put your iPad up, and listen to me, please!"

"About what?"

"A weird idea."

"The result of another dream?"

"Yes and no."

"This should be good." His disingenuous tone bothers her, but she continues.

"Listen, and you'll find out."

"Okay."

"I had an experience—sort of a conversation with a higher power. You want to know more?"

He puts his iPad aside. "Sure. First, let me get you some coffee." His newfound kindness surprises her. "How thoughtful.

Thank you."

"My pleasure." He pours her coffee and imagines what Julia might say. Whatever her story, he intends to listen earnestly since he just backslid slightly to his past antagonistic behavior.

"Here you go, hot and fresh."

Gino smiles most days now. Although unable to forget Sam Ellis's role in their lives, he accepts his inability to change the officer's impact.

"Thank you, Gino." Rich coffee aroma wafts from her cup. "Sure." He lowers to a chair. "Let's hear your story."

"Please hear me out before you comment, okay?"

"Hey, my iPad's off, our coffee is hot, and I'm in my favorite seat. Shoot."

Julia paces. He tracks her movement. "Every day after my accident, I focused on negative—like my pain and such. And you weren't shy to call me out."

"Right, you let circumstances, and your attitude toward them, paralyze you. My inability to accept your actions ignited most of our arguments."

"You didn't need to confirm my behavior, but thanks."

"I'm sorry, Julia. At least I accept my role in our arguments. Please continue."

"Each day my pain worsened, and I let agony beat me from physical, emotional, and psychological standpoints. I felt *poor me* and emphasized the wrong instead of right—what I couldn't do instead of what I could."

"You see this now?"

"I do. But people die in wrecks like mine or become paralyzed because of the surgeries I had."

"True."

"And people, as despondent as I allowed myself to become at times, kill themselves."

"Right again, and I worried about this with you."

"Honestly?"

"Sure."

"You never said a word."

"I wouldn't. I didn't want to plant seeds to suggest self-harm was a viable option."

"I would never—"

"I couldn't take a chance."

"Take my life."

"Your confidence in you exceeded mine."

"Are you serious?

"Please, let's not argue a moot point."

"You're right." Julia breathes deeply.

"Good. Go on with your story."

"I neither died nor became an invalid. And, although blessed, I focused on what I didn't have—a pain-free life—versus what I had—life at all."

Gino's wide eyes reveal surprise. "You've thought about this profound stuff a lot, haven't you?"

"Yes." Julia wraps her arms around her upper body. "My situation bothers me a lot and has for months. I wake up and plan to sew but allow my condition to limit me. People without hands paint beautiful pictures with their feet. Nick Vujicic, the guy without arms or legs, goes on stage and delivers messages of encouragement and God's love. I want to help others. There's—"

"Sorry for the interruption, Julia, but may I tell you a related story?"

"Of course, I'm interested in your thoughts. You seldom share them."

"A flaw I work on."

"Sorry. I didn't mean to criticize but to indicate I'm pleased to know how you feel."

"No apology needed."

"Go on with your story, Gino."

"It goes like this. A young couple, deeply in love for two years, decided to marry. Although the woman was blind, the man loved her unconditionally.

"Soon after they decided to wed, she learned her long wait for bilateral corneal transplant surgery ended. She scheduled an operation to restore her sight before her wedding. To her joy, she gained sight weeks before their wedding day—in time for her to witness the majesty of her ceremony.

"After surgery, however, the woman visited her fiancée and was stunned to discover *he* also suffered blindness, a fact unknown before she regained sight.

"Faced with this reality, she told her love they couldn't marry because of his affliction. Apologetic, her decision was final. He took the news gracefully.

"One week later, the blind man sent his former fiancée a letter. It consisted of only one sentence, which read, 'Please enjoy a happy life with *my* eyes. I pray they serve you well.'

"He gave *his* eyes so *she* could see."

Julia wipes her cheek with the back of her hand. Her chin quivers. "What a story. It touched me deeply."

"A sad story for sure, but a strong message. The man found joy after he helped his fiancée achieve her desire—her sight. He satisfied her without regard to personal cost."

"I'm amazed."

Gino must drive his point home. "The story demonstrates how far some people go to help others."

"Sure does."

"Julia, I don't suggest you sever a limb for an amputee, but I like your idea of helping others. You have super skills, great experience, and unequaled compassion."

"Yeah, and, on most days, I wake up and say, *'Oh, my back,'* and it's over. I need to change my pattern, Gino, and soon."

"I support you fully. You stand to gain plenty if you challenge your pain. I predict your health improves if you help others—like a reward you receive when you give."

"I agree."

To cement his message, Gino adds, "To focus on what's right beats fretting over what's not."

"I'm learning."

"Also, to focus on what you have is better than to grouse about what you don't."

"I understand this now too."

"And to concentrate on your value despite limitations is better than to let deficiencies define your worth."

Julia's chest expands high with a sigh. "I've taken so long to learn."

Gino reframes her negative perspective to positive. "But you learned. I'm happy."

Julia walks to Gino and places her hand on his shoulder. He stares without a word. She bends and kisses his forehead. He smiles, pleased he got through to her.

"Now tell me the rest of your story and what impact to look for with the new you."

"You're right about the *new me*. Here's what I want to do—to donate some of each day to a place called Caring Hands."

"Caring Hands?"

"Yes. The company specializes in transitional living skills for people recovering from spinal cord and other severe injuries. Their staff helps patients move from acute inpatient care facilities to their homes."

"What would you do?"

"I don't know. Who knows what I *can* do? But I intend to explore options."

"What interests you?"

"Any job that contributes to society—to our community—and makes it matter I lived. To continue how I lived the past few years would be sinful. I like Caring Hands because, but for God's grace, I'd have needed care in such a place."

"Did you contact them yet?" Gino asks, to gauge her interest.

He measures motivation by action.

"No. I wanted to run the idea by you first."

"I appreciate your consideration, but I support you all the way. In fact, if they need a volunteer handyman, I'll join you. To share our only true asset—our time—adds significance to our legacy."

"You'd work for free?"

"Julia, consider what Winston Churchill said. *'We make a living by what we earn. We make a life by what we give.'* I'll donate time to an organization like Caring Hands if you say it's worthy."

"Fantastic!" Julia's toothsome smile warms Gino's heart. "This might sound strange, but I dreamed I worked at Caring Hands already."

"You said fantasy played in there somewhere. In what capac-ity—what job?"

"Travel coordinator for out-of-town family members who visit patients. My dream felt incredibly real and vivid. I hope to do this."

"Do they have such a position?"

"I don't know."

"What's your next step?"

"Perhaps the most important step in my psychological rebound, I'll call there today."

CHAPTER 30

Robbed

Julia's partially paralyzed patient waits for direction. "Now grasp this with your right hand.

"Great. Squeeze harder to hold the spoon on your own.

"There you go.

"Good. Soon you'll pick it up without help."

Julia smiles at her patient's wife, who gushes over her husband's progress. This patient's case and other early successes provide Julia rewards beyond those imagined in her dream.

Soon after starting at Caring Hands as a visitation coordinator, company leaders recognized Julia's ability to establish rapport in every interaction. As a result, they created and trained her for a hybrid position to better use her skills. In addition to her coordination duties, she occasionally assists with dexterity rehabilitation. Julia's work thrills both her and company officials.

Although executives want Julia on its payroll, she declines, holding true to her objective—to serve voluntarily, not for pay.

Gino peeks into Occupational Therapy on his way to repair a leaky faucet. He hangs back to watch Julia work with her stroke patient, a broad smile on her face. He loves Julia's positive attitude, a considerable change from daily moans and groans at home. She still hurts but no longer allows pain to rob her of life. The value she derives at work offsets her discomfort.

Julia spots Gino at the doorway. He smiles, waves, and blows a kiss. Julia's heart melts. Her patient beams. Content, Gino leaves to complete his work order. Julia returns full attention to her patient.

† † †

Gino and Julia discuss their respective days on their drive home. As usual, Gino shares his observations on every aspect of company operations, but mostly about his and her work there.

He glances toward Julia, who is deep in thought. "I'm happy we volunteer at Caring Hands. And I'm glad we share each day's highlights on our drives home too. Most of all, I love the way you smile while helping patients. You have self-worth again, which means the world to me."

Julia responds introspectively. "I wish I listened to you sooner, but you never appreciated my challenges."

"I'm sorry, Julia."

"I hated our fights and my teary nights alone in bed. I felt you didn't care, but I now realize you helped me."

Her comment causes Gino guilt. "You don't need to apologize, sweetie."

"I feel I must."

"Well, don't. I acted like a jerk—often mad and incredibly selfish."

He glances at Julia again. She stares ahead misty eyed.

"I wasn't mad at you but about how your situation affected *me*. How your limitations limited our activities, whether socially or as husband and wife."

"I understand."

"Yes, but I intentionally made harmful comments."

"You hurt me a lot."

"I wanted you to realize pain doesn't have to end life—our life. I acted cruelly."

Both sit silently after Gino's admission. He comments further after Julia fails to respond. "Let me share a final thought."

"What?"

"I admire how far you've come and your convictions now. Pain no longer robs your self-esteem."

"*We've* come a long way, Gino. Not *me, we.*"

"Yes, *we've* come a long way."

†††

The slight man takes his goods to the counter.

"Will this be all?" a clerk asks.

"Yes."

"Do you need lottery tickets?"

"No. I detest games of chance."

"Me too. I never win."

"Be careful you do not lose tonight."

"But I don't play the lottery."

"Chance comes in many forms. Do not risk later."

"I beg your pardon?"

"When forced into options, choose wisely."

"I don't understand what you mean."

"You will."

The clerk stares into his customer's eyes. They say more than his words and leave him speechless.

"Excuse me. I will pay now."

"I'm sorry. Your total is $8.01."

"Yes, a significant time of night."

"No, sir, $8.01—your total."

The man pays his tab. "Be aware and reject urges for earthly glory. Remember, a man who swallows his tongue never gags on his words."

"Please forgive me, but I'm confused."

"Clarity follows. Watch and remember later."

The clerk shakes his head. "Thank you, sir. Have a good night."

"You do the same, Dwight." The man leaves the store.

Once the customer disappears, the clerk's associate asks, "Do you know him?"

"Never saw him before."

"But he knows your name?"

"I know, but how?"

†††

Two young men pull alongside the Circle K. Their car idles in darkness. The passenger harnesses his nerves. His bravery, fierce while crafting their caper, has since abandoned him. He trembles a frightened young man on the verge of a monumental mistake.

He irritates his cohort. "You okay?"

"Yeah—just nervous."

"Yeah, well, settle down. You know what to do."

"But what if someone enters the store?" The would-be tough guy's eyes fill with fear. "What do I do then?"

"Stop worrying. It won't happen. So get in, snag the cash, and get out."

"'Right. So let's go over our getaway again."

"Pay attention this time. We've gone over this a hundred times."

"Make it a hundred and one."

"You're serious?"

"Yes, tell me again. I need it down pat."

"Get the money and return here. We race to your parked car. You take the cash and go south on the 101. I go north. We meet at PF Chang's in Peoria one hour later. Got it?"

"Won't you call attention to us if you race?"

"It's a figure of speech, you idiot."

"Don't call me an idiot."

"Then don't act like one."

"Yeah, well, knock it off."

"Relax and focus on your task."

"I've got another question."

The driver cants and shakes his head. "No doubt."

"What do we do for a whole hour?"

"I don't care if you drive in circles. Just move your car and meet me at Chang's."

"Okay."

The young man removes his pistol from his pocket.

"You're loaded right?"

"No, I've only had a few beers like you."

With confirmation, his partner is, in fact, an idiot, the driver's shoulders slump. "Your gun. You loaded your pistol, correct?"

The young man's voice cracks. "Are you serious? Of course. If not, I might as well go in and point my finger at the dude."

"Settle down. We've waited too long for this for you to bone it up."

"Don't worry. I'm all right."

"Then breathe and relax. You must control the situation. If employees sense you're scared, we've got problems."

The young robber inhales profoundly and exhales foul beer breath. "I'm ready."

With a nod to the driver, the robber exits the car and checks for potential hot spots. He tucks his pistol in his belt behind his back and pulls his shirt over. He peeks around the corner to ensure an empty parking lot.

As his buddy takes a final look back, the driver waves him to proceed. He rounds the corner and approaches the front door. The clock reads 8:01 p.m.

† † †

Once home, Julia dons pajamas and relaxes on her bedroom chaise lounge. She reflects on her blessings and gives thanks for her life. She marvels at Gino and how, in spite of their arguments, he helps her. *My aches and pains robbed my happiness. No, I let them steal most aspects of life, period.*

Thirty minutes later over supper, Gino and Julia discuss her revelations about life and what it means to serve others. Gino proposes,

"Let's pledge from today to only focus on the current day and the future. Let's prevent the past from defining our tomorrows."

"Deal." Affection adorns Julia's face.

This agreement reveals the extent of their progress.

† † †

At the door, a tidal wave of emotions floods the robber and covers his face. His left eye twitches. After a deep breath, he steps inside.

The counter clerk bids good evening.

The nervous robber quickly looks around to ensure an empty store. A car's headlights penetrate the store's glass doors.

"Sir, can I help you?"

"Thanks, man. I need to check out your snacks. I've got the munchies."

The pudgy clerk chuckles. "Yeah, I get them too. Guess it shows, doesn't it?"

The emotionless man moves down a snack aisle. The clerk finds his behavior odd. A lady enters.

"Good evening. How may I help you?"

The young man watches with wary glances. The lady locates and pays for her merchandise and lottery tickets and leaves. His coast clear again, the robber takes a package of powdered donuts to the counter.

"Find what you needed?"

He puts the donuts down without a word. Eye to eye, the clerk senses danger. The customer's upper lip quivers as he removes his pistol and lays it on the counter in his right hand. He covers it with a bandana after the rigid clerk gasps and his terrified eyes lock on the robber's.

"Keep your mouth shut, and put all your money in a bag. Move fast and stay calm."

The clerk motions to the back of the store. His voice cracks. "All moneybags are in the office."

"Shut up and use any bag. Just hurry and put your cash in whatever."

"Okay, okay. Just don't shoot."

"Then don't give me a reason." Emboldened, the robber adds, "Do what I say, and no one gets hurt. And don't try any funny business, like pushing a panic button."

"No, sir, I'd never. I've got a family—kids, so please don't hurt me."

The thief finds his voice. "Then shut up, and do what I said. Hurry!"

The clerk fumbles as he doubles plastic Circle K bags. He looks up often at the hoodlum.

The crook rocks side to side, his head on a swivel to watch for trouble. A recheck of the parking lot allows the clerk to peek at the walk-in cooler. He expects a coworker to exit there soon.

"Come on, man. Pick it up. I didn't ask you to print the money."

"Yes, sir, I want to get it all, to include all the change and larger bills under the drawer."

The latch of the walk-in cooler door clicks loud. The tense burglar firms his grip on his pistol. The counter clerk's fear heightens.

A woman cross-wraps her arms around her shoulders. She shivers. "Burr. I'm still not used to the cooler." As she removes and hangs an oversized freezer coat, she notices her partner's tension. The counter clerk wants to alert her but can't.

"Get over here—now!" the brazen thief orders. The cooler clerk inches toward her coworker. "Say one word, and I put a bullet in your head." She raises her hands.

"Put your hands down. Nobody said to put them up." She trembles and complies, fighting back tears.

"Now stand there, and act normal while your buddy finishes." He turns toward and seethes at the counter clerk, who had stopped. "Step it up!"

The clerk trembles and drops some bills. He reaches down for them.

The robber leans over the counter to guard against funny business. "Now finish up. Damn, you're slow and clumsy." His right heel taps wildly, and his patience wanes. "On second thought, stop and give me—"

All eyes turn to the parking lot. A car, a patrol cruiser no less, enters the lot. His worse fears only seconds away, the criminal's mind scrambles in search of his next move. He visualizes several unhappy outcomes.

The thug moves his gun from countertop to his left pocket and tucks the bandana in his pants. His body swells with tension. His eyes pressurize in the face of this nightmare. "Three people die if either of you says a word. So be cool and act as if you know me. Talk about whatever—I don't care—but avoid stupid. Shut the cash drawer, and smile like you're happy I visited."

DPS cruiser 40733 rolls to a stop. A tall patrolman stretches, then enters the store. "How's everybody tonight?"

The nervous robber fights fear. "Super, officer, how about you?"

"Great. Not much action tonight, which I welcome."

"Can I help you find something?" The counter clerk works hard to talk calmly.

"No. Thanks. I'm here for coffee. I need a caffeine boost on slow nights, you know."

"We do likewise when we're quiet for long periods," the cooler clerk comments in a shaky voice.

Everyone hears the tension in her voice. The thief, with his back to the patrolman, mouths to the clerks, "Talk."

The cooler clerk contrives a chuckle. "So to continue, when I cast my line, my reel flew into the lake. There I stood, rod in hand, like an idiot."

After the men's exaggerated laughs, the officer relaxes and puts a lid on his cup. "I've got a twenty-ounce coffee. One twenty-nine with tax, right?"

"My treat tonight, officer," the now terrified thug asserts to keep the near-empty cash drawer shut. "It's to say thanks for all you do."

"I appreciate your offer, but it's not necessary."

"I insist. I'm seldom able to show appreciation for police, fire, or military personnel. Please allow me to honor you."

"Well, thank you."

"My pleasure." The robber offers an anxious double smile.

After two steps toward the door, the officer turns back. Pain stabs the thief's temple, and his eye twitches again.

The officer smiles broadly. "By the way, I love your fishing story. But don't feel bad. I had the same experience you described."

The lady swallows her fear on the verge of her riskiest move of her life. "Well, I felt embarrassed, but worse events happen in life, right?"

"For sure," the officer says through a smile.

"Heck, in my time here, we've never been robbed. Now a rob-bery warrants worry, not replaceable fishing gear."

"I need not tell you convenience stores are highly vulnerable. You never know who's a potential thief."

"I agree." The officer misses the terror in her voice.

"Enough cop talk. I just thought I'd mention I enjoyed your story."

"Thank you, officer."

He nods and leaves.

The robber waits for the officer to back his cruiser away before he gives additional orders. Once in the clear, he pulls his gun out again. "Forget what's left. Give me the bag—now."

He sneers at the lady clerk. "You're lucky I don't put you away for your stupid stunt. You're damn lucky the cop didn't catch on."

Tears flood her eyes, as her associate hands over the bag.

"If I see you push your panic button before I'm out the door, you're dead."

He backs out of the store. Once outside, he tucks his gun in his belt and runs to and jumps into the getaway car.

"Man, our luck. A cop shows up. How'd you handle him?"

"I'll tell you later. Let's get out of here—move!"

The driver jams his car into drive and splashes onto Olive Avenue. Peeling out, he barely avoids traffic in his lane.

Simultaneously, the counter clerk hits the panic button and races to the door to identify the getaway car. He notes the make and model but misses the license plate number.

As the getaway driver concentrates on traffic, the robber reflects on his success. A wry smile breaks over his face. *Someone called me sir, respect no one ever showed me—respect I never deserved but earned tonight, even though it took a gun to get it.*

Within three minutes, the pair arrives at the robber's car. He jumps out and confirms when they meet in Peoria. He slides into his blue Chevy Tahoe, and both head toward the 101 freeway.

† † †

Gino snuggles with Julia on their sofa.
"What a beautiful day." She sighs with contentment.
Gino squeezes her. "The best."
"I'm thankful we enjoy more days like this than before, Gino."
"Me too. I fell blessed by our progress."
"True."
They enjoy several seconds of quiet contemplation before Julia reflects further. "Most importantly, our compassion for fellow humans drives what we do, and we share our God-given gifts with others. In the process, we build heavenly treasures, which far outweigh earthly rewards. We offer our caring hearts to patients at Caring Hands."
"You're in a unique position to provide life-changing help, Julia. I believe you found why you survived your wreck—identified your destiny."
"Thank you. I give my best to everyone I serve."
"I know, and I'm proud of you."
"Thanks again, Gino. I'm thrilled with the new you."
"And I genuinely love the new Julia."

† † †

The getaway driver pulls over and idles on a side street. A patrol car tucks behind far enough away for its dash cam to record the encounter. The officer readies for a face-to-face with the Circle K robber. He approaches with a hand atop his sidearm.
"Good evening, Officer."
"How are you tonight?"
"Good, thanks."
"May I see your registration, insurance card, and license?"

"Sure." The driver reaches into his glove box. The officer watches for trouble. "Here you go. Can I ask why you stopped me?"

"Give me a minute. Sit still. I'll be back."

The officer runs a VIN and driver background check. The driver watches his rearview mirror unworried. He never entered the Circle K, and his motor vehicle records are clean.

After a few minutes, the officer returns. "I need you to come with me."

"What?" the incredulous driver asks. "Why?"

"Your car matches the description of a vehicle involved in a robbery earlier. You're not under arrest, but I need to take you to the scene."

"But I didn't commit a crime."

"Relax. I'd have cuffed you if I thought you did."

"This violates my civil rights."

"Sir, we can go there, or we can do things my way—your choice. You say you're innocent. It's my job to prove it. Help me do my job."

"I'll go, but it's a waste of time."

"Let's hope so for your sake."

The smart-aleck awaits his first ride in the back of a patrol car. Eased into the backseat, he smirks over his successful use of a drop car. It demonstrates even knuckleheads plan well.

† † †

"A table for two." The P. F. Chang's hostess notices how this guest fidgets. "A friend will join me soon. I'd like to wait for him at a table."

"Of course. Right this way."

The robber points to a booth with a view of the lobby. "I'd like this one."

"Certainly."

"I don't need a menu but would like a drink while I wait."

"Sure."

The robber orders a beer. He clasps his fingers to hide his shaking hands. He checks the time and scans the restaurant. Worry grows with each second his partner delays his arrival.

The server delivers the beer. "Would you like to order now?"

"No. My friend must be tied up. He'll be along shortly."

"Very well, sir. I'll check back a little later." The robber rubs his chin "Thanks."

†††

The cruiser enters the Circle K parking lot. A city of Phoenix police car indicates their investigation continues. The getaway driver checks the time on his phone, already late for his rendezvous.

The officer and suspect approach the store. Oddly, the driver's heart skips, a stress response even though no one there can link him to the robbery. Once inside, the officer confers with the city police-man. After, he addresses clerks. "Are you two okay?"

The counter clerk nods. "Yes, officer. We're shaken but other-wise fine."

"Good."

The lady clerk comments to the patrolman. "I didn't expect to see you again tonight."

"Me neither, but this guy's car matched your description."

The city officer interjects. "Is this the person who robbed you?"

To the officers' surprise, both clerks shake no. "No, sir, the guy who robbed us was the man we talked with, when he"—pointing to the DPS officer—"got coffee."

The suspect smirks at the officer, proud of his ploy. He props himself up with self-talk. *Just as I said.*

"I had to check since his car matched to a tee."

"No, Officer. He's not the man."

They talk further about the robber—his distinguishing marks, precisely what he said, and so on. The officer and policeman also confer again.

The driver's sneer sends chills up the lady clerk's spine.

"Thanks for your help. Your city police have jurisdiction and will complete the investigation."

The lady clerk shares her concerns. "Thank you, Officers. I hope you find the robber. He's scary and dangerous. You need him off the streets."

The suspect tilts his head slightly right to face the cooler clerk. His squinty stare rekindles fear she felt earlier.

The DPS officer and driver follow the counter clerk, who unlocks and relocks the door after letting them out. The driver glares back over his shoulder at the lady clerk, whose side cramps as she avoids eye contact.

Once back in the cruiser, the getaway driver relaxes. The patrol-man returns the suspect to his car, free to go. The driver rechecks the time and grits his teeth, too late to meet up with his robbery partner.

CHAPTER 31

Angry

The robber sits red-faced angry. He hails his server, pays his check, and exits the restaurant, concerned about his partner. To not show up or call signals trouble. If caught and he spills his guts, his partner's problems might soon become his. He must leave the rendezvous site—now.

The crook squeals his tires as he leaves the parking lot. His emotions amok, he accelerates and drifts through the banked on-ramp to the 101 Freeway South. He weaves around and between cars and forces his way through the gore point. His vehicle fishtails into the right lane, and he glances in his rearview mirror to check traffic.

A DPS officer notices this erratic freeway entrance. He follows the aggressive driver, and, within seconds, the vehicle's speed war-rants a stop. The officer sets his Circle K coffee in a cup holder and switches on his light bar. His siren blares as he punches his hemi-powered cruiser.

The robber notices flashing lights in his rearview mirror. He continues south as the patrol car advances. Both vehicles join westbound traffic on Interstate 10, where the thief pulls over, angry he failed to manage his speed. He fears his night might turn ugly.

The glare of the patrol car's spotlight reflects off the driver's rearview mirror. He squints and moves his pistol from his pocket to a hidden but reachable position. Stress triggers his eye tic. His stomach curdles and hands shake.

He waits and questions the officer's delay. His curiosity and angst grow with every second. Ready to burst, a tall man's silhouette appears in the bright beam. The burglar ensures the plastic bag of cash rests under his seat unnoticeable.

Window down and with a counterfeit smile, the robber says, "Yes, Officer? Oh, you."

† † †

Gino and Julia enjoy the news before they turn in. They learn about local and world events missed while they helped patients. An extraordinary story hits the airwaves.

"We have breaking news from the West Valley," reports the Fox News 10 anchor. "Moments ago, someone shot a law enforcement officer on a routine traffic stop on Interstate 10 near the Avondale exit. We're still learning details and will bring them to you once available.

"What we know now is a DPS officer pulled over a speeder at Mile Marker 133 on Interstate 10 westbound. According to a witness, she saw two flashes as the officer stood by the passenger's door. One flash, like a flicker, occurred outside the passenger's door. A second, more pronounced, came from inside the car. The officer fell to the highway's shoulder, and the suspect sped away, almost causing an accident.

"The whereabouts of the suspect's dark SUV remains unknown. Police ask you to call 555-555-1212 if you have information about this incident. We'll bring you more on this story if it becomes avail-able before we end our broadcast."

Julia turns off the television and tosses the remote aside. "All these shootings make me angry beyond words."

"I know. Cop shootings happen almost daily. So many officers shot across the country—and for what?"

Julia bursts into tears. "It's terrible. I pray the officer recovers and they catch the shooter."

"Yeah, people live a lifetime of despair if they fail to get closure, don't they?"

† † †

Gino scours news sources for updates on the prior night's story. He finds one on azcentral.com—an online news and current events site. The piece includes quotes from a Cracker Barrel waitress named Amanda, who observed the shooting. Gino smiles at how Amanda's choice when at her fork-in-the-road a year ago enabled her to witness this incident. He reads on.

A bullet struck patrolman, Sam Ellis, in the neck. The slug rested against his spinal column, fractions of an inch from his spinal cord. The officer underwent surgery during early morning hours, and his condition remains critical—his chance for survival uncertain.

Gino reflects on the irony. *The injured patrolman, Sam Ellis, the man I hated. A man I hadn't forgotten but suppressed in my memory.*

He sips his coffee and stares out a window. *The sun splashes bright in my yard, but dark days await the Ellis family.*

Gino replays past months in his mind. *What an unusual twist of fate. Someone shot Sam Ellis while he performed his job correctly. When he erred in Julia's accident, he escaped uninjured. Justice ignores norms— plays no favorites. Now Sam Ellis faces time to fret over his future while laid up in the hospital—a sad but fitting result. I can't let Julia know I know the officer.*

A prayer spills from Gino's mouth. He lifts up every fallen or wounded police officer, firefighter, and members of the armed forces.

Julia enters the room. "Who are you talking to?"

"No one."

"But I heard voices."

"Not voices—my verbalized thoughts on a news piece."

"Did they catch whoever shot the cop?"

"The Internet reports the shooter remains at large. The patrol-man has temporary paralysis from a bullet near his spine. Doctors question his survival or functional limitations if he lives. This tragedy makes me angry as—"

"Me too," Julia interjects empathically.

† † †

Doctors ready Officer Ellis, the person Julia prayed for fervently in past weeks, for his transfer to Caring Hands. He survived surgery and inpatient rehab, and doctors expect him to regain some functions. He needs weeks, if not months, of additional rehabilitation, however.

The Caring Hands revelation surprises Gino. *Our lives inter-twine with Sam Ellis again. I once went to kill him because he caused Julia harm, and now she might help restore his health after someone did to him what I couldn't. Justice—she's a strange lady.*

† † †

Julia and Gino talk over supper. "I hear you expect a new patient at Caring Hands."

"We receive new patients daily."

"No, I mean a unique patient—the injured patrolman. Sam Ellis."

"I'm not surprised. We specialize in treatment Officer Ellis needs."

"Makes sense."

"I wonder about his return to patrolman duties."

"It's a valid question based on your experience."

"Yes, unfortunately."

The cynic in Gino rises again. "I'll bet some people he ticketed off or arrested rejoiced over his injury. You know how people behave if aggrieved. I've been there. Trust me, some sick saps pray he suffers."

"I'm sure," Julia says, disappointed with humanity.

Months passed since Gino wished ill will on Sam Ellis. But with this Caring Hands news, his thoughts again teeter between good and evil. *Part of me says excellent—I'm glad someone shot him. Another part says too bad—a shame. My head takes me one place, my heart another.*

† † †

Caring Hands employees buzz over the patrolman's story. Julia fears the press, and Sam Ellis's celebrity status, might hamper his recovery.

The officer's notoriety angers Gino. He believes long-suffering means the officer will receive more *happy grams* from sympathizers, who, otherwise, hate cops. His rock star status keeps him in the news while Julia, whose life he hindered, helps him recover.

For Julia and Gino, Sam Ellis again causes a stir and robs others of attention they deserve.

† † †

Stella Ellis tries to lift her husband's spirits. He turns from her, which causes hurt and anger. Sam insists he wishes the bullet found his brain instead of his spine.

She believes him. She sees his struggles, hears complaints of pain and hopelessness, and experiences unwillingness to discuss his problems.

Stella also knows Sam carries a burden with painful regrets. She suspects his turmoil relates to the stress of law enforcement. Lately, however, he lives in silent depression, unable to open up or bury his demons. She risks another comment to reframe his perspective. "Sam, you'll be all right in time. We must be patient."

Sam stares into space. He turns slightly toward Stella, angry and distraught. "Someone robbed me of my career. And you think everything's fine—I should feel hunky-dory?"

"No, I don't. But your emotional funk started months before you got shot."

"When I recover, I'll tell you everything. I'll need your help to make matters right in our life."

"I wish I knew what you meant, but I don't," Stella says, frustrated. "What's this about?"

"You refuse to listen. I won't say now, because I can't fix my problem. But when able, I must."

"I can't understand what I don't know."

"Later, Stella."

"But you scare me, Sam. Everyday stress eats you alive. You appear unable to live with yourself for some reason."

Sam growls, "You overthink."

"I don't know what I think. I only know you act miserable and have for a few years. Your behavior brings me down in the process. I'm near the limit of what I can take."

"*You* can take? Did you honestly say the limit of what *you* can take?"

"Your tone hurts."

Sam stares at the wall and forms his thoughts. He turns toward Stella. "I'm sorry, Stella. Please know my dilemma doesn't relate to our relationship. I promise our situation will improve once I get rid of my troubles. I'll need your help."

"But why so secretive? Tell me how to help you do what you must. Don't let your situation continue to rob our happiness."

"Please, Stella. I know you're angry, but ride this out a bit longer. It will all make sense one day. I promise. It'll all add up on a guilt-free, feel-happy day."

CHAPTER 32

Meeting

Before Sam Ellis's arrival at Caring Hands, management names his rehabilitation therapists the *Alpha Team*. Because of relative newness there and the nature of this case, officials keep Julia Cavatelli off the team despite effectiveness in her expanded role. For training purposes, however, they assign her to monitor each of Ellis's meetings and upper extremity treatments.

Gino considers telling Julia about Sam Ellis. She often wonders about the other driver and why he fled. Julia once had wished to meet and question him. Today, Gino fears the truth about Sam Ellis might hinder Julia's recovery while she helps the officer in his. Unsure, he stays silent. If Julia ultimately learns the other driver's identity, she will do so on her own.

† † †

Gino and Julia leave for work. A routine day awaits Gino—a big one Julia.

"So you meet Sam Ellis today, right?"

"Yes. No big deal?"

"Oh?"

"Of course not." Julia's matter-of-fact tone surprises Gino. "He's like any other patient. No more—no less. I'll help him however I can if asked."

"Listen, we both know you two share much in common, so your words sound like company talk. You must be intrigued by Officer Ellis's backstory and notoriety?"

"You know how I work. I give my best to everyone."

"I know, Julia, but this is different."

She feels baited and scowls at her husband. "Gino, you seem again obsessed with Sam Ellis. If you ever change a lightbulb for him, get jazzed you brought light into his life. I expect to help him best I can if given a chance. But, remember, I'm only an observer in this case."

"I'm sorry, but you're a tad harsh."

"And I'm sorry I jumped you. But Sam Ellis means no more to me than Joe Blow. He's a man who suffers from an unfortunate accident. I experienced the same. So in that regard, I ache for him. Aside from those similarities, Sam Ellis arrived, simply another patient."

Soon after, they roll into Caring Hands' parking lot. They enter the lobby, and Gino watches Julia head for the treatment room with-out a word. *I wonder how long this man, who impacted her life so, remains merely another patient.*

†††

The meeting begins with much anticipation.

"Good morning, Mr. Ellis."

The cheery unit supervisor bugs Sam Ellis. He is far less chip-per. "Yeah, good morning,"

"I'm Samantha Quinto, supervisor of what we call the Alpha Team. My group's assigned to help with your recovery."

Sam Ellis nods, impressed. "Alpha Team, huh? Alpha's the top team in law enforcement and the military. So I get your best?"

"Team names might be different here. All our teams possess equal talent, even if our names suggest status we never intended."

Sam Ellis smiles. "I'm messing with you. It's nice to meet you, Ms. Quil—"

"Quinto."

"Quinto. Sorry, Ms. Quinto."

"No problem. It's not the easiest name."

Sam Ellis's attitude softens. "I promise to do better. By the way, call me Sam."

"Okay, Sam. You can call me Sam as well."

"Nice."

"I want to introduce team members who'll work with you."

Sam Ellis engages briefly with each person. He questions Julia's role but finally approves her involvement, which no one needs. The team, established to meet his needs and broaden the company's capabilities, has been set and oriented.

Before the meeting concludes, Sam Ellis shares his perspective regarding his treatment. "Allow me to thank you in advance for what you'll do for me."

Ms. Quinto leans forward in her seat. "Let me follow on your comment a minute. What we do here is get you to do for yourself. We aim for you to become self-sufficient—as close as possible to preinjury."

Sam Ellis ponders her comment a moment. "You didn't address one important issue."

Stella Ellis squirms, anticipating her husband's question.

"I'm sorry. What's your question?"

"Will I ever return to work?"

"I don't know, but that's our objective. The decision ultimately rests with your doctors, however, not anyone here. We'll confer with your primary care physician and specialists in your case, but their decisions, made in whole or in part based on our input, are theirs alone."

"Don't worry. I'll work hard to make my return happen—as hard as anyone you've ever seen." Sam Ellis knows from work on the force how efforts affect outcomes.

"Love the attitude. A person's recovery often depends on drive and willingness to work hard. It appears we need not worry about motivation with you."

"Not at all, I'm raring to go."

Ms. Quinto lowers her clasped hands to her lap, pleased. Everyone in agreement with Officer Ellis's treatment plan, they adjourn ready to begin his therapy at 10:00 a.m.

Sam Ellis looks at his wife, then back to Ms. Quinto. "Thank you. I won't let you down."

† † †

Gino taps the patient's door.

A gruff man's voice responds, "It's open."

"Excuse me, sir." Gino pokes his head past the door jamb far enough to see Sam Ellis in bed. "I'm here to tighten the shower grab bar."

Sam Ellis looks at Gino. "Beats me. I'm new here and know nothing about grab bars."

"I see."

"Well, if you see, you understand I don't need a bathroom."

"I'm sorry, sir. I'll go ahead and repair the bar. By the way, I'm Gino."

"Hey, Gino, I'm Sam. Sam Ellis."

"I'm happy to meet you."

"You too." Officer Ellis studies Gino's face and searches his memory. "Do we know each other? You look familiar."

Gino turns to face the officer. "Perhaps you're confusing me with someone else."

Sam Ellis grows insistent. "No, I think we've met before."

Gino cracks a smile. "Sad to say this, but I look like your average Joe."

"No, I think I know you."

"You meet so many people in your work I bet you've mixed me up with another person."

"You know I work for DPS?"

"Yes. I follow the news, so I know who you are."

"Then you know what happened to me."

"Mr. Ellis, I think you'll find our services exceptional."

"Call me Sam."

"Okay."

"Why'd you change the subject?"

"Sir, I'm here to fix a grab bar."

"You know where to find it." Gino's coyness bugs Sam Ellis.

"I'll finish in seconds. Good luck with your recovery. I think you'll do fine."

"Yeah, well, I hope. I've got a rocky road ahead." Gino pauses. "I bet it's rough."

Sam's eyes tear. "You have no idea."

"You're right, but I know someone who has. I learned from a good friend that hard work and emphasis on the positive smooths even rockiest of roads."

"Aren't you the optimist?"

"Optimism gives those disheartened their best chance for improvement. Other people often cause our problems, as in your case, but we choose whether or not to live with resultant misery."

Sam looks at Gino thoughtfully.

"Well, enough philosophy—I best get to my task. I enjoyed meeting you, and I'll continue to pray for your recovery."

"Thank you, Gino. I appreciate your support."

"You're welcome. Perhaps I'll see you around."

"Yes, let's hope. I enjoyed our talk."

"Me too. I've waited a long time."

"What?"

"You know since you arrived here, I've wanted to meet you."

"Oh."

"I'll make the repairs now and catch up with you later." Gino acts nervous about his slip up.

"Hope so."

"Oh, I'm sure of it."

Gino enters the bathroom.

Sam Ellis revisits his memory.

† † †

Gino contemplates Julia's chiding, morning comment about Sam Ellis. Her demeaning of his value at Caring Hands with her lightbulb remark bugs him still. He sees a deeper meaning, however. *Bring light to Sam Ellis. Perhaps I understand. The accident, meeting Travis, hatred left on a curb for forgiveness, and Julia's transformation from helplessness to helpfulness.*

Gino scratches his chin and questions events. *Perhaps Travis entered our lives to encourage us to more broadly bring light to the world, not just Sam Ellis?*

To reveal we receive when we give?

To teach we self-impose our limitations?

To live forgiven by extending forgiveness?

He understands Julia's opportunity through her work with Sam Ellis. He finds Officer Ellis open to deep conversation. After a change of heart, he must reveal Sam Ellis's identity to Julia for the officer to reap full benefits from his interactions with her. If not now, when?

† † †

Julia's contact with Sam rewards both. She admires his optimism about a full or near-full recovery. He finds her most compassionate and caring based on her questions while she monitors his first dexterity session.

Though silent on the point, Julia lacks optimism about Sam Ellis's recovery based on first impressions. She remembers, however, how erroneous perceptions cause problems. She frequently revisits the hospital therapist's indelible imprint on her memory.

As a result, Julia withholds her thoughts from Sam Ellis. She commits to shield him from the hopelessness she feels for him. To share too much now might cause two reactions: remorse and depression because of his accident, and gloom and doom about his chance for recovery. She guards against both.

† † †

After work, Gino wonders about Julia's first day with Sam Ellis. He avoids the subject on their drive home, however, because of morning sensitivity.

About halfway home, Julia stares at Gino. He never notices.

"Don't you want to know about my day?"

"Of course. I assume it was like every other day."

"Yes, but I had my first session with Officer Ellis."

"I'm surprised you'd single him out since he's *just another patient.*"

"So you want to argue?"

"No, but I want to make a point."

"Your point is *pointless*. There isn't one to make." Gino stares ahead.

"I assume you might be interested given your curiosity about Officer Ellis over past weeks."

Gino ponders. *Weeks? It's more like months—many months.* "I'm sorry. My snide comment wasn't necessary or appropriate."

"Apology accepted."

Julia sits quietly and stares out her window.

"So tell me about your day."

"Do you want to know or only ask to appear considerate?"

"Stop it, Julia. I want to know. I'm interested."

After several thoughtful seconds, Julia begins. "His session went well. He's a nice guy; I like him. I'm afraid, though, he might have false hopes about his recovery."

Her comment surprises Gino. "You can tell this soon?"

"Not always. And remember, as a therapy tech, I only monitor the officer's upper dexterity work. But I know when an injury's bad enough to alter one's life. Sam may have such an injury. My initial impression mirrors what I found in Sam's medical file."

"Sam's?"

"Yes. Officer Ellis encourages informality."

"Back to the issue, did you blindly accept what you read?"

"What's with you today, Gino Cavatelli? Why do you insist on sarcasm?"

"I don't. It's a weak attempt at a little fun. It would be a shame if Sam Ellis suffered permanent injuries."

"Yes, and next time you want a little fun, do so at your expense—not mine."

"Duly noted. I'm sorry." Gino fixes his eyes straight ahead.

"You should be. And, by the way, you've apologized too many times already today. So please stop."

Gino glances at Julia. "My last comment was meant to warn you to be careful with quick judgments. Remember the hospital therapist?"

"I'm way ahead of you. I thought of my situation when I observed Mr. Ellis. His problem with routine arm and hand movements, however, spells trouble similar to my situation. Odd, but I appreciate your reminder regardless of how poorly delivered. I'll not make the same mistake as the hospital therapist—ever!"

† † †

Two weeks into her husband's rehab, Stella Ellis questions its effectiveness. Early efforts fail to achieve *her* objectives, so she seeks to direct therapist efforts based on what *she* thinks will work best.

Mrs. Ellis, a continual pain in the rear, demands to meet with Samantha Quinto, the only person with whom she will speak. Ms. Quinto, aware of Stella's idiosyncrasies from earlier conversations, juggles her schedule to accommodate. She plans to meet Stella Ellis before real trouble arises.

Based on Mr. and Mrs. Ellis's request in the ensuing meeting, Julia Cavatelli's role on the team shifts from trainee/observer to the provider of upper extremity modalities. This transition surprises Mrs. Cavatelli given the high visibility of this case. Her bond with Mr. Ellis, however, exceeds that of other therapists, and Sam Ellis has more confidence in his chances for improvement with Julia Cavatelli active in his recovery.

† † †

Julia completes her tenth session with Sam. As expected, she likes and has a personal interest in him.

She wants the best for Officer Ellis but fears Caring Hands' best might not be good enough.

Julia decides to discuss Sam's accident to determine how his emotional state is affecting his chances for recovery. She must be careful but needs an avenue to open forbidden dialogue.

Then it dawns on her.

CHAPTER 33

Admissions

Julia Cavatelli knows not to talk with Sam Ellis about his accident. To do so threatens her role on the Alpha Team, if not continued employment at Caring Hands. Even so, she believes information about how *she* overcame personal hardship might help his psycho-logical and eventual physical recovery. She treads carefully.

"Sam, may I share a personal experience while we work?"

"Sure. Share away. I'm your captive."

"It's about an accident and its impact on me."

"Accident?"

"Yes. On November 8, 2011…"

Sam shuts down. Ugly images fill his troubled mind—the same vision he sees daily.

He relives a hard tug left on his steering wheel and jostling in his SUV.

He sees cars collide, one airborne until it lands on another. He remembers the aftermath grow small in his rearview mirror as he flees.

"And I was—"

"I'm sorry. Did you say November 8, 2011?"

"Yes. I was heading westbound on Interstate 10 near the—"

"Avondale exit?"

"Yes, the Avondale exit. How'd you know?"

Sam recognizes his error and stumbles for words. "Remember, I, uh, I work for DPS as a patrolman. We hear lots of stories about the interstates, and guys talk about their investigations."

"So you remember details of a random accident from over two years ago?"

"Please, Julia. Continue."

Curious, Julia asks, "Do you know other details?"

"I'm not sure. Tell me more."

"While in typical rush-hour traffic, I heard a crash, and a car fell from the sky and bounced off my van. After impact, it rolled down the interstate and landed on its roof. The irresponsible jerk, who caused the accident, fled."

"Honestly?"

"I'm sorry I called the person a name, but he must be one sick person."

Sam feels gaffed in his heart. Julia notices his demeanor change.

"Did anyone get hurt? Did you get hurt?"

"I don't know about other drivers. We never talked. I do know a lady lost her baby."

Sam's face contorts like after a gut punch. His head and voice both lower. "A child died?"

"Yes. A pregnant lady lost her son soon after the wreck."

"You okay, Sam?"

"Yes. I find this horrible and hard to hear."

"Beyond horrible. My husband, Gino, learned about the baby."

"Gino?"

"Yes. My husband talked with each driver when he searched for the other driver."

"The other driver?"

"Yes. Gino coined this name for the idiot who caused the wreck."

"I see."

"Sam?"

"I'm sorry I drifted, Julia. You never said if you suffered injuries."

"Yes." Tears build. "My neck and head hurt a lot, so paramedics took me to the hospital."

Sam fears the next answer. He asks anyway, "Any broken bones or cuts?"

"Believe it or not, no, but I had enough other problems.

"Don't overreach, Sam. Remember, small gains, not big leaps."

"Okay."

"I've meant to ask you about the mark on your left hand."

"A cross tattoo." Ellis has grown comfortable lying.

"It's unique."

"Perhaps one day I'll share with you how I got it."

"I'd be interested."

"Sure. Say, Julia, what do you mean other problems, if you can say?"

Julia wipes the corner of her left eye. "I bruised my cervical spine at three levels. I risked paralyzation from my neck down, so I had surgery and live with all sorts of hardware inside me."

"I'm sorry you had such a severe surgery."

"Yes, and I still live with awful pains and headaches."

"I feel for you, Julia."

"I don't mean to appear sorry for myself, but there's more." Surprise and disappointment grip Sam. "Really?"

"Yes. I underwent lumbar surgery eleven months after the first and another lumbar procedure eight months later. The doctor offered little hope for the rest of my spine."

The weight of Julia's comment gnarls at Sam's insides. "All those surgeries resulted from the same accident?"

"Sadly, yes."

"So much for one person to endure."

"Wait. I don't mean to burden you, but there's more."

"No, not at all. I'm interested and concerned."

Julia exhales audibly through her nose. "Muscle spasms started in my lower extremities—as many as twenty or more every night. With each, I get out of bed to stretch. Otherwise, they last forever."

"How do you sleep?"

"Ah ha, another problem. I seldom sleep well, so I'm always exhausted."

"Yet you work here and act perkier than other employees."

"I work through my pain. It took my husband months—no years—to convince me I can function despite physical limitations and exhaustion. What a battle."

"Did your situation cause conflict?"

"Yes. We fought hard and often. I once thought to leave Gino because he seemed not to care. It took a quote from a lady named Rikki Rogers to shake the crumbled dirt from my roots."

"What'd she say? Her message might help me too."

"She wrote, *'Strength doesn't come from what you can do. It comes from overcoming the things you once thought you couldn't do.'*"

"That's powerful."

"Yes, afterward, I read a similar inspirational quote on the Internet."

"And?"

"The adage goes, *'It doesn't matter who you were when you fell. It matters who you are when you rise.'*"

"That creates an image in my mind."

"May I ask what?"

"Oh, of me in Yuma. I felt down—bogged in the biggest mess I ever encountered. I admit I'm not sure I ever got up."

"I'm sorry." Julia places her hand on his forearm. "I lived a sad existence when Gino told me his adage. I hate to think what might have happened if not for these quotes. I only wish he told me sooner."

"I'm sorry about all this. It sounds as if life dealt you a horrible hand."

"Horrible understates my condition then." Her memories burn like freshly picked scabs.

"I appreciate your struggle. Based on my experience, weighty issues, like health problems, exhaustion, emotional stress, and relationship problems often cause depression."

"Right, I fought depression daily—still do today to a lesser extent. And the person responsible for all this lives unaware and probably doesn't care."

Sam asks in a guilt-laden whisper, "Do you think so?"

"Yes, no doubt."

"Can anyone be so cold?"

"Huh, I'm not sure. But I believe if the driver cared, he'd have accepted responsibility for his actions."

"Do you think the person has sufficient strength to step up and apologize years later?"

"I guess not. The driver hasn't."

Sam wishes to understand Julia's heart better. "Julia, does a person's non-apology necessarily mean he's at peace with his role in your accident?"

"I don't know. If not, when does the other driver own up—to say sorry to his victims?"

"It's also hard to know how much time a person needs to step up—"

"Yes, but—"

"To say sorry because everyone's different."

"True. And I doubt I'll ever learn who caused my accident. Too much time passed already."

"You never know. The human conscience seldom rests until cleansed."

"You talk as if from experience."

Sam snaps a smile as if caught in the act. "Yes, I suppose." He is disappointed he exposed his inner self.

"Then again you seem insightful on many levels."

"Well, let me invalidate your theory with a stupid question."

"Sure. Shoot."

"Can I assume officials never caught the other driver?"

Her expression reflects deep disappointment and sadness. "No. No one found the driver or his vehicle. I'm not sure how hard anyone looked. But I'm sure the person got off while I continue to suffer."

"Your story makes me sad."

"You know, I felt angry at first. And the more my problems unfolded, the more my husband's anger shifted to hatred. I think given a chance, Gino would've killed the other driver. I'm glad we allowed the adage *'Time heals all things'* to prove valid."

"Me too, I mean, from a law enforcement perspective."

"Of course. I moved from angry to wonder, and my husband no longer hates and obsesses about the other driver." Tears again fill Julia's eyes. *Reality feels more real verbalized.*

She observes Sam's eyes. *Their conversation moved him beyond what she would have expected.* "I'm glad your husband resolved his anger."

"Me too, I mean, from a humanity perspective."

"Even though the other driver didn't stop, I can't believe he lacks remorse for sideswiping the car and causing the wreck. Maybe he suffers pain too. It seems someone who fled an accident would feel remorseful the rest of his life."

Julia's eyes narrow and fix on the floor. *Sam expresses knowledge more than perception. And he said the other driver sideswiped a car to start the accident. How does Sam know? I never mentioned sideswiping—perhaps another detail he knows because of his job.*

"I can't answer your question, Sam. I'd have been miserable if I caused an accident and chose not to stop. I know that much."

"Yeah, I know, it's been hard."

Julia misses this admission—that Sam lives what she described. She fails to connect the dots about Sam's involvement in her accident. Sam joins those dots explicitly, however, and he despises the picture it reveals. She treats Sam to make him whole while his actions left her a fraction of her former self.

"All done for today, Sam." Julia looks satisfied. "How do your arms and hands feel?"

"Fine, but my heart hurts big-time."

Julia misses the degree of Sam's agony over being in a room with someone to whom he sought to apologize for years. Their conversation verifies his greatest fear, however—validates his worry. He ruined at least a couple of lives and now faces a crushed existence of his own.

Julia smiles softly. "Thanks for the patient ear, and forgive my lousy pun. I'm sorry for the messy details. I never intended to spill my guts this way."

"No, no, don't worry. I needed to hear what you said, if for no other reason than to know how I might feel toward the shooter. No apology needed. Your comments help me understand my status as an innocent victim."

† † †

Julia's discussion with Sam Ellis leads to an extensive conversation with Gino on their way home from work.

"May I turn off the radio?"

"Yes, of course. What's up?"

"Remember I said we couldn't talk to Sam about his accident?"

"I do. Your boss wants to avoid a circus environment."

"Yes—exactly. Well, I told Sam about some of my challenges since my accident."

"Why?"

"I thought it might change how he views his situation. You know, to see his shooting from a different perspective."

"You accomplish your objective?"

"I'm not sure, but I want him to understand what to expect as a victim of a tragic act."

"Is he still progressing? I remember your initial skepticism, but I sensed he improved through rehab."

"His bright picture dimmed recently. With each day his condition stays the same or regresses, the greater his chance for permanent impairment. Sam's sure to live in agony without a miracle."

"What a shame. Does Ellis know?"

"No."

"At what point do you tell him?"

"Not now. The jury remains out. Until we're confident Sam's clinically reached maximum medical recovery, we'll keep up his rehab. Any other action borders on irresponsible."

"No one wants to be reckless with Sam Ellis, right?" Gino's snide comment stems from how the staff has pampered Officer Ellis.

"What's with the comment, Gino?"

He shakes his head. "Forget it—just a stupid comment by a tired old man."

"No. I don't accept your cop-out. I think there's more."

"Julia, can we discuss this another time?"

"Sure—we'll talk another time, but we *will* talk."

Julia scratches her cheek. *What did Gino mean—his comments always secretive and mysterious? It's like he knows more than he lets on. I'm too spent to decipher his cryptic message, but I'll get to the bottom of this. At another time, I'll dig into what he knows—soon, but another time.*

I'm scared how he might react, but I must take the risk.

† † †

Gino stares out his windshield. *It's time to tell Julia about Sam Ellis. If not, she'll learn the person with whom she shared her story hides one of his own. Amazement awaits when she discovers their stories relate to the same accident—her heart sure to ache because he experiences ebbs and flows of emotions like hers. I'll start at the top and tell her every detail. I must act now, not later, but now.*

I'm scared how she might react, but I must take the risk.

† † †

Sam Ellis stares overhead. *I'm in a violent eddy of emotions, like water, which swirls and cascades over a waterfall with me in its vortex. At the edge, I see my fate if I remain silent, tossed into the foam and fury at the fall's bottom. So I must confess and seek forgiveness from Julia and her husband— tell them everything about my actions. I must do so now, not later, but now.*

I'm scared how they might react, but I must take the risk.

† † †

Travis and his helper observe activities at Caring Hands and beyond. The time for admissions and acts of forgiveness he started years ago nears.

"There is considerable angst at Caring Hands," Travis notes. "We finish our work there soon."

"Many will rejoice."

"And much weight will lift from burdened shoulders."

"The result of grace, mercy, and open hearts, Master."

"Yes, it will be as written despite how hard everyone tries to influence outcomes."

"As always for lessons that last a lifetime."

"Each person has learned much since opening their eyes and softening their hearts."

"Yes, Travis, and knowledge and understanding now embed in their minds and souls."

"We have positioned them well to help and inspire others they encounter in the future."

"The only way planet earth survives until the second coming." Travis proclaims, "Then we shall prepare for the finale."

"Shall we make ourselves known?"

"Will doing so change how events unfold?"

"No."

"Will the individuals fail to understand how circumstances meshed as they did?"

"Not likely."

"Then we have no reason to reveal ourselves to those who already know us."

"You honor me with your wisdom, Travis."

"One earns their honor. You serve me well."

"And I pledge to continue. We should move boldly. Many people fear perceived risks. Only you can help. Are you ready to enable forgiveness, which alters life, Travis?"

"I am."

CHAPTER 34

Clarity

After several weeks of therapy, Sam Ellis needs clarity about his condition. No more false optimism or smiles. Although improved slightly, medical specialists certify he is at maximum medical recovery. The once infallible officer suffers a permanent impairment with lifelong limitations and pain likely. Much like Julia and her job, Sam Ellis lost his ability to perform his duties or, perhaps, any functions. A compassionless stranger robbed his gifts like he did Julia's.

With medical verifications in hand, the staffing shifts to how to inform Sam Ellis. Based on her closeness with him, the team appoints Julia Cavatelli to advise the officer. She expects him to take the news hard.

† † †

Julia stares out her window more than usual on their drive home. After a while, she looks at Gino. Her eyes glisten. Words stick in her throat. She looks away again and presses her left palm to her cheek.

Her silence signals trouble and leaves Gino unclear if or how to approach her. He allows space and time. She whimpers. Gino asks, "Do you want to talk?"

"I need help."

"You know me. I offer solutions even when problems don't exist. So I'm good for a couple of suggestions when a legitimate need arises."

"It's no time for jokes. I grapple with a serious question and need a careful listen and honest answer."

"I understand. What's your question?"

"Would you withhold details from a patient once he maxes his medical improvement?"

"Let me guess, Sam Ellis?"

"Yes. In essence, staff charged me to tell Sam his law enforcement days are over. In fact, he might never do meaningful work again."

"I'm sorry for him, but you know how best to deliver such a message. The two of you are thick as a Dairy Queen Blizzard."

"It's worse. Sam's destined for a life of pain or pills the rest of his life—maybe both."

"Yeah, I figured as much."

"So how do I tell Sam and not devastate him?"

"When did you get this assignment?"

"This morning."

"Any chance the team's wrong?"

"Unlikely. Many specialists work on our team, and their clinical results suggest he won't improve beyond today—something about an unresponsive nerve. A tragedy, I know, but also reality."

"And you want what from me?" Gino asks for clarity.

"I respect your opinion, and I'm nervous about this. I never worked with a patient with such high expectations who has fallen so short. The news will destroy him."

"Why must *you* tell him?"

"Gino, he's my patient."

"I'm sorry. I didn't mean to upset you."

"I'm sorry too. Guess I'm edgy."

"I understand."

"Thank you."

"So if I read you right, you wonder what *not* to say?"

"I must avoid a rabbit hole from which I can't climb out. I care for the guy, and I'm about to break his heart. I have no way—"

"Julia, I must tell you—"

"Please, let me finish for once."

"I'm sorry. Go ahead."

"I honored the boss's request and never talked with Sam Ellis about *his* accident."

"A wise move."

"Yes, but as you know, we spoke about my wreck to prepare him should his results turn out badly."

"Wise again, I'd say."

"I never told you, but when we talked, he acted more concerned for me than I was for him. His actions defied description. He internalized what happened to me and experienced pain over my wreck. When I asked—"

"Julia, please stop. I must tell you something. My information provides clarity and answers your question."

"What, Gino?"

† † †

Stella Ellis enters her husband's room near 5:00 p.m. Sam faces his window. He looks to see who came in.

"Hello, Sam."

Sam turns back to the window; his silence reveals his sullen mood.

Stella hooks her purse on the back of a chair. Seated, she waits for Sam to speak. Sunlight streams in his window to profile the left side of his face. His moist left eye spells trouble, or so she thinks.

After several minutes, Sam faces her. "Hello, Stella."

She steps toward Sam but thinks better of it and moves back to her seat. Stella needs clarity about his disposition before she takes other actions.

"How's Wendy?"

"Fine. She'll visit you later today."

"No. Tell her to stay away. I don't want company."

"What's wrong, Sam?"

"Nothing, Stella." He aches, disappointed she ignores the obvious. "In case you haven't noticed, everything's great."

"Did you hear news about your recovery since we last spoke? What's got you so dejected?"

"Julia Cavatelli and I have a formal meeting tomorrow morning—not for therapy but on another topic. I doubt she'll invite me to a hoedown."

A nervous smile covers Stella's face briefly. "You expect bad news?"

"Stella! I'm no better than weeks ago. Don't you understand? Can't you see? Are you oblivious to my condition?"

She sits quietly stunned, then responds barely above a whisper. "I've buried the truth to suppress my pain. I sensed your recovery wasn't as good as you thought. I knew better than to challenge you."

"Challenge me?"

"Yes. I did what I could to guard against all negative, to include hiding my feelings from Wendy and anyone else who asked about you. Pretending helps my survival."

Sam glares. "*Your* survival? You worry about *your* survival?" He turns away in disbelief.

Stella's sobbing fills his room. "What did you expect of me, Sam?"

"Nothing, Stella. I guess I expected nothing. I'm tired and want to be alone. I'll tell you what happened after my meeting tomorrow."

Stella dabs her eyes. She lifts her purse and leaves without another word, not even a goodbye. Silence at this point helps her survival.

† † †

Gino tells Julia the whole story about Sam Ellis and his actions after the accident:

About tracking down the car and its owner's information in Yuma.

About his speeding ticket issued by none other than Sam Ellis.

About how his Cracker Barrel server Amanda witnessed Sam Ellis's shooting.

About his run-in with Phyllis Waddell, who planted the seed of forgiveness.

About his time on the curb waiting to kill Sam Ellis, and how a stranger sent by Travis convinced him to leave, into the light, no less.

About how his heart shifted from hatred to anger to awareness about the terrible mistake he almost made.

He shared every detail.

"Why didn't you tell me this sooner, Gino?"

"I tried but couldn't. You improved so much through your work at Caring Hands I didn't want to raise bad memories."

"But I made terrible comments about the other driver to the *other driver*."

"And he needed to hear them—to know how his actions affected our lives. But he must also know your heart. How you understand why the accident happened. Why all those circumstances on November 8, 2011, meshed to place you at the crash site at the time of impact."

Julia rakes fingers through her hair. "I suppose."

"Circumstances occurred like they did to place you at Caring Hands today to help the patients before and after Sam Ellis and to free him from his guilt carried since the accident. He knows the first part—how his actions changed your life physically and emotionally. He must now learn your heart of forgiveness.

"*Free him*, Julia!"

Tears stream down her face.

"How did this happen?"

"I suppose events occur because they're meant to happen."

"I don't feel I can discuss this with Sam tomorrow morning."

"Then don't. You found the right time to share information and stories with Sam before. Tell him when comfortable, but he must know the truth."

"You're right, Gino. He needs clarity. I'll tell him tomorrow."

"You'll do well."

"Thank you, Gino. Your support means the world to me. You're there when I need you most."

"I'm always by your side, but you only now see the truth." Julia bows shamefully. Gino lifts her chin softly. "I love you, Julia."

CHAPTER 35

Forgiveness

Julia's message of doom does not surprise Sam Ellis. Instead, it validates a motto by which he lives: *Verification of a single fact often diminishes a thousand rays of hope.* His reality dims with each day he stagnates. As a result, he…

Weeps instead of sleeps at night and contemplates his life's direction
Frets over what he cannot do more than focusing on what he can.
Worries about Stella's reaction to his lies.
His expression hides little, yet he refuses to give up.

Julia places her hand on his shoulder. "I know this stings."

"I've thought about this a lot—even cried at night. But despite how bleak my condition appears, I trust I'll improve. I know tests suggest otherwise, but I refuse to accept them as final."

"We agree—it's great to think positive. But we must also be honest, Sam. Your tests paint a dark picture."

Sam looks away as Julia continues. "I hurt subjectively. Tests can't validate or invalidate my pain. But we can't refute your clinically based results."

"I understand, but I *choose* to believe I'll improve."

"But how?"

Sam reflects. "I met a man once when I faced what seemed a hopeless situation. I felt doomed until he spoke with me. He urged I believe in a positive future even when hard to see or comprehend how. So I trust and commit to positive perspectives."

"I admire your optimism, but your encourager never knew someone would shoot you."

"You might be wrong."

"How so?"

"Perhaps he anticipated the event fully."

"Based on what?"

"He said one day I'd experience a situation, which challenges my core beliefs and constitution. I believe he meant this event."

"So you consider him a prophet?"

"I'm not sure, but he showed me impossible happens. In my case, he saved my life."

"I'm curious."

"I must leave it there. The details border on unbelievable, and I choose they remain private for now."

"I'm sorry I probed too deep."

"No—please, I gain much through our exchanges."

Julia sees an opportunity. "Related to our conversations, I must talk to you about another matter. Can we chat again—say 10:00 tomorrow morning?"

"Sure. I need time to process, so I prefer tomorrow as well."

Sam, despite his rah-rah front, understands Julia might be right about his recovery. Suddenly subdued, he said, "Please ask the desk to hold all calls and to intercept visitors today. I don't want to see anyone. And shut the door on your way out."

A tear finds Julia's cheek. Without another word, she exits and closes the door. Silence now is best for Sam's survival.

† † †

Gino and Julia pull into Caring Hands' parking lot the next morning. He looks at Julia, who sits forlorn. "You ready to meet with Sam Ellis again?"

"Ready or not, it's got to happen. I hope I hold my composure."

"You might not, but you're compassionate. You want more for Sam Ellis than he wants for himself. And full recovery can't happen. It seems natural to feel crummy."

"I guess."

"Look, hidden emotions in your voice and words won't conceal the pain on your face. Don't try. Sam Ellis knows you too well to fool him. Be you. You excel when genuine."

"I wish you'd join me."

"You don't need me or anyone else on earth. Tell him and hug Sam with the tenderness you've shown me throughout our life together."

"Will you see me later?"

"Yes, as time allows."

† † †

Gino heads to his tiny shop. A mundane day awaits him. Julia, with significant challenges, checks with the receptionist. Julia presents a chipper front. "Good morning. How's everything?"

"Amazing." The receptionist's bright smile and voice cause wonder.

"Really? What's got you so jazzed?"

"You work with Sam Ellis, right?"

"Yes."

"You won't believe the latest."

"Tell me."

"As you know, everyone agrees he'll not improve further."

"Yes, of course. I attended the staffing and delivered Sam the bad news yesterday."

"It must've been hard on him."

"Extremely."

"Well, let me tell you the latest. It seems a miracle happened sometime in the past eighteen hours."

"What do you mean miracle?"

"Ellis's neurosurgeon scoured his medical file yesterday after-noon. We needed his sign off for discharge, and he wanted one final time through Ellis's records before doing so."

"Unreal. I thought everyone signed off before I talked with Sam."

"Apparently not. But what the doctor found smacks of *unreal*."

"Go on."

"He noticed a possible false negative on a critical test. The results appeared extreme compared to earlier assessments—sort of an outlier."

"And?"

"He ordered a retest, which happened yesterday."

"And?"

"He blew a fuse neither he nor anyone else noticed the mistake earlier."

"What mistake? What happened?"

"We retested with positive results."

"Which means?"

"Maybe they were negative results."

"You confuse me."

"You know, a better negative result produces a positive outcome."

"Ah…yeah. Tell me the impact."

"The nerve thought permanently damaged isn't."

"Are you're positive you understand this correctly?"

"Yes. And what's more, Mr. Ellis had a near standard exit physical later yesterday."

"So let me get this straight. Sam improved from yesterday morning to last night?"

"Yes."

"Are you sure staff didn't goof again—perhaps mix Ellis's results with another patient's?"

"Yes, I mean no. Team members triple checked since results varied so much from the last test. They're Sam Ellis's—no doubt. The neuro scheduled an Alpha Team meeting for early afternoon."

Julia considers a greater force is responsible for Sam Ellis's improvement. "When did your shift start yesterday—7:00 p.m.?"

"Yes, but I arrived a bit early."

"Did anyone visit Mr. Ellis between the time the doctor noticed the questionable result and his physical?"

"Apparently so, even though Officer Ellis requested no visitors. The person I relieved said two gentlemen stood at his doorway on and off."

"Did she describe them?"

"Yes, she said these guys looked unusual."

"How so?"

"One guy, who left by himself a couple of times, looked fairly normal. He came and went without her ever noticing, and she said she monitored everywhere carefully. In fact, she peeked around the corner often to check for them down the hall toward the restrooms."

"And the other guy?"

"She went on and on about the second man and said he was skinny and different."

"Different how?"

"I guess he's pale—like he needs a shot of iron, or maybe a little sun. But she gushed over his eyes."

"What about them?"

"Mind you, this girl's prone to exaggeration, but she said the thin guy's eyes penetrated hers—as if to see deep into her soul."

"Did he speak?"

"I guess not. And after doctors announced Officer Ellis's good news, he too was gone."

"Did he pass the reception desk?"

"No. The guy vanished."

"Vanished?"

"Apparently so. All of a sudden the man was gone, and no one saw him leave.

Julia's emotions soar, and joy overtakes her expression. "By the way, the skinny man's a friend. He's a bit mysterious and pops in and out unexpectedly to help people. He's a good guy."

"I'll say this, he left quite an impression on others here."

"I have no doubt."

† † †

Julia darts to Sam Ellis's room, hardly able to contain her exuberance. She knows how and why Sam Ellis improved. She sticks her head in his room. "Got a minute for a friend?"

Sam's voice is happiest since his arrival. "Julia. By all means, come in."

"How are you today?"

"Haven't you heard?"

"Tell me."

"I got good news."

"Oh?"

"Yeah, I heard late last night they caught the guy who shot me, thanks to a tip from a Cracker Barrel server. He's a small-time hood who robbed a Circle K I visited earlier that night. I spotted him on the freeway an hour or so after the robbery. Lucky me, right?"

Julia wonders why Sam mentions the capture instead of his exciting medical news. She comments from experience. "Sometimes people end up in the wrong place at the right time, and bad things happen. I know firsthand."

"Yes, you do, Julia Cavatelli. Yes, you do. Let me tell you what else I found out from investigators."

"Sure. I want to share your excitement."

"This might be hard to believe."

"Try me. I've been through a miraculous event or two in my lifetime."

"Hear me out before you comment."

"Agreed."

"Have you heard about this guy Travis?"

"Yes, I'm familiar."

"Someday, I'll tell you a related story, which might amaze you."

"Likewise."

"What do you mean?"

"Tell me what you found out. We'll share our stories another time."

"Only if you promise."

"Yes, of course."

"Well…supposedly someone close to Travis provided police details about my accident. My witness Amanda mentioned two flashes before I fell to the shoulder. Everyone knew the second one came from a gun in the SUV. No one knew what caused the first outside the vehicle. It happened fractionally before the first."

"I remember news stories about a mystery flash."

"It's no longer a mystery."

"What did you hear?"

"Get this. Travis's associate told authorities the first flash happened when he, Travis, nudged me an indiscernible distance to the right before the thug fired his shot. Doctors said if true, he saved me from the bullet severing my spine.

Julia sits speechless.

"Your smile intrigues me, Julia."

"I'm overjoyed for you. And it's hard to imagine I'd meet some-one personally impacted by Travis. Thank God for him.

"I'll say. So you believe this story?"

"It's hard to disbelieve based on what you read about Travis."

"I tell you, God answers prayers."

"You don't need to convince me."

"Sam, you're weeping." Julia wipes his cheeks.

"Tough guy, right?"

"I've always thought you a softie."

"Like mush when you're around."

"I'm flattered, but enough about me. Tell me about last night's other big story. I hear you got great news on the medical front?"

"Yes. Doctors say I'm better than in the past few weeks. They don't understand what happened from a few days ago, but my neu-rosurgeon assures me I'll be okay."

Julia smiles and listens without a word.

"It's quite a different story from what you said yesterday—likely the result of your work with me." His impish smile pleases Julia.

"Funny, my thoughts exactly."

"Really?"

"No, I jest, of course."

"I don't."

"You're too kind."

"You're too good."

"Stop before my head swells."

"That's not your style."

"Again you shift the conversation to me. Enough already!"

"Fair enough."

Julia's expression turns serious. "Since we don't need to rehash yesterday's meeting, I'd like to discuss another matter."

"Can I share something first?"

"Sure, right after me."

"Okay." Sam shares a grateful smile.

Julia looks away momentarily, then turns her eyes to meet his. "I find this as hard to do as it should be easy."

Sam's smile fades. "What is it, Julia?"

"I know who you are, Sam."

"Well, I hope so. We've worked together several weeks."

"No. I mean I *know* your identity."

"Pray tell, by all means, tell *me* who I am." Sam's playfulness gives way after studying Julia's face.

"You're the other driver. You operated the SUV and caused my accident."

Sam's turns mournful. He squints at Julia slightly and sighs deeply. "I wanted to tell you yesterday."

"Really?"

"Yes. I figured it out with your story, which crushed me. Here I struggle to regain my life, and I almost cost you yours. Perhaps I did in a way since your once vibrant existence is now little more than hell from a physical standpoint."

"Sam—"

"No. Let me continue, please. I agonize daily because of my horrible mistake, causing and fleeing the accident."

"Sam—"

"I'm not that guy. My parents raised me better—not to be a villain or coward. But I was both on November 8, 2011, and I've hated myself since."

"I'm sorry." Julia's heart burns with this confession.

"You're sorry. From within every ounce of my being, *I'm* sorry. I'm sorry about the accident."

Julia tightens her lips in sorrow.

"I'm sorry I hurt other drivers and cost a baby his life." She lowers her head in remembrance. "I'm sorry you had those surgeries."

Julia thinks of painful days and rehabilitation. "I'm sorry my actions impacted your relationships." She envisions Gino angry and sleepless nights. "I'm sorry it's taken so long to apologize."

She prays God lifts Sam's spirits and removes his agony.

"I have many regrets."

"Sam—"

"My words might sound empty, I know, but they're all I have." Julia remembers pleading with Gino to understand.

"I've lived in anguish—teetered on the brink of insanity, and my best days are like an average person's worst.

She recalls days on the razor edge of sanity.

"I've wanted to say these words to you and the others." Julia wishes Sam felt her forgiveness. "I've struggled with what to do."

She recalls her uncertainty.

"I wanted to contact all of you but lacked the courage. There I was, a big, tough highway patrolman, and I couldn't find strength enough to say I'm sorry."

She remembers days incapable of mustering strength enough to combat her pain.

"Heck, I'm such a coward I'd probably try to commit suicide by slitting my wrists with an electric razor."

Julia chuckles.

Sam smiles.

"Sam, all you ever had to do is what you just did. But I forgave you long ago. I didn't know your identity but couldn't let anger linger and turn to hatred."

Gino, who stands hidden outside Sam's doorway, sighs. He enters. "Neither could I, Sam."

Sam's eyes grow wide. "Hey, you're the maintenance guy."

"Yes. I'm Gino Cavatelli. I'm Julia's husband."

Sam covers his nose and mouth with his cupped left hand. "I can't believe—"

"I've known your identity a long time. At first, I hated you." Sam Ellis lowers his eyes.

"I wanted to make you pay for how you ruined our lives."

The officer's nod demonstrates he understands.

"But you didn't cause our problems. We messed up our own lives."

Sam looks to speak.

"No. Wait, Sam."

The officer closes his eyes and listens.

"In anger and hatred, I presumed to know why Julia's crash happened and why you fled."

Sam looks back at Gino, in pain from his words.

"But I didn't know. And I had no right to question why and judge your motives or to hate you because of them. I'm sorry for how I felt about you."

"Mr. Cavatelli, you—"

"It's Gino."

"Okay, Gino. You don't need to apologize to me. I must apologize to you and Julia. I beg your forgiveness."

"We forgive you, don't we, honey?" Gino asks while he walks toward Sam.

"Of course." Julia moves to Sam's other side. "It's what we know is right in our hearts."

Julia and Gino each grasp one of Officer Ellis's arms. She looks intently into Sam's eyes. "You're worthy of forgiveness, Sam Ellis. And we both forgive and free you."

Just then, a thin man with pale skin, who listens from afar, turns and walks away. The lean man's smile indicates satisfaction to Caring Hands' receptionist as he passes. Struck by his appearance, sudden calm and unexpected peacefulness overwhelms her.

After a second-long trance, she turns toward the building's entrance for another glimpse of the fascinating stranger, but he isn't there...but gone, as if vanished—gone as if never there.

ABOUT THE AUTHOR

Greg Casadei is a retired insurance executive from Surprise, Arizona. He is the author of *A Gun and Cherries in the Bucket of Blood*, a 2014 book about his response to the Americanization of his Italian ancestors. His friendly yet compelling style draws readers into his work as if they shared experiences presented.

www.ingramcontent.com/pod-product-compliance
Lightning Source LLC
LaVergne TN
LVHW041909070526
838199LV00051BA/2557